A Minister's Ghost

By Phillip DePoy

A Minister's Ghost

PHILLIP DePOY

ST. MARTIN'S MINOTAUR ✽ NEW YORK

www.minotaurbooks.com

Library of Congress Cataloging-in-Publication Data

DePoy, Phillp.
    A minister's ghost : a Fever Devilin mystery / by Philip DePoy.—1st ed.
      p. cm.
    ISBN 0-312-33934-8
    EAN 978-0-312-33934-0
    1. Devilin, Fever (Fictitious character)—Fiction. 2. Railroad accidents—Investigation—Fiction. 3. Appalachian Region, Southern—Fiction. 4. Mountain life—Fiction. 5. Folklorists—Fiction. 6. Georgia—Fiction. I. Title.

PS3554.E624M56 2006
813'.6—dc22

                                      2005050403

First Edition: January 2006

10 9 8 7 6 5 4 3 2 1

This book is dedicated to the memory of the real Hiram Frazier. I met him at a bus stop at 5:30 in the morning in 1969. Instead of asking me for a quarter, he wanted to tell me what had happened to his life. I hope he's resting in peace.

This book is also dedicated to the little person in Central City Park, who, late at night that same year, fought off four attackers with his walking stick and then quietly got on the bus with me less than three minutes later. I hope he's still kicking.

Maybe I should have dedicated the book to those bus stops.

Acknowledgments

Acknowledgment is made to the Georgia Council for the Arts. In the early 1980s I was a writer-in-residence for the Council in Tifton, Zebulon, and Rabun, Georgia. I was able to collect and record the manuscript materials called *Thunder in Omega,* from which some of the stories in this book were taken.

Grateful acknowledgment is also made to Lee Nelson Nowell for her reading and editing skills, genuine encouragement, and lemon mousse.

A Minister's Ghost

One

Transparent as moonlight, silver hair made wires by the wind, an old man stood at the railroad crossing. Midnight had come and gone, a freight train roaring, trailing littered leaves all around him. A cold November air built autumn's derelict mansion with those leaves, his home for the evening, but it was gone with another gust. No shelter for the helpless.

I watched him from my pickup, trying to decide if I should stop and give him a ride. He was shivering, bone white in the damp, dressed in black tatters. The primary shame of our century is that a propensity for human kindness is often kept in check by suspicion, disgust, and fear. I had an impulse to help, but I hesitated.

Just as I determined to offer him a lift, the lights of a semi rose over the ridge in the gathering fog. My eye was distracted for an instant; when I looked back, he was gone, one more old leaf blown away.

The semi clattered by. I turned left to cross the tracks, scanning the trees for some sign of the vagrant traveler. He'd vanished.

Another failing of human beings in this century is an almost complete inability to recognize an omen, even one so obvious. A November ghost is always an omen. I'd been out all day collecting old stories for a new book, ancient lessons for the young millennium. One more lost apparition seemed a fitting punctuation to a long day spent in the past.

The ride up the mountain took longer than usual. Mist turned to rain and slowed my progress. The year was old, the night was long, and there's no darkness like a moonless midnight on Blue Mountain. My headlights made valiant effort, but only emphasized the black trees, black road, black air. Occasional lightning made shadows dance in the woods; thunder rattled my truck's windows.

I was glad to see my cabin come into view. The rain was falling harder, and I dashed to the front porch, shielding my ancient Wollensak tape recorder. Inside quickly, fumbling for the switch by the entrance, I managed to hold back the gloom of the night with a little kitchen light and some extra noise setting down the bulky machine.

It was a ridiculous indulgence in nostalgia, the Wollensak, when modern technology was so much more convenient and infinitely more efficient. But Alan Lomax had used a machine just like it to record music and stories that had once filled the mountains, but only existed in the Library of Congress by the end of his lifetime. Sounds that were gone from the American hills forever were captured by that recorder for generations to hear. I fancied my mission was the same: a kind of sonic archaeology, sifting through the sand of boring reminiscence hoping to catch a glimpse of a rare, priceless artifact. Alas, most of my day had been sand, now soggy, and I was exhausted with little to show for my efforts. All I wanted was bed.

No matter how long I stayed away, a few hours or the long years of my university life, I always had the same sensation when I came back to my family's cabin. Inside those walls the past was not gone, memories of my deceased parents were as real as furniture, unsettling as an autumn storm. I'd been home for nearly two years and still felt strange, dripping onto the floor, to think of the place as mine. The downstairs had changed little in years: small, bright kitchen to my right, muted living room to my left. The rugs were old, but the floor was clean; everything was as my father had left it.

I locked the door behind me, turned out the kitchen light, and headed for the stairs. Lightning illuminated the windows, muffled thunder vibrated the roof. I would have made it safely into the harbor of dreams in my bedroom upstairs but for the pricking pin of red light blinking on the phone answering machine.

I halted my lumbering. *What could there possibly be in my life that couldn't wait until morning?* I thought. *What message would be important enough to keep me from well-deserved rest?*

Still, I pictured myself lying in bed, eyes open, staring at the ceiling, wondering who had called, what they wanted.

Insomnia has a million evil assistants.

The phone machine was on the kitchen counter next to the espresso machine. Three steps took me to it. I tapped the button and was delighted to hear Lucinda's voice.

"Fever? You still out?"

I tensed. Her voice was filled with trouble.

"I'm calling a little after midnight," the recording continued, "so maybe you're already asleep, but if you get this anytime tonight, please, please call me. I've gotten some bad news. I guess I just want to hear you tell me it's all right, or something foolish like that. Please call me. I'll most like to be up all night."

I could hear the distress, the torn syllables. She'd been crying, was trying to sound composed or brave. Something serious had happened.

I dialed her number. She answered on the first ring.

"Yes, hello?" Her voice cracked.

"Lucy, it's Fever."

"Oh, thank God." She fought to keep herself even. "Could you come on over here, do you reckon? I really need somebody to lean on."

"What is it? What happened?"

"You know my little nieces, Rory and Tess?"

Teenaged girls, sweet as cider, Rory and Tess were popular with everyone who knew them. What came into my mind at that particular moment, for some reason, was how proud Rory, the younger, had always been of never missing a day of school. She delighted in recounting endless new lessons—Platonic thought, the heroines of Thomas Hardy, the mysteries of algebra—almost as much as lording her attendance record over her older sister. Tess had forever lost a perfect attendance award early in her scholastic career as a result of an *incident,* as it later came to be known, involving the school play.

Tess was supposed to have played Betsy Ross in a Fourth of July pageant. She would meet George Washington at his home and say, "It is I, Betsy Ross, bringing a new flag for a new nation!" and everyone would sing "You're a Grand Old Flag." I'm told the rehearsal went smoothly. The day of the show, however, Tess was pacing nervously backstage, saying her line over and over, when the *incident* occurred. In a matter of seconds her elaborate costume caught on a nail, ripped, and fell off. Two sizes too big, held together with pins, the dress was a pile of rags on the floor.

She stood at the door of George Washington's home clutching the American flag, dressed only in a bonnet and underwear, and began to cry.

"I can't come in," she yelled when she heard her cue, "because I'm back here *necked*!"

That concluded the play, and Tess skipped school the next day.

It was a story often told. I'd heard it at least five times at church meetings or family gatherings, but I never tired of it. Tess was a blond, serious and hilarious at the same time; Rory's hair was chestnut colored, and I couldn't remember ever seeing her when she wasn't laughing, or about to. They were unusually filled with light, joyous all the time, the kind of children rare enough in the mountains and unheard of in the city. Lucinda wasn't as close to her own sister, the girls' mother, as she was to the favorite nieces.

"Of course I know them. Are they all right?"

Her moment of silence made me swallow.

"Lucy?"

She was crying and trying not to let me hear it.

"They're dead, Fever," she choked out.

I don't remember what I said to her, but I was in my truck before the next clap of thunder, skidding down the wet, black road toward her house.

A thousand things to say flew through my mind as I sped along the highway; none seemed good enough. Part of my problem came from the fact that I didn't miss any of my own departed relatives, who fell primarily into the *good riddance* file. There was also my abiding belief that death was welcome, kind, the end of a slope; a new horizon. I was steadfastly more frightened of a lingering life than a quick death. Although the image of the girls being hit by a train was something I wanted to avoid, the event, nevertheless, seemed to me a spectacularly efficient way of dispensing with the inevitable. I rejected that tack as a way to comfort Lucinda, however. Not everyone shares my views.

The rain around her house was steady, the night was ink, liquid and opaque. I could barely make out a single living room light through curtained windows, orange the color of jelly sugar candies, a comforting glow.

I was surprised not to see any other cars in front of her house. Bad news in Blue Mountain generally provoked a battalion of well-meaning friends and curious acquaintances with great food and lame comfort.

I was barely out of my truck when her silhouette appeared in the doorframe, arms crossed, Kleenex in hand. Her loose dress was nearly devoured by a huge, gray, open cardigan. Her auburn hair fell around her shoulders like autumn leaves.

"No one else is here?" I called, closing my door.

"It's one in the morning, Fever," she answered patiently. "Besides, you're the only one I called."

"Oh." I pocketed my keys, bounded through the rain and onto her porch. "Well, here I am."

"Thanks," she managed, frozen in the door.

Given my general discomfort with affection, we could have stood that way for a while, awkward, not knowing what to do or say. Luckily the drive had afforded me time to compose my words, and I took charge. Three small steps and I held her in my arms.

"I love you," I said plainly, "and it'll be all right."

The accident happened in Pine City, only a few miles south of Blue Mountain. The girls had been to the movies; their ancient Volkswagen Bug stalled at the railroad crossing on the edge of town, and a train hit it. Our mutual friend Sheriff Skidmore Needle had called with the news, which seemed a little strange to me, but he knew how close Lucinda was to the girls and I let it go under the circumstances. Details were not related, thank God; Lucinda's nieces were pronounced dead at the scene.

"Even if they were stalled, why didn't they just get out of the car?" she said for the third time, pulling another Kleenex from the box on her lap. "I don't understand."

We sat in her living room and talked about the issue for nearly two hours. It was a calm room, a reflection of Lucinda's spirit in general. The walls were a pale ocean blue, the sofa was a perfect gray contrast. A dark, ancient Oriental rug covered the wooden floor. Over the stone fireplace: a three-hundred-year-old family portrait of distant relatives, a Scots landowner and his brood who claimed kinship, by marriage, to Robert Burns. The painting was old, but the smile on the wife's face always seemed modern and mischievous to me. I stared at it to keep myself from giving in to Lucinda's dismal mood. I felt I needed to stay lighter in order to help her.

"Oddly," I told her toward the end of the second hour of my visit, "I wrote an article last year about train hopping, *hoboing* some people still call it, and you'd be surprised at the statistical incidence of accidents like this one. At crossings, I mean. Dozens of interviews on tape talk about it, and I got the statistical information from the Federal Railroad Administration." I put my hand on her forearm; my voice lowered. "And of course you realize that quoting statistics at a time like this is a sad attempt on my part to distance us from the emotion of the moment."

I thought she might smile.

"How many?" she sniffed.

"What?"

"How many people are killed at train crossings?" She dabbed her eyes.

"Oh. Over four hundred in 2001."

"Four hundred people," she said, shaking her head, "didn't have sense enough to get out of their cars and they got hit by a train?"

"No," I told her, "nearly half of those four hundred were what they call 'trespasser fatalities,' people who were trying to jump on or off the train illegally."

"The ones you were studying for your article, the hoboes."

"Right."

"Are there still *hoboes*? Seems like something from the Depression." She set the box of Kleenex down on her coffee table, a converted antique trunk.

"Plenty," I said. "We call them homeless people, now."

"Oh." She closed her eyes. "Well, we do have those in abundance."

"There you are."

She yawned; a good sign, I thought.

"Could you sleep?" I ventured.

"Fever," she said as if she hadn't heard me, "I don't believe in statistics. Numbers. My little girls are people. Were. They were smart. They would have gotten out of the car when they heard a train coming. Something happened to them."

"Lucy," I sighed, moving closer to her, "you're tired; you need some rest."

"No," she insisted, gathering strength. "This isn't right. It wasn't their time." Her eyes shot into mine like searchlight beams. "You have to find out what happened."

"What happened," I said as gently as I could manage, "was a terrible, unbelievable accident. You'll make yourself crazy thinking anything else."

"I already made myself crazy," she shot back, the beginning of a vague hysteria edging her words. "That's why you have to do this for me. I can't rest until I know what really happened over there in Pine City."

"I don't see how it will help."

"If you look into this and say there's nothing to my fears," she told me, attempting to collect herself and sound reasonable, "then I'll leave off. But I have a feeling about this thing, a bad feeling I can't shake." She drew in a sobbing breath. "I can't think that a thing like this could just *happen*."

7

There it was, the fear behind the fear. She meant: How could God allow it? I should have realized that would be her overwhelming darkness, but I often forgot her basic religious underpinning. Still, I found myself wondering something along the same lines. If there was nothing more than blind fate and cold statistics involved in the loss of such beautiful children, what sense did anything make?

"Okay," I said softly. "You go to sleep, and I'll speak with Sheriff Needle first thing in the morning."

"Then you'll go to Pine City."

"Then I'll go to Pine City," I affirmed.

"Good." She let out a long, branching sigh. "You know that's the first time you ever said you love me. I mean, when we were on the porch earlier tonight."

Her head found its way to my shoulder.

"Is it?" I smoothed the hair from her forehead.

She was already asleep.

Two

The next morning was biblical: a polished, open sky after the storm, a perfect sign of God's promise to the earth. We'd both fallen asleep on the sofa.

I got up as gently as I could manage and tiptoed into Lucinda's kitchen, dressed in yesterday's black jeans, black T-shirt. Sun shouted in through closed curtains, chickadees clattered in the birch outside.

Standing by the window, I was already lamenting Lucinda's lack of appropriate coffee accoutrements. All she owned was an ancient percolator best suited, in my opinion, for a museum or an antiques show. Espresso is the only genuine beverage for eight in the morning. Still, caffeine was needed, and the percolator was gurgling.

I did my best to keep quiet, closing the kitchen door. Lucy's house was larger than my cabin, better appointed. The living room was to the left of the front door, dining room to the right. A long hall took me to the kitchen at the back of the house; beside it was a sort of den or parlor, home for her television and large bookshelves. Three bedrooms were upstairs, a full bath on each floor.

Her backyard was a half-acre English garden where she spent hours every day. Some Saturdays she delighted in directing me as to what I should dig up, how it should be moved, and where I should plant it next. She rearranged the garden more than she did the living room. It was a spectacular example of the agricultural arts.

While water became coffee, if the brown water I was about to drink deserved that appellation at all, I dialed the telephone on the wall, blue powder and hospital clean.

"Morning," the familiar girl's voice answered. "Sheriff's Office, Melissa Mathews speaking."

"Sheriff Skidmore Needle, please, Melissa." Even though Skid and I had known each other since boyhood and it had been nearly a year since he had been elected sheriff, I still delighted in asking for him that way on the phone. I liked the fact that he was sheriff, it made the entire county seem saner. I also thought it was somehow amusing to tease Melissa.

"May I tell him who's calling, Dr. Devilin?" Melissa asked me zealously.

"No, you see, Melissa," I began, "if you know who I am, you don't need to say that part. I mean, you already know who's calling. It's me."

"Oh, right."

"But you can tell him it's someone else calling if you want to."

"Okay." She put the phone away from her mouth and shouted, "Dr. Devilin's calling!"

The phone clicked and Skidmore's voice was on the other end.

"We have an intercom, but Ms. Mathews still likes to shout." He took the phone away from his mouth. "I got it!"

There was another click, and the telephone circus was concluded.

"And she still hasn't quite mastered the whole *telephone answering* part of her job," I said, hoping to lighten the initial moments of my call.

"Fever." His voice shifted to low tones. "You're calling about Lucinda's little nieces."

"I'm at Lucy's now, in fact. She's still asleep on the sofa. I'm in the kitchen."

"I understand," he surmised. "You want me to do most of the talking in case she walks in."

"Mm hm."

"I know she's got to be really upset." He sighed. "It was terrible at the scene, and that's a fact. Their car was nearly flat. That train hit it good. Girls died instantly. Thank God."

"Still wearing seat belts?"

"Yes."

"So they hadn't even tried to get out of the car."

"Didn't look like it." He shuffled some papers in his desk. "We're still trying to figure out exactly what happened."

"But no evidence, that you saw," I whispered, "of anything out of the ordinary."

"No," he sighed. "It was a really bad accident."

"Lucinda wants me to look into it," I said quickly. "I understand that you don't want me in your way. All I need to do is go over to Pine City, take a look at the crossing, see the car, examine the bodies, that sort of thing."

"I could have guessed she'd want you to do this," he said, a slight irritation growing in his words, "but I have to ask you not to. I don't want her upset. And I *don't* want you in my way."

"Of course." I'd heard that tone a lot recently. He was tired, pressed—and it was only eight in the morning.

"Believe me," he allowed, "you don't want to look at the bodies. What's left of them is seriously messed up."

"I've seen worse. We've seen worse together."

"Right," he agreed after a moment.

We were both thinking about the decomposed bodies we'd found little more than a year before in the woods close to the town mortuary.

"I still don't like to think about that," he said quietly.

"So you'd understand," I pressed, "if I just had a look into this for a day or two, completely out of your hair. To appease Lucy. I know it was just an accident."

"What did I just say?" he snapped, irritation growing for some reason. "I don't want you in this mess. I'm really busy."

"I know," I cut him off.

I didn't want to hear the litany of troubles I was afraid he might recite. Not because I was uncaring, but because I knew the effect they were having on him—and his home life. His wife, Girlinda, had called me in tears several times over the summer.

"Keep me posted, then," I said, clipped.

He knew I'd look into things for Lucinda's sake, but he was so strained I didn't want to press it then.

"Right," he agreed, but clearly didn't mean it. "'Hey' to Lucy."

"'Hey' to Girlinda."

We hung up.

The kitchen door swung open and Lucinda stood sleepy-eyed in the doorway. "That was Skid?" she managed.

"It was."

"How's he doing?" She yawned.

"He said 'hey.' But he sounded shot. He worries too much."

"Or something." Her syllables insinuated what the whole town gossiped: Skid and his secretary, Melissa, were seeing one another.

"I don't want to have this discussion again about Skidmore," I said, turning toward the percolator. "He's my oldest friend, I trust him, and there's nothing to all the talk about Melissa and him. Plus, you know that if Skidmore was seeing anyone but Girlinda, she would kill him, then call the doctor to revive him *just* so she could kill him again."

Lucinda didn't seem in the mood for levity.

"Where there's smoke, there's fire," she said hoarsely, ambling into the kitchen.

"A stitch in time saves nine," I intoned.

"What?"

"Sorry," I sniffed, "I thought you wanted to talk in clichés."

That, of all things, made her smile.

"Very funny. Are you drinking my coffee?" She was content to change the subject. "That's a warning, a danger sign."

"I know," I agreed. "It's the last days."

She shuffled to the table and sat; I poured coffee into her favorite mug. The sun insisted on tidying the room, making it clean of any shadow the night had left behind. Walls were washed in amber morning light, and everything seemed better when I sat beside her, even to drink the awful brew.

Silence spoke volumes; our eyes didn't meet. It was the sort of conversation we'd been having, on and off, since we were both fourteen. Some things are understood between two people who know each other that well and don't need to be said. Unfortunately, other things that yearn to be said sit silent too and make a palpable wall of longing.

"Will you be all right if I just slip over to Pine City for a few hours now?" I stood and took my cup to the sink.

"Of course," she said firmly, staring out the window. "I want you to go look into things. I'll be okay."

"I know, I was just making sure you were ready for me to leave.

Her chair scraped a harsh yelp across the floor as she turned to look at me.

"You know I'm never *ready* for you to leave, Fever," she said softly, "not to go to college or off to teach, not even to walk into the next room most of the time. I wouldn't mind it if we were never much out of sight. But I don't expect that's what you meant."

I set the cup down in the sink, didn't look at her.

"I'm here now," was all I could think to say, staring down at the stainless steel faucet.

"I didn't mean . . . ," she began, but fell silent.

"You meant," I told her, swinging slowly around, leaning back against the counter, "that you're glad I'm back, glad I'm here now. You meant you missed me when I was gone. You meant you like it better when I'm here than when I'm not. You can put me down for all of that too, in spades. You think I don't understand something mysterious or secret about our relationship, but I do know a thing or two. I know, for instance, that I'm the only one you called last night. And you know what that means?"

"What?"

I looked down at the clean old linoleum floor.

"I believe you're sweet on me."

"How much more complex is it than that?" she asked, her eyes brighter. "In your mind."

"Enormously," I shot back. "A genuine adult relationship is supposed to be dense; the primary sin of popular culture is a lack of complexity. I consider it our duty to help ameliorate that situation by indulging in the most complicated emotional miasma of the current century."

"We've certainly got a head start on *that*. And well begun is half-done."

"A bird in the hand," I said, launching my frame away from the counter, "is worth two in the bush, and I'm off."

"I'll just wait here, then, shall I?" She didn't move.

"Maybe we could have lunch when I come back." I suggested. "What's today?"

"Saturday."

"Are you on call at the hospital?"

"I'm supposed to go in," she said hesitantly.

"You're taking the day off. That's not a question."

"All right," she agreed. "I'll call them right now."

"I'll see myself out." I headed out the door without looking back.

"I might be in the garden," she called out, "if you phone."

I smiled at that: Saturday gardening could mean that she felt better.

I paused a moment in the living room to pick up my black leather jacket and to get a good look at one of the photographs on the mantel. Two teenaged girls stood side-by-side holding a carved pumpkin and a blue ribbon between them. Autumn light brushed their faces, and the clarity of their eyes was piercing, even in the photograph. It was signed at the bottom, "To Aunt Lucinda, love Rory and Tess. Look, first prize!"

Pine City isn't far from Blue Mountain as the crow flies, but if you're forced to take the main road, it twists around for nearly half an hour before you see their town hall. I pulled my ancient green pickup to the side of the road close to the railroad crossing and got out. I hadn't been there in a while, but everything I could see was exactly the same as it had been since I was a boy.

The road I parked on was the axis of town, the railroad crossing about five hundred yards shy of the square. The cross street where I stood had been a gravel road when I was a boy, but blacktop had long since replaced gray rocks. The rails toward town veered off sharply to the right, away from the square, just after the crossing, and rhododendrons twice my age had grown high enough to hide the trains as they passed. The other side, the direction from which the train would have approached the night before, sloped downward from where I stood, making it impossible to see anything coming until it was less than fifty feet away.

Like a lot of other towns in Appalachia, the railroad had made a city out of a gathering of scattered farms and businesses. The train station, only a little farther on down the tracks after the curve and the rhododendrons, had once been a palace where exotic treasures from strange places arrived on boxcars, where soon-to-be grooms stood on platforms waiting, a bunch of red roses in hand, for strangers to arrive from Atlanta or farther-away towns.

For me it had been a place from which to leave home, glad of freedom; a place to return when the world was too wild.

I left home when I was seventeen, graduated early from high school and shot from Blue Mountain like a cannonball, or a fast train leaving from the Pine City station. My best friend, Skidmore, was the only one there to say good-bye. I could always see that moment in my mind's eye, Skid barely managing not to cry, shaking my hand and telling me he'd never see me again.

And I had agreed with him, smiling, glad to think it was true. I would miss my boyhood chum, no doubt, but the rest of the place sloughed off my spirit without a single thought more than *Thank God I'm getting out.*

I leapt onto the train, threw open the window, let the air rush past me as the train picked up speed, headed for Atlanta and my real life, blowing away all the bitter dust from hearth and home. I couldn't think of a strong enough phrase for my sense of freedom. I'd not yet learned to curse.

But I had come back, of course. I stood at the side of the tracks, leaning back against the hood of my truck, still hearing the train that had carried me away roar in my mind.

I gazed at the rhododendrons and compared the path of my life to the railroad tracks. The steel lines bent off suddenly in an unexpected direction, but they were cast with iron spikes, as unyielding in their direction as the course of the sun and moon, or the planets spinning in space.

You never leave home, I thought. *You just think you do. My house could be in the south of France and I would still live in Blue Mountain.*

Home isn't a place as much as a cellular memory, a collection of experiences that trail out behind you.

Like railroad tracks.

The business at hand was a gloomy, one and the day obliged by shutting up the sky with gray clouds and a light, cold drizzle. I was glad I'd worn the black leather jacket, it shed the rain and stayed warm; regretted the black high-top tennis shoes—liked the look but the feet were already wet.

The town square turned to Renoir for images in that mist: the courthouse became a sheet of brick-red light, the lawn in front a yellowing field of wheat. Thick, black vertical lines played the part of oak trunks, topped with dabs of rust and ocher. The Confederate war memorial statue seemed to wave at me in the shimmering air, and the rest of the shops in the recently revitalized downtown area were obscured by a low patch of fog or poor eyesight.

I should get glasses, I thought, turning from the square to the more immediate task.

The formerly gravel road, called Bee's Crossing, was slick. It was lined on either side with weeds and dead wildflowers.

I gazed up at the railway warning post. There was no arm to come down to keep a car from crossing the tracks, but the tall post sported two red lights on top of a black bowl the size of half a basketball that would be the warning bell. I wondered how I could find out if it was working besides, obviously, standing there until a train went by.

Nearly leaden with reluctance, I heaved a sigh and pushed myself away from the hood of the truck to wander the scene of the accident. The worst of the wreckage had already been cleared, but the inevitable diamonds of broken window glass glittered in the road and on the tracks. There were a few small pieces of twisted metal and torn rubber, unrecognizable as anything having to do with a car or a train, but everything else had been impressively scoured. I had no idea what to look for.

I wandered across the tracks, feet more than a little cold.

Bee's Crossing ran straight away from me for two blocks, lined on either side with lots of trees and a few big houses, before dead-ending. One of its cross streets went to the rail station if you turned left, or to the shortcut back to Blue Mountain if you turned right.

The girls were going to take the shortcut, I thought, but I immediately regretted bringing their image to mind.

I saw them, late coming home from the movies, worried about the parents yelling at them, deciding to go the back way home.

The shortcut was faster than the highway if you didn't mind risking the dirt roads that went up the cemetery side of Blue Mountain. If you had no trouble, you could cut fifteen minutes or more off your travel time, but the roads were treacherous if they'd turned to mud, and you ran the danger of getting stuck and ending up hours late.

The girls had decided to take the chance. If they'd been less concerned with getting home, or earlier out of the movie, they would have gone back on the main road, the way I'd come: past, not across, the tracks.

I made a mental note to check and see what was playing at the Palace, and what time the movie had let out. Pine City had an old movie house, built in the thirties, abandoned in the seventies, restored in the new century and showing old movies.

It was a popular place with tourists because the building's age matched the entertainment offered, and to visitors from the big cities it was an opportunity for time travel: sit in the dark eating a bag of nickel popcorn and watch Jimmy Stewart talk to an invisible rabbit. The place was also a popular dating destination with high school students who had never heard of Jimmy Stewart and felt they were discovering some ancient artifact, a darkened part of the pyramids where no one had ever been before. That sensation was exacerbated by the restoration decor: someone's vision of Solomon's Temple. Clearly a biblical scholar had not been consulted.

The lobby was part Moorish, part Hollywood: tall wooden columns painted gold, frescoes copied from the Sistine Chapel, and wall hangings obviously purchased from the Bela Lugosi estate. Inside the theater, the seats were upholstered with what appeared to be leftover scraps of abandoned "Oriental" rugs. The ceiling had been painted with a "midnight in the desert" theme, stars (twinkling Christmas lights) swirled around a bold full moon (a large auto headlight). In front of the screen, gold curtains closed and opened before every show.

When Lucinda and I had gone to see *Lawrence of Arabia* there, the place was packed. She asked me why I thought so many people had troubled themselves to come to a movie house to see a film they could rent for less at a video store. I told her I thought human beings in the twenty-first century were hungry for communal experiences. She told me she thought coming to the theater was a better date than sitting at home. Most of the audience were couples.

I wondered if Rory and Tess had met anyone at the movies.

I turned around and retraced my steps back across the tracks, paying more attention to anything off to the side of the road. Wet sheets of newspaper, rusted old cans, more broken glass—there was nothing that seemed related to the accident at all.

I decided to wander the tracks. It was clear from the direction of the glass on the street and the other bits of debris that the train had been coming from out of town and going toward the station. It would not have been slowing down much, the old railway station had long since closed. Trains only rattled through town now on their way north with long boxcars and freight piggybacks. The rails were slippery, so I resisted the urge to tightrope-walk the way I always had as a boy.

A few feet from the crossing, headed toward the abandoned station, a glint of something caught my eye, a reflection. I stepped over the rail and skidded a little on the wet grass. About six feet from the tracks I found two plastic CD cases. One, by someone named Jane-Jane, was empty; the other had a sticker on it that said "from Aunt

Lucinda." It was the sound track to the movie *O Brother, Where Art Thou?*—which made me smile in spite of the circumstances.

Every once in a while something comes to the mountains that reinvigorates our ancient traditions. In the late sixties and seventies it was the Foxfire project, reintroducing teenagers to their folk heritage. By the turn of the century it was a Hollywood movie reminding America about some of its original music. People all over the world who had never heard of Jeanie Richie or The Skillet Lickers could finally understand, in a context they could accept, the music I considered seminal to our culture: rural, rough roots; simple melodies and age-old stories.

God Bless the Coen Brothers, I thought, picking up the CD cases, *for making that movie.*

A few other bits of trash were around the cases: a crushed lipstick, several Diet Coke cans, a hairbrush. I thought they might have belonged to the girls too.

Just as I was thinking that, the tracks thumped twice, not loudly but hard enough to make me jump. A second later the bell on the warning light by the crossing banged out a message that could have been heard in Vermont: a train was coming. I stepped well back from the tracks, could see the red lights flashing madly.

Then the train blared out its horn and I dropped everything I had just picked up.

The horn shot through the marrow at the center of my bones. I tried to get farther away from the tracks, but the rhododendrons proved a solid wall. I actually began to shiver a little, from the adrenaline or the cold I couldn't tell.

The train called out again, much closer this time, and the bell and lights on the warning pole seemed to intensify. The rails began to shake and the roar of train noise filled the air. I rarely consider praying, but just as the engine shot past, it occurred to me I might take it up. By my estimation it was going seven hundred miles an hour.

Fear might have hyperbolized the estimate a little.

I couldn't move. The rush of wind that the train dragged along battered me, threw sticks and leaves and bits of trash at me. I folded my arms, lowered my head, and closed my eyes against the on-slaught. It was a long train and the assault continued unabated.

After what seemed an hour, the caboose finally shook and rumbled, and noise began to fade; the warning pole fell silent and red lights blinked off.

I couldn't help thinking about an old song called "In the Pines" with its declaration of the longest train in Georgia: "The engine passed at six o'clock and the cab went by at nine."

I let out a long breath, stooped to pick up the things I'd dropped, and headed back toward my truck.

Well, the warning light works, I thought to myself, trying hard not to consider what a train like the one I'd just experienced would do to a Volkswagen stopped in its path.

A moment later I dumped the CD cases, lipstick, cans, and hair-brush on the passenger seat when I got into my truck. I wasn't sure where to go next, the local junkyard, where I knew Skidmore had had the Volkswagen taken, or the morgue. Neither seemed any good.

Distant thunder encouraged the sky above to darken to charcoal, and the rain picked up a little. Unable to face the morgue, I started the truck and headed through town toward Waldrup's Cash and Tow.

Pine City seemed deserted in the rain, and even the courthouse looked empty. Cars were parked in front of one of the tourist shops, an imitation general store, but the customers were apparently huddled inside, unwilling to face the cold and damp.

Waldrup's was the only towing company in the county and would have made no money at all except for the addition of a thriving junkyard business. It served as a meeting place for teenaged boys with pretensions of automobile prowess. They bought spare parts and swapped fantastic lies about how fast they'd been going when the police caught them.

Once you got any car over about forty on most of our roads, in fact, you'd be off the pavement, onto the shoulder, or flying down a mountain with little hope of stopping until you hit the valley floor.

Anyone who said they'd taken those curves and slopes at more than fifty was lost, himself, to hyperbole.

By the time I got to Waldrup's, the rain had abated, though the sky had grown darker.

The first thing I heard when I opened the door of my truck was a cracking adolescent voice saying, "One hundred and twenty, on two wheels, almost all the way."

Three skinny boys were standing around a wrecked Mustang, its hood up. I thought one of them might be Nickel Mathews, the cousin of Melissa, Skidmore's deputy/secretary. All three of the boys were staring at the engine the way doctors study a patient on an operating table.

"She's gonna need a valve job," one boy said quietly, "but I believe she'll make it."

I walked by them without speaking. The yard occupied three acres, and every inch was covered with something that had once been automotive. The owner, E. P. Waldrup—whose initials did not stand for anything, and whose friends called him Eppie—was asleep in a sagging brown armchair ten feet from the Mustang, next to his "office." He was decked out in his usual extralarge, grease-stained indigo coveralls. A man of considerable girth, he threatened to break the substantial chair in which he shifted, snoring.

The office was a shack the size of an outhouse that held a desk, a phone, and seven hundred boxes of paperwork that no one in the universe could make sense of except Eppie himself. Beside him, stretched out between the office and a telephone pole, was a heavy metal clothesline wire hung with a bizarre array of metal car parts. That sculptural conglomeration of refuse was the main reason I knew Eppie Waldrup.

Long ago this strange, uneducated man had constructed a rare musical instrument, a sort of junk xylophone. He'd strung up twenty-three various car parts on the metal clothesline just to the side of his one-room-shack office. These car parts hanging in the air were a kind of miracle. If he was in the right mood, and sober enough, he would treat the odd guest to a concert on those scraps of metal. There being no guest odder than I, Skidmore had persuaded him to perform for me several years previously, and I was enraptured. The sound had unearthly beauty. I had come back to record him twice.

He played with two tire irons and moved, when he played, with a grace that belied his bulk. He was carried on wings of music. Each piece on his line was a perfectly tuned musical note; combined, they made almost two octaves. And he prided himself on his ability to play just about any song requested. I tried to stump him the first time I met him by suggesting he play Bach's "Jesu, Joy of Man's Desiring," and he only had to thump out the first three bars or so before I conceded that he was playing the melody line perfectly, if a little slower than the norm.

"You'll have to do better than that, college boy," he'd taunted me. "I got a education in music from my childhood piano teacher, Miss Phelps. Can't nobody take that away from me."

Occupation and accent are not always indications of mental content.

I had to remember not to be startled by the sound of Eppie's voice. For reasons no one knew, it had never changed. Despite that he was over forty, past six feet tall, and weighed nearly three hundred pounds, he had a voice like Shirley Temple's.

I'd interviewed him twice as a kind of lunatic-fringe/primitive genius, a musical Howard Finster. Both times we'd had a good laugh at what his voice sounded like on tape. He seemed to have a sense of humor about everything in life, his own foibles included. I thought we liked each other in a casual way, and I was hoping he would tell me things that Skidmore might not, under the circumstances.

I approached the armchair gingerly. If you woke up Eppie too quickly, he was liable to swing something at you or call his dog on you, which was worse. The dog, Bruno, was nowhere to be seen, but I knew it was lurking.

I stopped five feet from the sleeping giant.

"Professor Waldrup," I announced.

He smiled, eyes still closed.

"Doc," he squeaked. "That you?"

"I'm afraid so."

"Christ." He looked me up and down. "You look tired. Up all night?"

The boys at the Mustang stopped talking so they could listen to us, but were still pretending to look at the car.

"I came to see you," I told him.

I knew what a figure I must have cut, over six feet tall, hair prematurely white, skin pale from too much indoor thinking, and dressed in black. I always tried to give the illusion of having casually thrown on whatever it was I wore, but the truth was more embarrassing. I enjoyed presenting a strange image. The details and origins of that enjoyment provided a lifetime of introspective analysis.

"You come to tape-record me playing something again?" He sat up and blinked hard three times.

"Sadly, no," I said slowly.

"Oh." He sniffed, looked away, and shifted in his seat. "You come to see that Volkswagen I got back there."

I was always surprised at the leaps Eppie's logic took, and the accuracy he enjoyed with them. He surmised that I was helping Skidmore with the accident investigation, as I had been known to do in the past.

"Don't get up," I suggested, "just point."

"Naw," he told me, twisting sideways in preparation to throw his bulk forward. "You gonna have some questions."

"You saw something questionable?"

"Me?" He laughed. "No. But I know you. You can't shut up with them questions."

"I have a lot to learn—" I grinned—"so I have to ask."

"That's the damn truth," he groaned, leaning forward.

His hands strained on the arms of the chair, turned white as he pushed himself up and away, launching himself in my direction.

I followed behind him as we rounded the office. The boys allowed themselves to watch us, silent.

I cleared the corner and was stopped in my tracks by the gnarl of orange metal that sat in cleared space with police tape around it. It looked like a giant, crumpled autumn leaf.

The next thing that struck me was that one of the doors was completely ripped in half, as if a chain saw had torn into it.

Eppie leaned against the back side of the shack and I approached the wreck, a little light-headed.

"Train ripped the door like that?" I managed.

"The police did that, or fire department, one," he said softly, "to get the bodies out."

The bodies. How could there have been anything left to get out? The car was a concave orange *C,* nearly two-dimensional. The engine had been ejected out the back end and was lying on the ground behind the wreck. The steering wheel had popped through the windshield. I couldn't even image how that had happened.

"Took 'em two hours to get the bodies out," Eppie said, anticipating my line of thinking. "The good thing is, that curve in the tracks had the train slowed a little bit, I guess, and the direction of the hit pushed the car off the tracks so the train didn't carry it all the way until it stopped."

"Where did the train stop, did they say?" I asked.

"It didn't completely come to a halt until it was past the old station." He took a deep breath and started my way. "They told me it would have been a whole lot worse if the train had been going at full speed."

I turned toward him, glad to take my eyes off the wreck.

"First, I don't know how it could have been worse, but second, the train wasn't going full speed when it hit? Who said that?"

"Nobody." Eppie shrugged. "But the train's got to cut to near half speed to make that curve, don't it?" He let his eyes drift in the direction of the wreck. "Still."

"Exactly." I followed his gaze. "What made it slow down?"

"They saw the car on the tracks?" Eppie ventured, roughing his curly brown hair with a thick hand.

"No. I was just there. The way the tracks slope down in that direction, the engineer wouldn't have seen anything until he was nearly into the crossing. But the girls would have heard the train coming."

"Or the crossing bell."

"Right," I agreed. "It's loud."

I tried to make myself go closer to the car, but couldn't seem to get my legs to work. I was afraid I might see something inside that I wouldn't want to see.

Reading my mind or my face, Eppie cleared his throat.

"The police had me wash out the car after they did all the technical crap," he said. "Washed it out good. And when they left, I did the same thing. It's pretty clean now."

"That's an old VW," I began slowly.

"It is."

"It wouldn't have a CD player."

"No," he answered. "I don't think it even had a radio. But definitely no CD."

"You wouldn't know when the accident happened, would you?"

"Well," he offered, "let me see. They called me to come haul the wreck around one thirty. They said it took nearly two hours to get the girls out. But how long before the accident was reported and everybody got there, I have no idea."

I forced myself closer to the wreckage.

Upon closer inspection, the interior of the car was battered but not entirely crushed. I could see the seats were folded but not destroyed, their springs poking out. There was, indeed, no radio in the car. The simple dashboard sported a primitive heating system based on blowing hot air from the engine into the car, and there was a cigarette lighter. Otherwise, it was bare. The gearshift had been bent in the direction of the driver's seat, the steering wheel jutted at an odd angle out the front windshield. What caught my eye was the ignition, because it made me think of something.

I backed away from the wreck.

"No keys in the ignition?" I asked.

"What?" he said, taking a step my way. "Keys?"

"They're not in the ignition." I looked down. "Wouldn't, ordinarily, the police leave the keys in the car, in case you needed them?"

"Ain't much I can do for this car," Eppie said slowly. "Maybe the cops took them, or maybe the keys got knocked out when the train hit. You see what it did to the steering column."

"I do see," I told him, though I wasn't looking.

I didn't feel I could look at the wreckage for one more second, and I still had to go to the morgue.

"Thanks, Eppie," I sighed. "I'll be back."

He was still cocking his head at the orange mass when I left the yard. The boys had gone; the rain was starting up again. The sky was bruised with rain clouds, and a cold wind snapped hair across my forehead.

The last thing in the world I wanted to do was visit the county morgue.

Three

Morgue might be too strong a word for the loose arrangement between the county and the Deveroe Brothers' Funeral Parlor. All three brothers were barely smarter, collectively, than a butter knife. Still, they had taken over the town mortuary after the previous owner had been indicted on hundreds of counts of illegal improprieties including "misuse of a corpse," a charge that would not bear much scrutiny on my part.

The boys had managed to pass all their classes at mortuarial school, or wherever a person learns such a business. They'd been registered, certified, and bona fide for nearly six months, and their business seemed to be running smoothly.

I remembered them only as wild boys whose main occupation was capturing feral swine and rounding up poisonous snakes for our more primitive church services. Still, the county allowed bodies to be taken to their one examination room for autopsy and for study to determine the cause of death in any questionable circumstance.

The cause of the girls' death was not in question, but because of the nature of the accident, a certificate from the county coroner had to be issued. So the girls were lying in state at the Deveroe Brothers' Funeral Parlor in Blue Mountain.

As my old green truck rattled over the highway toward the place, I tried to distract my mind. Was Skidmore really having an affair with his secretary? Would he really participate in such a cliché? Had I really told Lucinda that I loved her? Would that obligate me to accelerate the relationship? Alas, none of these thoughts worked as a distraction. The only image in my brain was a picture of two mangled bodies.

It was close to noon when I finally pulled up to the parking area on the side of the yard at the Deveroes'. I was so reluctant to go in that I could barely find the strength to turn off the engine. Rain was thumping frenzied syncopations on the roof and hood of the truck, and I could just make out the funeral home through the downpour. I decided to sit a moment, hoping the rain would abate.

All around, sheets of gray rain painted a melancholy veneer over ruby leaves in the old oaks, obscuring their color, demanding a more muted hue to surround the old funeral parlor.

Before I could reach for the door handle, I heard someone call my name; I made out a black shape moving toward me. Before I could see who it was, I heard Donny Deveroe's voice.

"Stay right there, Doc," he demanded. "I got you."

A moment later he was beside the truck, huge black umbrella sprouted above his head, opening my cab door for me.

"Saw you pull up," he said. "Thought you might like to stay a little dry."

Donny was the size of a linebacker, but his face was scrubbed and cherubic, his brown hair slicked back, and he wore a clean black suit. I'd never seen him in anything but overalls, and for a moment I thought he might be a distant relative of the boy I knew, that I'd mistaken him for Donny.

"All part of the service," Donny said cheerfully.

I managed to pocket my keys and climb out of the truck under the protection of the skillfully handled umbrella, keeping its wrangler amazingly dry in the torrent.

"Donny?" I finally asked.

"Yup," he said as we headed for the front porch. "It's me, all right."

"That suit looks good."

"I know," he said proudly. "Truvy picked it out."

Truevine Deveroe was the only sister in the bunch, our local witch until she and her husband, Able Carter, had moved away to Athens, Georgia, so that Truevine could get her GED and then go to the university there.

I climbed out of the truck and under the protection of Donny's umbrella; we headed for the porch of the funeral home.

"What do you hear from your sister?" I asked.

"She's good," he said hesitantly. "But she and Able still ain't had no baby yet. That worries me."

"They've only been married a year," I reminded him.

"A whole year," he said, shaking his head. "And still no baby."

"Maybe they're waiting until she's done with college."

The porch was dry and solid. Donny folded the umbrella, careful to keep it away from me, and shook it hard, ridding it of water.

"Maybe." He leaned the umbrella against the wall. "I reckon you come to look at your friend Miss Lucinda's nieces."

"Yes."

"You helping out Sheriff Needle like you always do?" He was speaking uncharacteristically softly, something I felt he had learned in mortuarial school.

"Soft of," I conceded. "But I have to tell you, I'm not looking forward to seeing the bodies. Lucinda was very close to those girls, and I knew them slightly myself."

"Oh," he said, opening the door for me, "don't worry about that. We took care of everything."

We entered the quiet of the funeral parlor itself. The hallway was immaculate. Polished golden floors glistened in every direction. The room to our left was gleaming, a perfect Victorian sitting room. The staircase that led to the office upstairs had been given new black-and-white tapestry-like carpeting depicting, as far as I could tell, scenes from Shakespeare. The banister had been polished to a mirror's perfection. In front of us the spotless hallway was lined with old photographs framed in thick antique gold.

I didn't know what I'd expected, but the last time I had been inside the boys' own house, there had been dead, gutted animals in the kitchen, flies everywhere, and a stench that could have been used as a military weapon. The funeral parlor was, on the other hand, cleaner than I'd ever seen it, still as a church, and softly lit, like an early sunrise.

"You boys surely have done a nice job with the place," I said, trying to keep the amazement in my voice to a reasonable level.

"We take our work very serious, Dr. Devilin," he said sweetly. "I know you remember what we was like in the old days, but we're all grown-up now."

The old days were barely more than a year before, but sometimes a great change engenders a rip in time. Donny did seem to have matured by a decade.

"I see—" I began.

"Come on back," he interrupted. "I think you'll be pleased with our efforts."

Our efforts. I could barely contain myself.

The room at the end of the hall was lit by candles, outside light through a stained-glass window, and a snapping blaze from the small fireplace at the far end. The effect was soothing until I thought about what I might see in the two coffins on skirted tables at the center of the room.

"We worked all night," Donny whispered, "all three of us, getting them ready in case someone came this morning."

I slowed my walk. Donny obliged by moving away a step or two, surely another trick learned from his recent schooling.

The two chocolate-colored coffins rested side by side. The lids were open. The skirts around the tables were black, and in the soft light the coffins appeared to be floating on shadows.

I allowed a glance to creep over the rim of the one closest to me. My eyes were amazed; my heart was broken.

Rory lay sleeping, dressed in a white gown, one hand resting at her neck. She was made up for her high school prom: hair perfect, cheeks blushing, lips an immaculate natural gloss. I had the sensation that I could wake her if I took that hand.

I turned to Donny. "My God."

"Yeah," he said, a glimmer of the rougher boy I knew, "but I wouldn't get too much closer if I was you. We had to put a lot of that face together."

"Put it together?"

"Putty mostly," he offered. "Some of it's wired plaster. What we got in here last night? You wouldn't have recognized it."

"Oh." I swallowed.

"Sorry," he said quickly. "That was unprofessional."

"You certainly did work quickly." I tried to pry my eyes away from the caskets, with no success.

"The family." He shrugged. "They were in a hurry. We even had a sort of hassle with the new coroner. He seems to think there was more to all this than a train wreck. But in the end he let us do our work."

"What's his name? The new coroner, I mean."

"Millroy."

"He thought this wasn't an accident?"

"I don't know what he thought," Donny said softly. "Our first obligation is to the family."

"Right." I'd have to check in with our new coroner.

Donny folded his arms.

"I can't get clear in my head," he began, "if you're here to pay respects, or you're doing an investigation."

"Right," I answered, looking down at my wet tennis shoes. "I can't get that straight either. Just trying to find out what happened to these girls."

"They got hit by a train," he said before he could stop himself.

"I know," I said steadily, "but Lucy thinks there was something else. And now you tell me this Millroy has doubts."

"Well," Donny said, almost to himself, "it's not unusual, you know. I've found that lots and lots of folks come in here thinking that."

"Thinking what?"

"That there must be some other explanation for the . . ." He groped for words.

"Death of a loved one," I ventured.

"Exactly." He folded his arms. "It's not good enough to know it was a heart attack that killed your husband, you want to know what caused the heart attack. I don't see how that matters once you're dead. Dead is dead, 'scuse me for saying so."

"No," I confirmed. "You're right. But what Lucy can't believe is that the girls wouldn't move the car when they heard the train coming."

"Maybe the car stalled," he said simply.

"Why didn't they get out, then?"

"That's a point," he conceded. "Why didn't they?"

"I don't know, but *that's* not unusual. I tried to tell her: four hundred people a year are killed just like this. It happens."

"Uh-huh," he allowed, "but when it happens to someone you know, you want more than that."

I looked up at Donny.

"You have grown up," I said softly.

"Thanks, Doc." He offered me a curt nod, still trying his best to play the part of the funeral parlor director.

I glanced back at the coffins, took a quick look at Tess. She was even more beautiful than I remembered, dressed in white too, and holding a small bouquet of dried lavender.

"Can we go somewhere else?" I asked quickly. "I don't think I can stay in here."

"Of course," Donny responded immediately. "Let's go back to the parlor."

I don't remember walking back toward the front of the house, I may have had my eyes closed some of the way. I just remember finding myself seated in a soft leather chair, close to another fireplace. Donny was on the sofa opposite me, a practiced look of sympathy on his face.

"You boys did a great job with the bodies," I said, collecting myself and struggling toward objectivity, an investigator's persona.

"We only had time to do the faces," he corrected. "The rest of the bodies is still a great mess. Sorry."

"They were in pretty bad shape when they came in, I suppose." I leaned forward.

"Are you sure you want to hear about it?" he asked gently.

"I'm really wondering about a few things that maybe you can help me with. For example, did the girls have keys on them, or were any keys brought in?"

"Keys?"

"Car keys, house keys, a key ring," I prompted.

"Nope. We put all the little effects together in a little basket, like an Easter basket. No keys at all. Why?"

"Just a nagging detail, probably. What *effects* were there?" I wondered. "I mean, what did you put in their basket?"

"Wallets," he began, rolling his eyes upward, trying to remember, "a pack of Tic Tacs, some change. Not much."

"How about a personal CD player?"

"Oh." He nodded. "Sure, now that you bring it up. Rory sort of had on headphones, and the CD player was in her coat pocket."

"Really? Is it still here? Could I see it?"

"It's in back." He stood. "I think we put the headphones down in her coat pocket with the player."

I followed him out the room and down the hall to another room at the back of the house. This one was gray, more clinical, lit by fluorescents, and antiseptic smelling. The two chrome tables in the center had drainage holes at the sloped bottom edge. I tried not to stare at them.

A rolling clothes rack was against one wall. Donny went to it, found a fluffy blue coat. It was at least 50 percent stained a rust color that I wished I hadn't seen. He fished in one pocket and produced a miraculously unharmed CD player the size of a bread plate.

"Here it is," he said, holding it up, headphones trailing behind, dangling toward the floor.

"Is there anything in it?" I didn't want to touch it.

He popped it open. "Yup." He took out the shiny disc. *"Tonka Toys.* By somebody called Jane-Jane."

"Ever heard of her?"

"Nope." He held out the CD.

"Do you have a player? I'd rather not put on those headphones."

"I understand," he said, nodding. "We like to have soothing music playing when we have visitors. It's in the other room."

He put the player back in the stained blue coat and headed for the viewing room. I followed, steeling myself against the sweet sight of the girls, hoping to keep my eyes averted.

The room's dim light was, indeed, comforting, and the crackle of the fire was reassuring.

Donny went to a small hutch in the corner of the room, opened it to reveal a hidden stereo system. He turned it on and put in the CD.

An explosion of petulant blaring filled the room, an adolescent girl's anger.

"Okay," I told him over the din.

He touched a button and the room fell mercifully quiet again.

"Loud," Donny said.

"Could I use a telephone here?"

"Office upstairs," he answered. "You want this?" He held out the CD.

"Better put it back in the player in Rory's coat," I said. "You wouldn't know if Rory was driving, would you?"

"No." He started back to the other room.

"The office is the first room at the top of the stairs, right?"

"Exactly," he confirmed. "You can go on up. I'll let you have your privacy. You calling Sheriff Needle?"

"Right." I turned to give him a smile. "Were you always this bright?"

"No," was all Donny said before he disappeared into the overlit room.

I headed along the hallway and up the stairs. The banister was so polished I was afraid to put my hand on it, I didn't want to smudge the finish.

Directly at the top of the stairs was a door that opened into a room with floor-to-ceiling windows in the outside wall. The other three walls were completely occupied by dark-stained oak bookshelves. There were few books still in evidence, but plenty of papers, stacks and stacks, neatly arranged. Ages ago when the funeral parlor had been a private home, the room would have been a library. Even darkly overcast, there was enough light through the windows for me to see the huge oak desk, top well organized, and the phone close to the far corner.

I walked slowly in, letting my eyes adjust to the lower light, rounded the desk and picked up the phone, dialed Skid's number by heart. I was surprised to hear him answer. He rarely did that since he'd been elected sheriff.

"Sheriff's office," he said tersely.

"Skid, it's Fever," I told him quickly. "I'm at the funeral parlor. Have you seen what the Deveroe boys did with the bodies?"

"No." He was in no mood.

"Great work. They look wonderful. The girls. And sad, you know."

"Fever," he broke in, "I'm kind of busy."

"So I went to the scene of the accident," I hurried on before he could continue, "and found two CD cases that belonged to the girls, as well as a lipstick, Coke cans, and hairbrush that may have been theirs. Then I went to Eppie's and saw the wreck, and I have a few really fast questions."

"You found some things you think were in the car with the girls?"

"They were down the tracks from the crossing, about fifty feet or more, off to the side, under the bushes," I said. "No one would have seen them in the dark last night. I wouldn't have seen them except for luck. But here are my questions: Do you know who was driving last night?"

"What?"

"Which girl was driving," I repeated, "do you know?"

"Tess. Why?" His voice had relinquished a touch of its frost.

"And Rory was wearing headphones at the time of the accident," I went on, "listening to a CD."

"The headphones weren't on Rory's head, exactly," Skid sighed, "but that doesn't mean anything, given the circumstances of the accident. They were attached to a portable player in her coat pocket, so it's a good bet she was listening to it, yes."

"Did you hear the music?"

"Did I listen to the CD?" He bristled. "No."

"It was loud," was all I told him. "My last question is, did you or somebody last night take the car keys, the keys to the Volkswagen?"

There was a beat of silence.

"They weren't in the ignition," he said slowly.

"Right, and no one found them last night?"

I heard him shuffling papers on his desk.

"No." He seemed to be thinking.

"Okay, that's all I needed," I said briskly. "I'll give you a ring tonight."

"Fever, damn it," Skid said, a small taste of his real voice creeping into his words, "that's not all. What's on your mind? What are you doing?"

"I'm just *collecting* at the moment," I said honestly, "trying not to come to any conclusions. But it is strange that the keys are missing, don't you think?"

"It's strange that I didn't notice it," he said ruefully.

"I'm going to talk to the girls' parents in a while," I said softer, "and before you tell me to leave them alone, I'll promise not to pester them long. I only have a few questions. You should really come and take a look at what the brothers did over here at the funeral home. It's remarkable."

"You're going to call me tonight." It wasn't a question.

"After I talk to the parents," I agreed, "and give the Palace a call."

"The movie house?" He was irritated again. "What do you want with that?"

"Do you know what movie the girls saw?" I asked slowly.

"No."

"What time it let out?" I shot back, picking up speed.

"No."

"Do you know if the girls met dates there last night?" I concluded.

"Fever—," he began hotly.

"That's why I'm calling them, Skid," I answered defensively. "Why are you so weird about all this? What's the matter with you?"

For a moment I thought he might have hung up. Then I heard him sigh.

"Being sheriff is a lot different from being deputy," he told me, all his steam gone. "There are things about this situation that I can't tell you; it's more complicated than you think."

"What are you saying?" I rested myself on the corner of the desk.

"I'm saying there's more to this whole mess than just a train wreck," he said stonily.

"*Just* a train wreck?" I shot back.

"I can't *talk* to you about it, Fever." There was iron in his words. "You're not a policeman, you're an ex–college professor. Leave it be. I won't be responsible for what happens if you don't do what I say. I mean it."

"All right," I answered slowly through tight lips. "I'm going to talk to the girls' parents for Lucy's sake, and then I'll stay out of it."

More silence ensued.

"I wish I could believe that," he said at last. "Look, I've got to go."

"Bye."

He hung up.

It wasn't much of a fight, but it was the worst communication Skidmore and I'd had since we were in high school. We never fought. Something was really bothering him.

What was all that about not being responsible for what would happen if I didn't leave the investigation alone? I thought as I sat there on the desk. *Was he threatening me? Am I in some sort of danger? The train wreck wasn't the only thing that happened last night, that's clear.*

The only effect any of my thoughts had at the time was to convince me to step up the investigation.

I looked around for a phone book, ended up calling information for the number of the Palace movie theater.

The phone rang a while before someone answered.

"Palace."

"Hello," I began, "This is Dr. Devilin calling. I have a few questions about the movie last night. Did you work?"

"Last night?" the teenaged boy said. "Uh-huh, I work every night. What is it you want to know?"

"What's your position there?"

"Position?" he grunted. "I do everything: sell tickets, work concession, clean up. It's just me and Chester."

"The projectionist?" I guessed.

"Yes, sir."

"So what movie was playing last night?"

"*Vertigo,*" he said in a bored voice. "Hitchcock."

"You're not a fan."

"It's almost as stupid as *Psycho,*" he complained. "If you want good Hitchcock, you have to go back to *The Lady Vanishes,* in my opinion, or *The Thirty-nine Steps.* Before he went Hollywood."

"You're a student of film," I said, doing my best to take him seriously.

"I'm going to make films," he said plainly.

"Really? I think that's great." I took a different tack with him. "I've made a few films myself. Just documentaries."

"You're the folklore guy, right? You came to our high school once. You're all *Nanook of the North* and stuff."

That a young man from the mountains knew enough about film history to appreciate early Hitchcock and to remember the movie I'd shown two years before was impressive even to me and belied every stereotype in the book.

"Who are your influences, cinematically?" I asked him.

"Claude Lelouch is the main one," he fired back. "He could tell a story that didn't depend on the budget."

"*A Man and a Woman,* right?"

"That was his commercial success, yes," the boy said sagely. "What else do you want to know about last night? I've got a lot to do before we open."

"Sorry," I hurried on. "What time did the movie let out?"

"The early show on Friday's over at around nine; second show's done by eleven thirty at the latest."

"You wouldn't know the Dyson girls, would you?"

"Nope." I could hear him clattering something in the background, maybe getting the popcorn machine ready.

"All right, they're two high school girls," I began, "one's around eighteen with blond hair, the other's got brown hair, a year younger. They're sisters, pretty, very outgoing."

"Okay."

"You don't remember seeing them last night?" I pressed.

"Mister," he sighed, "on Friday night we're packed. There were probably a hundred people here. I can barely keep up."

"I understand," I said calmly. "What's your name, do you mind my asking?"

"Andy Newlander," he whined. "I'm going to change it. It's not a good filmmaker's name."

"Would you mind if I came by sometime this weekend and showed you their picture? See if you remember them?"

"Why?" He was suspicious. "Are they in trouble?"

I took a deep breath.

"Did you hear about the train wreck last night, over there in Pine City?"

"No."

In as little detail as possible, I explained to Andy Newlander why I wanted to come and see him. He agreed, more subdued than he had been, and we hung up.

Outside the rain was clattering at the window, a wandering spirit demanding sanctuary. Distant thunder sounded, absent any lightning I could see, like muffled timpani played slowly. The room grew darker, and in the distance, I heard a train whistle blow.

I made my way downstairs, wandered to the back of the funeral home again looking for Donny. I was doing everything I could to get images of Tess and Rory out of my mind, but they wouldn't leave. Like the girls themselves, their memories clamored for attention, each one cheerfully vying for full appreciation.

The recollection that won out and occupied me as I stood in the doorway staring at their coffins and wondering where Donny had gone concerned the snapshot on Lucinda's mantel.

Several years ago there had been a carnival in Blue Mountain just before Halloween night. Everybody in the county was there. In some folk communities, schools are often one of the gathering places for secular entertainment. Nearly everyone had children or grandchildren in the county school, and if they didn't, they knew someone who did. So the Fall Festival was held on the school grounds.

The air was crisp as an apple, filled with the scent of burning leaves. Trees in the school yard were riotous: red leaves, rust reeling downward in crazy spirals of autumn air. They rained onto wooden booths, pony rides, milling crowds. A huge hand-painted sign that said *Welcome to Your Fall Festival* stood tall in the yard. It was decorated with red witches, white goblins, and happy orange jack-o'-lanterns, a product of the cooperative efforts of the lower grades.

Down in the cafeteria, teachers had assembled a haunted house, a sad affair of torn sheets, darkened windows, and grown adults dressed in Halloween costumes. Bowls of grapes passed for eyeballs, plates of cold cooked spaghetti masqueraded as conquerer worms. Lucinda wanted to go, but I demurred.

"Do what you like to a school cafeteria," I told her, "it requires more than imagination to forget the smell of coleslaw hanging in the air."

Skid, a lighter version of the man with whom I'd just spoken, had dressed himself as a reptilian monster wearing a clerical collar and black suit. Billed as the "Preacher from the Black Lagoon," he occupied the festival's dunking booth.

For a dollar, anyone could throw a baseball at the target, and if that target was squarely hit, it might send the monster plummeting into a tub of icy water. The monster would howl, and the children would scream.

I considered the situation from the monster's point of view. There he was, minding his own business, not bothering anyone. One second he's sitting warm and dry, the next he's dunked in cold October water, without a warning or a prayer.

Such is life.

Just before sunset everyone had gathered near a bonfire to judge several contests, among them the jack-o'-lantern carving. I fought my urge to tell anyone who would listen that originally the purpose of the carved pumpkin had, indeed, been to make a lantern, and the lanterns were used throughout the autumn months. Only on All Hallows' Eve were the lanterns made into faces, and then the idea was to frighten away the spirits of the dead, or to light their way so they wouldn't get lost.

Instead, Lucinda and I wandered among the quarter acre of severed orange heads, marveling at the craftsmanship and enthusiasm all contestants had mustered.

There were nearly fifty entries, arranged in rows and glowing in the fading evening light. Some were nearly as big as doghouses, carved mean: scowling eyes, razor teeth, howling mouths. Some had old felt fedoras on, making them look like hoboes, vacant wandering souls. One had a patch over its left eye. One was carved to look like a medieval hellmouth, as I explained to Lucinda, and inside it were melting toy plastic soldiers playing the part of tormented sinners.

The biggest, fiercest one had been made by the son of Pastor Floyd Davis, the Methodist minister. It was as terrifying an image of Satan as I had seen anywhere, complete with carrot horns, a rotted-eggplant tongue, and peeled white turnips embedded in it that looked very much like blind eyes.

Tess and Rory had stood at the far end of the last line, a small cardboard box between them. They refused to let anyone look in until the two judges—Pastor Davis and a school science teacher whose name I didn't know—got to them.

The judges made their way up and down the long rows of jack-o'-lanterns taking notes, conferring humorlessly, and measuring. Everyone had stopped whatever they were doing and come to watch. Booths were shut down. Skidmore stood close by, wrapped in a blanket. The cafeteria was empty.

The scene was, in fact, something to see: fifty leering pumpkin faces lined up, candles glowing warm inside, everyone standing around, silent as the grave, waiting for the decision of the judges.

Someone standing beside Skid said, in hushed tones, "Usually the bigger the pumpkin, the better the chance of winning. That's why they're measuring."

Contestants really wanted to win. The main prize was from E. P. Waldrup's Cash and Tow: a month's worth of free gas, an oil change, a tune-up, and a choice of one item, any item, from anywhere in the yard. This was quite an offer, because some of the "items" in the yard were entire cars.

The Palace had thrown in four free movie tickets, good anytime. And Miss Etta's diner was offering free pumpkin pie for a year, in keeping with the situation. That Miss Etta only made pumpkin pie once a year did little to dampen enthusiasm for it. Miss Etta made very good pie.

Many of the local boys had put a good deal of effort into winning.

My eyes were on Tess and Rory and their little cardboard box. It was like a baby coffin. They were barely able to contain their excitement, laughing and whispering to each other. Pastor Davis was still measuring his son's hellmouth when the science teacher made it to the end of the line and demanded to see the girls' creation.

Rory sighed, leaned down, and opened the top of the box.

"Floyd," the science teacher gasped, her face transfixed. "You'd better get over here!"

Pastor Davis wound up his tape and hurried over, clearly irritated by the disturbance in the solemn proceedings. But his expression took on a beatified look of wonder when he peered down into the cardboard container.

"Lord Almighty, girls," he said softly.

People around began to close in, pressing on every side, trying to peer down into the box.

"What is it?" someone whispered.

"You're not going to believe it," the science teacher intoned.

The girls beamed.

Slowly Pastor Davis bent over and pulled out the carving the girls had made.

It was no bigger than a child's head, made from a baby pumpkin. Everyone froze.

In the fading light, licked by amber cast from the bonfire, every one of us witnessed a living, human face. The pumpkin had smiling eyes, a gentle expression filled with love. The fire's glow gave the eerie impression that the face was constantly changing features, shifting, looking around at everyone. It was clearly alive.

"It's Judy," Lucinda whispered.

The girls had not carved a demon or a devil, but one of the kindest faces I'd ever seen, apparently the perfect image of their favorite babysitter, Judy Dare, a little person from Chattanooga who lived in Blue Mountain. I'd met her once at Lucinda's church, barely four feet tall, beautiful. The jack-o'-lantern that depicted her face was not a contrivance to scare away evil spirits, it was a hand-carved tribute, a labor of love; a sacred object designed to invite saints and angels. It was a work of art.

We stood transfixed. None of us could believe what we were seeing. Judy's orange face smiled, winked, sighed in the flickering light.

"Well," Pastor Davis said finally, "you girls really did something here."

Tess lit the candle inside, and Cousin Judy's face radiated the joy of life, beamed like the soul of a real woman.

Lucinda rubbed her eye and sniffed.

"This is just like those girls," she managed. "Everybody else was trying to see who could make the scariest, the meanest—that wouldn't even occur to them. All they've got in them is love and kindness. They carry on so about Judy; they still visit her all the time. I mean, look at that little face."

I think I put my arm around Lucy then, or maybe I just had the impulse to.

Ordinarily the winner of the pumpkin-carving contest would have been shouted out by the judges, rejoined by much cheering. That year everything was quiet. Pastor Davis fished in his coat pocket and simply handed over the paper that gave the girls their prizes.

There was a lot of smiling all around.

Lucinda got the girls to stand with their carving in between them. She took a quick snapshot. Everything went slowly back to normal: the pie booth sold pumpkin pies, caramel apples were stuck on sticks, girls held hands with their boyfriends; the sun began to set. Everyone took a turn walking by the Judy pumpkin.

After the sun slipped past the horizon, a chill wind came up. It suddenly blew over the large sign in the school yard, and everybody began to gather things up, in a hurry to get home.

"Might rain," Pastor Davis offered as he passed us, helping his son carry the fantastic devil head to their truck.

"Judy is the girls' babysitter, right?" I asked Lucinda as we headed for my pickup. "Do I remember that correctly?"

"Yes." Lucy nodded. "They call her their aunt, but she's really just a neighbor, lives on the same street as they do."

"I have met her, haven't I? She's the one you introduced me to at your church."

"I believe it was at a church dinner once," she told me, nodding.

"Can you believe I barely remembered that?" I fumbled for my car keys. "You'd think I would remember a little person at that church."

"Judy's shy. Probably why she isn't here tonight. Sometimes even when she's around, you don't notice her, which isn't hard to imagine, little as she is."

"I hope she sees this pumpkin, though." I opened the passenger door. "The carving, I mean. Don't you think she'd be flattered?"

"I can't imagine she wouldn't be," Lucinda said, climbing into the cab, "but I don't really know her."

Thunder rattled the sky, and thick, cold globs of rain began to pelt my truck. I got in quickly, cranked the engine. In the rearview mirror I caught sight of several men, Skid included, making sure the bonfire was out. Beside them I saw Tess and Rory carrying their little cardboard box, running, laughing, stumbling toward their little orange Volkswagen parked under a chestnut tree.

"Don't they look peaceful?" Donny said from behind me.

Startled, I turned his way quickly.

"Sorry, Doc," he went on, "I didn't mean to sneak up on you like that."

"That's all right, Donny," I said, recovering. "I was just remember-ing them, something they did a couple of years ago at the school."

"The pumpkin-carving contest." Donny nodded sagely.

Even though I grew up in Blue Mountain, knew most of the peo-ple there as family, I never ceased to be amazed at the way everyone knew everyone else's business. Or that everyone occasionally exhib-ited a rough clairvoyance.

"You remember that?" I asked.

"Me and Dover had a entry," Donny said simply.

"The year the girls won, you and your brother entered a jack-o'-lantern?" I found it hard to believe. It wasn't the sort of thing the boys were likely to do in those days. *Steal* a pumpkin, throw it at a passing neighbor, even give one to their sister, Truevine, in the hope of talking her into making a pie—these were more in line with their general wont.

"We had the biggest one there," he said in hushed tones. "We were sure we'd win. We wanted the stuff from Eppie's yard. You know. Funny what you want when you're a kid."

I turned again to look at the side of his face. In his dark suit with the glow of the fire from inside the room painting his face with am-ber light, I saw a new man, different from the wild boy who'd hunted pigs and snakes. This was someone of substance. Sometimes the job makes the man.

"Would you be offended if I said I was proud of you, of the transformation you've made, Donny?"

"What?" He tilted his head. "You're proud of me?" His face went boyish and I wasn't sure if he was going to smile or cry.

"You and your brothers have really done something here," I went on quickly, "and I expect there are quite a few people in town who see the changes you all have made. In yourselves and in this place. It's good work and it deserves to be recognized."

"Thanks, Dr. Devilin." He studied his shoes. "That means a whole lot."

"You got the girls ready in a hurry," I said, stepping away from the coffins. "Is the family coming soon?"

"Anytime now."

"Oh." I jumped. "Well, I'll be going, then."

I headed toward the door. It wouldn't do for me to run into the parents at the funeral parlor. I was hoping to catch them at home, maybe the next day. I had some questions for them, but I certainly didn't want to intrude on their moment with the bodies. No need making the investigation any more difficult than it already was.

"When's the funeral?" I asked Donny, fishing in my pocket for keys. "Do you know?"

"Tomorrow," he answered, following me. "At noon. You want me to walk you back to your truck?"

The rain had let up a little.

"That's all right," I assured him. "I can dash for it."

I pulled open the door, gathered my collar around my neck, and jogged down the steps.

"Okay, then," Donny called from the doorway. "Take care."

Thunder sounded again, louder than before. A gust of wind drove orange and rusty leaves down all around me as I dashed for the truck. Leaves stuck to my face, my arms, my chest, as if autumn had decided to claim me for its own, wrap me in its shroud; cover me over with a cold embrace.

I brushed them away before I climbed into the cab and pulled the door against a chill draft. But one leaf had followed me in, rested on the dashboard: orange, the color of a pumpkin, a crumpled wreckage of the year's end.

The coroner's office was only a five-minute drive, on the same main street as Skid's office and Miss Etta's diner. I thought I'd drive by to see if Millroy might be there.

The door was open; I pushed it. A stranger in a black suit wended my way down the short hall and came to a stop three inches too close to me.

"You're Dr. Devilin."

"I am."

"My name is Davis Millroy, the new county coroner," he said. "I know Lucinda Foxe from the hospital, and she seems to be a fine person, so I try to keep on her good side. That's how I know you. I'm new in town, so I try to get to know people before I meet them."

"Yes," I said, holding out my hand. "Welcome to Blue Mountain."

"I've been here six months."

"I'm hoping you'll talk with me about your findings concerning these girls."

"What girls?"

"Tess and Rory Dyson?" I suggested. *How many girls are you currently investigating.*

"Oh." He looked around. "Naturally. Ms. Foxe is the girls' aunt, I believe."

"Correct."

"Which is why you are here." He squinted oddly.

"Can you tell me about your autopsy," I said, not looking at him. "Do you mind?"

"I enjoy talking about my work," he answered completely expressionlessly. "You aren't the only nonofficial personnel interested in my report. I probably shouldn't be telling you that, but I consider it a professional courtesy."

"I'm sorry?" I had no idea what he was talking about.

"One medical man to another."

"Oh, right," I agreed. "Absolutely."

No point in my telling him that my doctorate was in folklore, it would only have embarrassed him. After he'd been in town for a while, he'd realize it all on his own anyway.

"I'd expect the same," he told me, stone-faced.

"Of course."

"Won't you have a seat?"

He indicated two worn chairs in the tiny reception area. They were made of nicked wood and natty fabric, thirty years past any sense of fashion.

"Who was it that came to you?" I asked. "I mean, the other 'nonofficial personnel.' "

"I'm really not at liberty to say." He sniffed.

Then why did you tell me about it at all? I wondered to myself.

We sat. Gray light somehow found its way into the room through the windows. It only made the room seem ancient.

"So your autopsy?" I prompted.

"Standard," he answered curtly. "Sudden trauma. Both girls died instantly."

"Nothing out of the ordinary?" I prodded.

"Like what?"

"No evidence of anyone else in the car with them," I suggested, "like hair or skin?"

"No." He held his breath a moment. "But there was a strange anomaly. Something you don't ordinarily see in a case of sudden death or in any accident of this order."

"What was it?" I caught his eye.

"I only found it by accident. I wasn't satisfied with the toxicology report." He stopped, at a loss.

"You mean you thought the girls might have been drinking," I allowed. "Why else would they let a train run into them?"

"Not exactly," he said slowly. "The report had already been run and eliminated that possibility. But the brain chemistry of both victims seemed to indicate elevated 5HT. An excess level of serotonin."

"I'm not certain what that is," I confessed, though it somehow sounded familiar.

"The brain chemical serotonin," he lectured, "is the main one that LSD, PCP, and other psychedelic drugs mimic in order to produce the hallucinogenic effects."

"That's right," I remembered. "During certain folk ceremonies in Mexico, peyote buttons are sometimes ingested and *they* increase serotonin. I did some research—"

"So I performed a few more tests," he interrupted impatiently. "But I didn't really get a chance to finish everything. That's what's got me worried."

"You think the girls had taken some sort of hallucinogen?" I didn't even take the question seriously, knowing the girls.

"Not exactly," he admitted. "It's a tricky thing. Elevated 5HT levels can mean anything from schizophrenia to psychosis, autism, Alzheimer's disease, anorexia, even blood clotting."

"I see," I responded contritely. "What was your conclusion?"

"After careful reconstruction of what I believe was their blood chemistry before the accident," he droned on, "it appears that both girls had a rush of endorphins and neuropeptides, blood vessels were dilated, and blood pressure went down *in addition to* high levels of serotonin."

"You can tell all that?"

"Or infer it.".

"And that indicates?"

"Extreme, prolonged laughter."

"Really?" I hadn't meant to sound so surprised. "They were laughing when they died?"

"Yes."

"I can see that you'd want to know why." I nodded.

"I mean, I've asked around. These girls weren't the type to have been experimenting with hallucinogenic drugs, but it's not unheard of that someone might have slipped them something in a soda pop. These teenagers do it all the time at their parties."

I realized then that his demeanor reminded me of Jack Webb from the old *Dragnet* television series. That, in turn, reminded me of my friend Dr. Andrews. Tall, blond Manchester native, a great Shakespeare scholar and a vicious rugby player, Andrews never failed to find himself perpetually fascinated by American television. He had forced me to watch dozens of episodes of that police drama, each, to him, more hilarious than the last.

"What was your final ruling?" I asked him point-blank. "I mean about the death?"

"Accidental," he sighed. "But the boys at the funeral parlor were in such a rush to get their job done for the family, and they can be intimidating. I'm not entirely happy with the finding. I told the sheriff I'd like to run some more tests. Why would they have been laughing like that? I mean, wouldn't you like some kind of answer that's better than that?"

"For example?"

"Well," he suggested casually, "if, in fact, someone slipped them a drug at a party, say, then my finding might change from accidental death to murder, you understand. The drug being the actual cause of their untimely demise."

Millroy got a phone call then, before I could ask him anything more about his theories. I excused myself with a wave. The phone call was from Skidmore.

I spent the rest of that Saturday with Lucinda. She had called in sick to her hospital duties. The rain kept her from gardening, so she turned to her indoor variant of the same impulse: cooking. I sat in the kitchen, helping when I could. Mozart French-horn concertos filled the house; we played them over and over, round, golden sounds that were perfect for November rain. We didn't speak, the music and the rain eased us of that obligation, and I saw no reason to upset her with Millroy's suspicions until I was more certain of things.

She was making apple tarts. The pastry was so simple I always marveled at the luxury of the final product. How a cup of flour, an eighth of a teaspoon of salt, a stick of butter, and three tablespoon-fuls of ice water could accomplish perfection was beyond me. I attributed it to Lucinda's touch.

The apples were fresh-picked, rock-hard Red Delicious, cut in paper-thin crescent slices. Two drops of vanilla and two tablespoon-fuls of sugar were added, along with a tiny squeeze of lime. The tarts themselves were less than half an inch thick, cooked to gold. The production of these miracles occupied us well into the early part of the evening.

Only once, when the horizon turned the same gold as the pastry, did Lucinda stop her work. She looked out at the setting sun and spoke to me without turning.

"The girls used to love these apple tarts."

"You can do this if you want to," I said as gently as I could manage, "but I can't see that it does you any good."

"Do what?" she asked, still staring at the sunset.

"Pick at the sore place, needle yourself with thoughts about Tess and Rory. I've been doing it too, a little, but it doesn't help them, and it's certainly not improving your spirits."

"Listen." She turned. "If you have to try not to grieve about this so you can concentrate, I understand that. But I *have* to grieve or mourn or whatever you'd call it. I have to do it in my own way and let it wash over me. If I deny it now, it'll only come back to bite me sometime later."

Her eyes were red, her hair uncombed. She sniffed. Her apron was spotless, a deep blue that would soon match the night sky. She had completely given herself over to her spirit, and she was beautiful.

I envied everything about her in that moment.

"I wish I could do that," I confessed softly. "I can't, but I would really like to be able to let feelings take me over that way and have done with them. My style is more in the way of holding on to pain, pushing it deeper down until it's a block of granite that dynamite wouldn't budge."

"You're a deeply troubled individual," she answered, the whisper of a smile on her face for the first time all day.

"Exactly what makes me so fascinating."

"Is *that* it?" She returned to her work. "I've been trying to put my finger on it."

"I'm going to talk to their parents first thing tomorrow," I said, trying to return to business, "and then to the movie theater to show their picture to a person who was working there."

"Why?" She crimped the crust of the tarts to an artful frill.

"Make sure they actually went to the movies."

Lucinda stopped what she was doing, didn't look at me.

"Teenaged girls," I began before she could object to my plan, "you may be amazed to hear, sometimes tell their parents one thing and do another. It doesn't make them bad people, it makes them teenaged girls."

"So you've got to check up on them." She took a breath to say something stronger, but settled on "I'm too tired to argue. You do what you think's best."

There was proof of just how sad she was. Any other day of her life she would have debated the merits of her nieces until I ran screaming from the house.

"I'll stay here again tonight if you like," I went on, scrupulously avoiding eye contact, "or go on home. Whichever you prefer. Do you want company or peace and quiet?"

She went back to her work, about to put the tarts into the oven.

"I don't like to ask," she said hoarsely, "but I surely would appreciate it if you'd stay again tonight. I know you don't have clothes or your things here—"

"Lucy," I said, stopping her. "I'm happy to stay."

She scooped up the apple tarts, swung open the oven door. It creaked, a pleasant, warm sound.

"We wouldn't have to sleep on the sofa again, you know." She slid the pastries into the oven and closed the door. "You've never seen it, but I've got a perfectly nice bed upstairs in my room."

Four

Lucinda's husband had been dead seven years, and my last relationship, with a graduate student at the university where I'd been teaching,
had been gone for more than three. Incredible as it might have been to
admit, neither of us had slept with anyone since. Lucinda always bus-
ied herself with work at the hospital; I'd been back home in the mountains for two years writing or researching, occupied with my work.
Hollywood movies or New York television about urban sociology paint
a picture of human sexuality that would shame a bacchanalian. But
I've found that the genuine experiences of most honest Americans
who live in small towns is much more sedate, slow moving—and se-
cretive. Lucinda and I were in a glacially paced courting mode.

Until the events of that night sped up the pace of our interaction
significantly.

Suffice it to say that the details of our mutuality will go to the
grave with me, except to report that the process was gentle, silent,
and slow enough to take up the entirety of that night.

I was out of bed at dawn. Lucinda had just fallen asleep. I wanted to
get an early start on the day, and I knew if I allowed myself to fall
asleep, I wouldn't continue my investigation until the middle of the
afternoon.

Lucinda's bedroom was dark, the curtains drawn. A painted
wooden angel hung over the headboard of her oak Lincoln bed. The

rest of the room was stark, clean. The wooden floors were polished glassy. The only other piece of furniture was a large antique wardrobe with deer carved into the top piece.

The promise of morning sun tantalized through the edges of the curtains. I crept into the bathroom, took a quick shower. I put back on the same clothes I'd been wearing the day before and tiptoed downstairs.

I considered for a moment that I wouldn't make it through the day without going home and making my requisite espresso. I finally opted for an English muffin and three mugs of Earl Grey tea.

Ten minutes later, only slightly invigorated by the breakfast, I made it to my truck and slipped off the parking brake. In relative silence the truck rolled far enough to make it out of Lucinda's yard before I had to start the engine.

The morning was dawning much more pleasantly than the day before. Clouds were few, birds were abundant. The sky was turning blue quickly, the hard blue of November days.

I had debated over and over about contacting the girls' parents. I wanted to ask them a few questions, and a phone call seemed too cold. I was afraid to call them at all, in fact, because it's easier to hang up on a person than it is to turn that same person away from your door. I thought if I showed up on their front porch, I could be done with my work and leave them alone in short order.

I knew as I was driving to their house that my plan was ill-advised, but I couldn't see an alternative. On the other hand, I knew well that I was sleep-deprived, caffeine deficient, and generally insensitive. Confusion was my only touchstone.

I considered then that I ought not to be allowed to roam freely, that some sort of county ordinance should be passed requiring me to stay a hundred yards away from most decent folk.

The Dyson household, the only home Tess and Rory had ever known, was a grand, white construction, Victorian and stately. It was close to Blue Mountain's courthouse, on Main Street, only several blocks from the business center of town. Mr. Robert Dyson was head of our county school system if I remembered correctly what Lucinda had told me about him. I couldn't recall his title. Lucinda and Robert were not especially close, and for that reason there had always been some tension between Lucinda and her sister Sara, who had married Robert when she was too young. Tess and Rory were the only children, and the true link between the sisters. Mrs. Sara Dyson, née Foxe, was a tireless churchwoman in Blue Mountain's tiny Catholic community. Lucinda always said that Sara had converted to irritate her husband. Mr. Dyson was a Baptist. The religious disparity had raised eyebrows in town twenty years ago, but the dispute was an old, tired one when the century turned.

The Dyson house was pristine from the outside, a small front yard with a brick walkway that ran from the street to the large wraparound porch. The door was dark red, the only spot of real color: the trim was battleship gray and the gingerbread frofrou on the facade was charcoal.

There was no sign of life in the house. I parked on the street and got out of my truck. Instantly the blinds in the front room fell, as if the house were squeezing its eyes shut.

I stood a moment in the street, uncertain what to do. I realized that I probably looked a fright, no change of clothes in three days, black leather jacket, strange high-top tennis shoes still a little soggy. Before I could make up my mind, the front door flew open. A burly man in a white shirt, sleeves rolled to the elbows, appeared in the doorway.

I waved. He stood frozen.

"Is that Mr. Dyson?" I ventured, heading his way.

"I'm certain you can understand, Dr. Devilin," he began coldly, "that we're not really in the mood for company. We're preparing to go to a funeral. I don't mean to be rude."

"Yes, sir," I interrupted, heading up the walkway. "I only have one or two questions. It's really more for Lucinda than anything else."

"I can't fathom what questions would help my wife's sister understand this any better than I do," he answered, his voice hardening.

"Lucinda's got it into her head——," I tried to explain, but he wouldn't hear it.

"I know what she thinks. She's called. And to tell you the truth, I think she's right. There's not a chance in this world that my little girls just sat there and let a train run into them. They were deliberately killed."

He stepped back, about to close the door.

"Let me help find out what happened, then," I said quickly, picking up my pace toward him. "That's exactly what Lucinda wants."

Deliberately killed? I was thinking.

"Sheriff Needle said you might come by," Mr. Dyson said, his voice rasping. "He told me not to talk to you. He said the same thing to Judy, I'm sure. Go home. This is a police matter. If you don't leave now, I'll have to call someone and tell them you're trespassing here."

He slammed the door. There were low voices inside, then silence.

I stood, foolishly, on their front lawn in a golden autumn morning, trying to figure out why my best friend, Sheriff Skidmore Needle, had warned these people against me.

It seemed clear to me that Mr. Dyson was serious, that he would surely call the police if I didn't leave.

I got back in my truck, sat for a moment thinking what to do. Though it happened rarely, I had been run off from mountain cabins a few times when I was trying to collect folk material, even shot at twice. But the shock of a professional man in one of the grandest homes in town all but booting me off his lawn had me momentarily stunned.

All that came to me, thanks to Mr. Dyson's mentioning her, was the memory of the pumpkin-carving contest the girls had won, and Lucinda telling me that the fabled "Aunt" Judy lived on the same street where I was parked.

What was her last name? I fumbled, closing my eyes to concentrate.

After a moment, mostly to ease the Dysons' minds, I started my truck and pulled away from in front of their house. I turned the corner and parked on the side street, got out, and stared down the street.

Her name is Judy Dare, I remembered in a flash.

Pleased with my powers of memory, I started down Main Street again, hoping the name *Dare* would appear on a mailbox.

Hope proved unnecessary. Before I had surveyed half a block, another door on Main Street opened, and a child's voice called my name.

"Dr. Devilin!" A stage whisper.

The house with the open door was a brick Tudor-style, half-timbered above the door. A screened-in porch to one side was obscured by floor-to-ceiling bamboo blinds. The front door, rounded at the top, was painted red. It was on the other side of the street from the Dyson house, and two doors down.

The lawn was perfectly manicured. A fieldstone walkway led straight from the sidewalk to the door through a thick carpet of weedless grass. I could not make out the figure in the doorway, she stood back from the entrance.

"Yes?" I finally answered, trying my best not to sound startled.

"Come on in!" A little hand beckoned furtively, adding urgency to her voice.

I looked around. I was alone on the sidewalk; not a car was in sight on the street. I crossed and headed up the walk.

"I'm hoping that you're Judy Dare," I ventured.

"You know perfectly well who I am," she chided lightly, stepping into the doorway.

She stood three feet and eleven inches tall, a blond, attractive woman in her late twenties. She wore a chic blue dress, very adult couture for such a child's frame. When I got closer, I was able to see a more mature face than I had expected. There would have been no mistaking her for a little girl. Her eyes were filled with seven or eight lifetimes; her expression betrayed a complexity of mind I had rarely seen in the mountains *or* in Atlanta.

"When I saw you pull up in front of the Dysons'," she began before I had made it to the doorway, "I knew they wouldn't see you."

"They've been through quite a lot."

"We all have." She didn't look up at me.

Immediately I began to worry about eye contact, concerned that my size would make her feel uncomfortable. How would I look at her? Where would I sit? Was all the furniture in the house her size?

"A lot of people worry about that," she said matter-of-factly.

I froze in the doorway.

"Did I say something?"

It wouldn't have been the first time I'd spoken a thought out loud without realizing it. Crawling through the caverns of my brain has always been a little like spelunking without a light.

"I read faces," she said softly, "not minds. Lots of people worry about where to sit, where to look when they first visit me. I choose to think it's sweet: people are concerned about my feelings. Don't worry."

The house was my size. To the right there was a living room with a stone fireplace, built-in bookshelves on either side. To my left a pair of French doors led to a study. Beyond the living room lay the dining room through a large, rounded archway. A grand art nouveau chandelier hung over a dark, mahogany Empire table.

The living room was immediately comfortable: a worn leather chair, a sturdy sofa from the 1930s, an expensive Oriental rug on the floor, burgundy and blue. There was even a fire in the fireplace. I shed my leather jacket.

Judy took the chair, indicated the sofa for me.

"You're looking for answers about my girls," she began before I had settled in on the sofa.

"I am."

"You're having trouble with the sheriff in that regard." she went on. "Which is troubling to you, because he's your friend."

"You *say* you're not clairvoyant," I told her, smiling, "but if you keep divining facts like those, I'll never believe you."

"Given your father's profession," she sighed, staring into the fire, "I wouldn't imagine you'd need to be told the tricks of the trade."

I wasn't entirely surprised that this woman would know my father's occupation. Lots of people in Blue Mountain still remembered my parents' odd traveling show. It had been disbanded for over a decade, but stories still circulated about my father's magic act, and my mother: his lovely assistant. They'd performed several tricks that had never been explained and were the subject of some conjecture in the world of professional magicians—a world I knew nothing about.

"What's the surest way to guess the outcome of any problem?" she went on.

"To already know the answer before someone asks the question." Clearly.

"I feel I already know you," she said, a strange non sequitur. "You look a little like my beau. He has white hair, though his comes from being an albino whereas yours comes from worry."

"I look like your boyfriend?" I shifted on the sofa, trying to get a little eye contact.

"Same jawline, same lips." She finally turned my way, smiling. "Of course, he's cuter to me, but you're both pretty fine." She locked her eyes on mine.

"Thanks," I said, taken aback by her bold stare.

"He's Orvid Newcomb."

"Your boyfriend is a Newcomb?" I didn't even bother to hide my surprise.

The Newcomb family had been our most prominent one when the area around the mountain was first settled. The town had, in fact, been called Newcomb Junction until the 1920s. The family had grown gothic and spooky by then, and a quasi-incestuous relationship had produced several children who were born small. One of these offspring, Tristan, the famous, self-named Newcomb Dwarf, had owned the traveling show that had employed my parents. Blurting out the particulars of their family always seemed odd to the casual visitor in Blue Mountain, but to most natives it was nothing special, like people who live in New York and take the Empire State Building for granted.

"Orvid's the reason I live here." She returned her gaze to the fire. "We met in Chattanooga, but he wanted to come home. Maybe you can understand that."

Once again I had the eerie sensation that she was inside my mind.

Like Orvid, I was an odd prodigal, gone from our town for years, always swearing never to return. But something had drawn me back—was it really only two years ago? I told myself I'd come back to collect folklore, even admitted that Lucinda had been a part of my decision. But as I sat in Judy Dare's living room, I suspected that Orvid and I might have returned to Blue Mountain for other reasons. Maybe we'd come back to see if the town was ready to accept us for what we were, take us in. Maybe we were hoping the place would seem like *home*—at last.

"What makes you think I'm having trouble with Sheriff Needle?" I asked, mostly to shake darker thoughts from my mind.

"He came by. Told me not to talk to you. That seemed odd. Didn't you two work together on that mess with Truevine Deveroe?"

"We've worked together on things since we were boys," I answered her solemnly. "But that was before he became sheriff."

"It's a big responsibility," she agreed. "But he's missing a bet with you. You're the one to do it."

Her eyes welled, and she sniffed twice, finally reaching in her pocket for a tissue.

"Do what?" I leaned forward a little.

"You're not as ignorant as most around here," she said, dabbing her nose, "but you've got the same kind of stubbornness with words and ideas."

"What are you talking about?"

"Getting folks to admit they know the time of day around here," she shot back, "is like pulling hen's teeth."

"Oh," I sighed. "That. I do find it frustrating."

"But you do it yourself," she insisted. "You're doing it right now!"

Her voice was getting higher, and her face reddened.

"You can't be wandering around town picking up trash on the side of the railroad tracks and visiting these old fat boys and the junk-yard." Her voice was iron. "You have to help me!"

"Help you do what?" I implored, at sea.

"You have to help me get who killed my girls!"

Five

It took several moments for Judy to calm down, and even then her hands were still shaking.

"There's no evidence at this point that anyone killed those girls," I said as soothingly as I could manage.

"Don't insult me," she snapped. "Don't insult God. God does not take away a treasure, only something evil will do that."

"The girls were something special," I had to admit, mostly to veer her away from her emotional gestalt.

"You don't know how they were," she sniffed. "The first night I was ever in their house, had dinner with them, they were nothing but tads then. I was supposed to be the babysitter. We were all sitting around, looking down at the dishes and talking about this and that, and Rory spoke right up and said, 'So, Judy—pardon me for saying so, but you seem to be a midget.' I thought her mother would die."

"Sara is easily embarrassed." I grinned. "What did you say?"

"I let out a big old laugh." Judy's face was transformed with the memory of the girls. "'Well, I'll tell you, Rory,' I said, 'I am. That's just what I am, although most of us prefer to be called little people now days.' She says, 'Like the leprechauns?' Her mother made her apologize to me but I said, 'Being little isn't a disease; it's okay to talk about it. In fact, I kind of hate when people don't talk about it and try to pretend it doesn't exist, you know—I mean, I *am* shorter than anybody here.' And Tess stands up and says, 'I don't know, I might have you beat.' "

Judy looked up at me.

"Children get right to the heart of the matter, is my point." Judy sighed. "They don't mind talking, don't beat around the bush."

"I understand you were close to them."

"You don't understand a thing," she said plainly.

"All right, then explain it to me."

"Explain what?" she growled.

Asking the right questions in a situation where you don't know the answers is as much a matter of psychology as anything else. For years I'd asked people as ornery as Judy about their lives the same way. I knew there was treasure to be had, but I didn't know what it was, or how deeply it was buried.

Ask a question, then be quiet and listen, I always used to tell my students. *You can miss a lot if you're trying to think up your next question when the informant is talking.*

"Tell me about Orvid." I sat back. "You brought him up for a reason."

"He's little, if that's what you mean," she said, but it was nothing more than a statement of fact, "and he's what they call *albino,* white as milk. His hair's snow white, and his eyes are pinkish, and he can't go out in the sun long or it would kill him."

"You met him in Chattanooga," I prompted.

"I was standing at the bus stop in front of the Aquarium in the middle of the afternoon." She smiled unconsciously. "There was a kind of a gang of young tough boys and they were bothering me. Big, tanned college boys from Florida, I think. They were drunk. They would run at me, and at the last possible moment, they'd leapfrog over my head. So close it would mess up my hair. I was scared."

"Unbelievable. Were they saying anything?"

"Calling me names." She shrugged. "I'd heard them all before."

"Terrifying." I shook my head.

"Then," she said sweetly, "out of nowhere comes Orvid. His legs are kind of bowed out the way a lot of little people's legs are, and he walked with a cane. It was quite stylish: a wooden stick near as high as he was tall, with a shiny silver knob at the top and a metal cap of some kind at the bottom. I was scared to death, but Orvid seemed completely calm and even looked at his watch to see what time it was as he came to stand beside me at the bus stop. He told me, real quiet, that the bus would be along any minute and not to worry. Said he'd wait with me. I felt better."

She sat back, her smile bigger.

I had in my mind the image of the white-white, little man and the big, tanned boys leaping. I resisted the urge to comment.

"The college boys kept on saying things to us," she went on, swallowing, "and I was afraid they might do something worse when one of them made the mistake of going to jump over Orvid's head. Now, I didn't even see Orvid move except kind of out of the corner of my eye, but just as the man cleared the top of Orvid's hair and before his feet even hit the ground, Orvid grabbed ahold of the silver knob at the top of the cane and drew out the longest, meanest-looking knife blade I ever hope to see."

"The boy landed on top of it?" I leaned forward.

"Astride," she said casually. "Orvid turned that blade up so that the boy was kind of frozen, straddling the blade, and afraid to move. The other boys stopped talking all of a sudden. I mean, I'm sorry to say this, but that blade was a quarter of an inch away from making that boy a gelding."

Judy didn't look me in the eye.

"I was so scared, I couldn't speak," she went on, "but Orvid said to the boy, more calm than ever, 'Don't you think you should apologize to my date for scaring her?' and the boy said, right away, 'Absolutely. Ma'am, I am heartily sorry for disturbing you.' And at that exact moment the bus pulled up."

She grinned at me then.

"What did you do?"

"I jumped on the bus!" She smoothed her hair behind one ear. "Orvid put his cane back together and followed me right on. We sat all the way in the back and he escorted me to the house where I was staying."

"You were living in Chattanooga?" I asked.

"Studying. I was taking my degree."

"Really?" I leaned her way. "What was your course of study?"

"Dental assistant for juveniles," she told me confidently. "That's my line of work."

"And Orvid saw you home that afternoon," I coaxed.

"And he asked me out right away." She blushed. "I'll tell you what's the truth: I surely did let him kiss me that night. I thought he was about the most dashing man I'd ever seen, even in the movies."

"You let a stranger kiss you?" I teased.

"A stranger is only a stranger until you get to know them," Judy answered. "And by that time, they're a friend."

"You've dated him ever since?"

"We're engaged," she said, uncharacteristically girlish.

She held out her left hand and displayed a ring, antique, ornate, covered with diamonds.

"That's a family ring," I guessed.

"The Newcombs surely do have money," she acknowledged. "But I'm proud to say that Orvid works for a living. I help him with it, in fact."

"What's his business?"

"Cutlery salesman," she answered, mesmerized by the glitter of her own ring.

Six

"You know that Tristan Newcomb owned my parents' show before they took it over from him," I said, my voice husky.

"The Ten Show," she drawled. "Yes. These Newcombs, they own near about everything, don't they?"

Her voice betrayed a vast suspicion and a subtle hatred. Both were common in Blue Mountain where the Newcomb family was concerned, but I found it odd coming from a woman who was in love with a member of that cursed family.

I steered myself back to the issue at hand.

"Well, I'm telling you, Judy," I said, my voice a little flinty, "just as I told Lucinda: it's most likely that this was a terrible, terrible accident. No one tied them to a railroad track and ran over them with a train."

"Bullshit!" she snapped.

I confess to being taken aback by such an adult word in a child-sounding voice. I started to apologize for the phrase *ran over them,* but Judy went on before I could gather my thoughts.

"Would *you* sit on a train track and let the engine run you down?"

"Not deliberately," I confessed, "but if my truck stalled, the door was stuck; I misjudged the time I had—if I had been drinking, say, or taking drugs."

"Rory and Tess don't drink!" Judy stood. "And they don't fool with the drugs like a lot of these kids around here, so don't even start up with that mess. Somebody's responsible for this, somebody bad. I have proof. I swear to God, I'll get the person that did this, and you'd better help me or you'll regret it!"

Her voice had gone shrill.

"I know you're upset," I began, soothing, "and I'm unbelievably sorry for your loss—"

"That's it!" she screamed. "Orvid!"

A dark form appeared in the doorway.

Orvid Newcomb was made of white fire. His eyes shone like lanterns; his wild, pale hair seemed to crackle about his face. He was dressed in a light green linen shirt, rolled to the elbows, and black pants. On his frame, the clothing seemed mythic.

He stood in the doorway, both hands on his silver cane, a smile creasing the right corner of his mouth slightly upward. As an afterthought I realized he was barely four feet tall; it was hardly the first thing anyone would have noticed.

I could not take my eyes off him.

"I've so looked forward to this meeting, Doctor," he said softly.

His voice was hushed, deep, richer than complex Bordeaux.

"He makes a nice appearance," Judy said softly, "don't you think?"

"Certainly startling," I managed.

"Take your pick, Dr. Devilin," he whispered.

"My pick?" I still stared.

His pale eyes flickered, his smile increased.

"When Odin made the world and the sky," he told me, taking a step in my direction, "from the body and skull of Ymir, the first giant, my people lived under the earth, master craftsmen, great artists in steel and wood."

"Ymir?" I stammered. "That's Norse mythology."

"Or would you prefer the *little people*?" he shot back, his accent touched with a perfect brogue. "Fabulously wealthy drunkards whose special art was, I believe, shoes."

His stance took on a vague menace.

I exhaled and looked him squarely in the eye, realizing he was testing me: a challenge. He was trying to scare me, intimidate me with his grasp of my own discipline. As luck would have it, I knew what he was doing.

"Right," I said, settling back on the sofa, not rising to the bait. "I see show business is the curse of your family as well as mine. Nice entrance, though."

He and Judy exploded in laughter.

"You have to admit," he said, coming my way, "it would impress the rubes."

"It's your easy-reference world mythology that impresses me," I said, coming to my feet and offering my hand.

He grasped it. His thumb and little finger barely made it around my palm, but his grip was a vise.

"Odin," he said, "the father of the Norse gods, killed the giant Ymir and made the sea from his blood, I believe. The bowl of heaven was his skull. I like this vision of the gods and my imaginary ancestry much better than the sort of drunken shoemaker dwarves of Ireland."

"You do fit the Norse mold," I answered, "if you had anything to do with fashioning the cane you have. The Norse dwarves had a genius for metalwork and jewels. That cane's beautiful, and, if what Judy told me was true, potentially deadly?"

In answer, he took a step back and drew a long, thin silver blade from the hollow of his cane. It was at least three feet long with one dull side and one sharp side, coming to a needle point at the tip.

"I did create this myself," he said confidently. "Thanks for asking. Makes for a great demonstration at trade shows."

"You said you'd been looking forward to meeting me," I went on, taking my seat again.

Orvid put his blade away and sat on the table in front of me, his hand on Judy's.

"My cousin Tristan, who owned the show for which your parents worked, was my hero," he began. "He stood on his own two feet, eschewed family money, made a name for himself on his own terms, and retired rich without help from anybody."

"I thought you might be thinking about the rumors concerning Tristan and my mother," I said directly.

No point in beating about the bush. My mother had slept with half the population of our county, and her most notorious liaison was said to have been with Tristan, giving rise to the gossip that Tristan had been my father. He had not been, my father was the magician Fletcher Devilin, but rumors persisted.

"No." Orvid said slowly, "I don't think we're related, if that's what you mean, but we do favor one another in several ways."

"I noticed that," Judy interjected. "I told him so."

"I heard, sugar pie," he said sweetly to her, then turned to me. "But I've been looking forward to meeting you because Tristan told me so much about you."

"He did?" I'm certain my voice sounded skeptical. "I only met him once or twice, when I was quite young."

"He kept in touch with your mother for a long while," Orvid said, a light in his eyes. "You might not realize how much your mother bragged about you to other people."

"I generally prefer not to discuss my mother," I told him, shifting uncomfortably on the sofa. "I knew her better by reputation than by experience, and her reputation remains something of a scandal here in Blue Mountain."

"That's putting it mildly," Judy said, grunting a single laugh.

"All right," Orvid said, "I'll let it be for the moment, except to say that I've heard stories about you for many years. You're a strange, complex man, and I think that we're brothers of another sort even if we're not related in any biological way."

"This whole matter of family," I told him, clearing my throat, "it's not something I can talk about."

He heard the clenched nature of the words, saw the tightened muscles of my neck. I watched him observe, assess, and decide.

"I only bring it up," he went on breezily, "because I think we could work together to find who murdered Rory and Tess Dyson."

I leaned forward a little, looked from Judy's face to Orvid's.

"May I speak freely?"

They both nodded, assuming I was about to reveal something important.

"I think, Mr. Newcomb," I began, "that you and I are alike at least this much: we're both interested in helping someone we love deal with a traumatic event. Lucinda loved those girls, clearly Judy did too. I think the best way to help is to face facts: a train hit a car. Sad to say."

"Ordinarily I might be inclined to agree with you, Dr. Devilin," Orvid answered, inclining his head toward the darker part of the room, "but not in this case."

"Why not?" I tried to hide my irritation.

He smiled indulgently.

"Because in this case, I saw the murderer."

I managed a wry tone despite Orvid's insistent gaze.

"Have you told Sheriff Needle?" I drawled, smiling.

"That presents something of a dilemma." Orvid's voice was calm, but he suddenly looked to the floor, as if something there had caught his eye. "He was there."

"Skidmore saw the murderer too?" I pressed, still completely unconvinced that Orvid had seen anything.

"Not exactly," Orvid sighed. "He was busy."

"What was he doing?"

"Watching me." Orvid sniffed and finally turned his face upward. "But that's another story for another time. I did see something, and I'm convinced that there's more to this situation than meets the immediate eye."

"You saw something," I said hesitantly, "*where,* exactly?"

"I saw something happen at the railroad crossing," Orvid reported, "just before the girls pulled up to the tracks."

"Another car?"

"No, I was trying to conclude my business quickly and had to fetch something on the other side of the abandoned station, but I could hear the girls laughing. I assumed everything was all right. The car sat at the crossing for as long as two minutes that way, and I think the engine was off."

"But you didn't see any of this," I said, absolutely certain he was lying.

"I had some business to attend to," he repeated at a louder volume. "The next thing I heard was the train leaning on its whistle. Then the crash."

Orvid shuddered without realizing it.

"You stayed to talk to the investigators, of course," I said, eyes half-closed.

"I did not." Again Orvid avoided my eyes. "My business was of a certain nature, a delicate nature, and I was not interested in explaining to the police why I was there."

"Especially since Skidmore was there watching you."

"Well, yes, but the train wreck distracted him."

"I see." I sat forward. "Is any of this remotely true?"

"What?" Orvid snapped back.

"Skidmore was there?" I ignored his ire. "He saw the accident?"

"No," Orvid growled. "He heard it, exactly as I did."

"Only he went running toward it," I sighed, sitting back, "and you ran away."

"Dr. Devilin," Orvid said slowly, "it's really ill-advised to take a tone like this with me."

"What was your business?" I asked him point-blank.

"That's off the point!" He stood, his volume cranked. "We have to get clear what happened at that crossing, what the girls were doing just before the train came! And you haven't yet heard the most salient fact concerning the sheriff!"

"Sweetheart," Judy whispered gently.

Silence dropped over everything in the room like a sudden darkness.

"Yes, all right," Orvid trailed off, realizing he was losing his temper. Judy sighed.

"Different people," Judy began meekly, looking down at her fingers, "deal with death in different ways. I look for who's to blame. Dr. Devilin has more of an acceptance of things, Orvid. Most likely the better path. Maybe we should let this go. It was just an accident."

"You know you could talk to Lucinda," I said softly. "I think she'd get a lot out of speaking with someone who loved the girls as much as she did."

"That would be nice." Judy stood. "I'll see you to the door."

Orvid had locked his eyes on Judy's profile. He didn't move, but a razor-thin smile was on his lips.

As Judy walked me out of the living room, and she exchanged the same hint of a smile with Orvid, I realized that she did not actually believe acceptance was a better path than blame.

She had suddenly given up on asking for my help. She was just getting me out of the way, making ready to wreak her revenge.

Seven

I was out the front door, down the sidewalk, and into my truck—still trying to fathom Judy's dark thoughts—when it began to rain in earnest. It was a cold rain, brushing a gray metal sheen over everything, making all nature impenetrable.

The truck rumbled, I turned on the headlights. I took a last look at the Dyson household. As I did, the front curtains trembled. Someone in the house had been watching me. I assumed that Mr. Dyson was deciding whether he should call the police. *The police* in this case meant an old friend of mine, or was he an ex-friend?

The day had already filled with a sufficient amount of sadness to warrant a quick escape from that thought. I focused my mind instead on Orvid's assessment of the facts surrounding the train accident.

Obviously he had been engaged in some illegal activity along the train tracks and was inventing material to appease his girlfriend. I was interested in what his nefarious business might have been, and under ordinary circumstances I would simply have gone to Skid and asked him why he was investigating Orvid. But there it was: the infamous "circle of thought," and a tighter one than usual. Running away from an idea is always the surest way to run right back into it. Before I'd shifted the truck into first, my mind had already come back to Skidmore.

I'd always been his staunchest supporter, and the innuendo that swirled in the town's gutters about his relationship with his secretary,

Melissa Mathews, seemed ridiculous to me. Skid loved his wife, Girlinda, who was not only the best cook in the county but the best shot as well: two primary ingredients of their marital bliss. Still, guilt makes a man behave more strangely than a rabid dog. A guilty man will contort his body to accommodate the thorns that grow on his soul until he's hobbled and bent.

And Skid had begun walking with a slight stoop.

Such thoughts almost made me pass the hitchhiker by.

When I was fresh out of college, I'd spent a year in Europe thumbing rides. I'd sworn then that I would never pass a fellow traveler without stopping. Even though years and an increasing malevolence in the world had separated my oath from the man I saw on the road, I hit the brakes nonetheless.

I could see him in my rearview mirror. He wasn't even looking my way. I'd passed him by, so he was waiting for the next car or truck. I backed up a little and honked the horn. It seemed to startle him. He looked all around, not in the direction of the noise.

When he realized I was waiting for him, he nodded and walked, slowly, to the passenger side.

As he drew nearer, I was glad I'd stopped. He was an older man, grizzled, white-haired, unshaven, dressed in black. And drenched from head to foot.

I leaned over and opened the door for him.

"Come on in."

He stood his ground.

"I don't want to get your seat all wet." His voice rumbled so deep and hollow that it startled me. It sounded weirdly amplified, even in the jagged white noise of the rain and my truck's engine.

"I don't care about the seat," I told him honestly. "Where are you headed?"

He hesitated, then nodded again and climbed in slowly. I could smell cheap alcohol oozing from every one of his pores.

"Down the road," he intoned.

"You're in luck then," I said amiably, eyes back on the road. "That's exactly my destination."

"Name's Hiram Frazier." His vacant eyes stared nowhere. "I'm a preacher, and the Lord's whipping boy."

"A preacher." I pulled onto the road, falling into my folk-collecting mode without realizing it.

"Had a church in Pistol Creek, Tennessee, many years back. Good congregation: sober, plain, and mean. But the Lord took me as his testing scourge. I awoke one morning to find my wife, my jewel, stone-cold dead in the bed beside me. No warning, no word of farewell."

"I'm sorry." I wanted to tell him that his story sounded familiar to me, somehow. Maybe I'd collected it somewhere. But he cut me off before I could completely search my memory.

"Sh," he snapped. "I'm not finished. Damn. Now I have to start over. I had a church in Pistol Creek, Tennessee, many years back. Good congregation: sober, plain, mean."

"I don't need to hear the story," I sighed.

"She was *dead*," he snarled, leaning forward, hands on the dashboard. "You'd best hear the story. We all come to death, brother, one way or another. This is my calling: to be a traveling creature, a beacon to woman and man. If you would shun that burning hell, you'd take a warning by me."

His vehemence took me aback. I stole a glance at his profile. He was staring out the window, eyes wide, face white and glassy as marble. I had a sudden realization.

"I think I saw you the other night on my way home," I told him. "Waiting by the railroad tracks in Blue Mountain."

"I ride the rails. I preach to those who do the same, poorly sojourners. But I have never been in this town before. I stay shy of Georgia. Had a bad experience once."

"What sort of experience?"

"What?" He turned my way.

"You had a bad experience in Georgia."

"Never been to Georgia before," he shot back angrily. "I've had many a bad experience elsewhere, though. My wife, my jewel, she was stone-cold dead."

"You were a preacher, you say?" I lowered my voice, trying to calm him.

"I'm the Lord's whipping boy," he said, slightly more subdued. "I take a warning with me wherever I go. I was in South Carolina yesterday. Or day before yesterday. That's how I know I was not in Georgia. Preached a sermon there that set many a heart to fear. Fire on my tongue."

"In South Carolina," I confirmed.

"Had a vision," he went on, mostly oblivious of my presence. "Two virgins in a pumpkin carriage. Happy children. Laughing. God smote them. For no good reason. Just took these sweet girls. Sent them a black snake belching smoke, which roared over them like an iron thunder. They were gone before the noise of it left the air. Gone."

I slowed the truck.

"Wait," I managed. "This was a vision you had?"

"In a train yard." He nodded curtly, then his voice rose, a grating crescendo. "The vision set my tongue ablaze. Words rose up like sparks from a coal. What the Lord would love He first rebukes. What God cherishes, he punishes. Good works are scattered like pearls before swine in this earthy prison. Evil deeds latch on. Evil deeds make a pallet where all the lost may lay a weary head. You do Evil in this world, God turns a blind eye. You do Good, it's a magnet for His ire. This is a Universe of opposites, brother driver. God will not allow Good to go unbalanced. This is the message of Jesus Christ: Jesus came into this world shining such Grace that it soiled the lake of humanity. We cannot accept that much white light. We must be plunged into the depths of darkness lo these long years since His ascending to make a balance on the land. Excess of Good provokes excess of Evil. That's the trick of our God, the God of Abraham. He sends us his Goodness, but it burns too bright and attracts the darkness. A black moth to a white flame. Do *not* perform good works in this world of woe, brother driver, or you risk the thunder of dark balance, the tipping of the scales. There is much work left to be done."

Instantly he fell silent.

Shaken by the power of his voice and the absolute surrealism of his speech, I nearly stopped the truck. I realized I was shivering a little.

"Here," I stammered. "Let me turn on the heater. You must be cold."

"Don't feel cold." He sighed. "Nor heat. Nor hunger pangs."

"I'm sorry about your wife," I said softly, hoping to rein him in.

"Stone-cold dead," he muttered.

"What's Pistol Creek like? Your hometown."

"Have not been there in many's the long year," he whispered. "But in my childhood there was red honeysuckle, I remember. You could eat the whole flower. Used to do that."

"It's in the mountains?"

"Hilly," he acknowledged.

"What else?" I prompted, attempting to keep him calm.

"Long ago, people there knew me." His voice was lead. "Someone knew me enough to love me, marry me. People were happy to ordain me into a ministry. Sold me a house, said *hey* to me in the grocery store, went fishing with me. Long ago."

"But you have the memories of that life," I said slowly, encouraging him to recall the human being inside the shell.

"You couldn't tell it now, but they say I used to be good-looking." He smiled. His face softened. "So good-looking, in fact, that it saved my life."

"How?" I smiled back.

"When I was a young man," he answered, settling back in his seat a little, "I was in love with a girl name of Frannie. We ran off one weekend and got married. Didn't tell the families, just ran off. Of course, we went right on living at our parents's homes, both of us. Hid the truth from our folks. But we'd see each other on the sly every day, somehow."

"Why didn't you just tell everyone you were married and live together?" I knew the answer, but I wanted him to keep talking.

"You don't know what a little town is like. Her father would have shot me dead."

"I suppose"—I laughed—"but he would have shot you twice as dead if he'd caught you with his daughter and *not* known you were married."

"That's exactly what did happen!" He slapped his knee.

"My God."

"That's the point of the story." He lowered his voice. "You understand, we behaved as married people do, and by and by Frannie found herself with child. At first we could keep it hid, but by the sixth month it was beginning to be obvious."

"I'd imagine."

"Frannie was bigger every day. Of course, her father finally realized it. Confronted her in the kitchen one suppertime. Says, 'You're pregnant, by God!' Which was a shock to one and all. You did not say the world *pregnant* in those days. It wasn't polite."

"In my hometown," I agreed, hoping to turn our exchange into something like a conversation, "you could never say the word. Once when I was six or seven, I heard my parents were talking about a girl in church and shaking their heads. They said she had *broken her leg,* that's the phrase they used. I suppose they thought it would explain why she hadn't been in church in a while. But they all raised their eyebrows and nodded knowingly."

"Broke her leg." He grinned. "Never heard that one."

"The problem was," I went on, glad my passenger was mellowing, "I saw the girl the next day at the grocery store, and she wasn't wearing a cast or walking with crutches or anything. I was very little, as I was saying, shopping with my mother, and I turned to her and said, very loudly, 'That girl didn't break her leg at all, she just got fat!'"

"Oh, Lord." He laughed. "Bet your mama wailed the tar out of you."

"It's the only time I ever recall her giving me a whipping. And I believed even then that it was more for the benefit of the girl in the store than it was for me. The girl was quite embarrassed. I think she might have even started to cry. I had no idea what I had done, but for a considerable time after that, I thought that breaking a leg was something bad; wrong to talk about in mixed company."

He nodded. Even chuckled.

"But I interrupted your story." I turned the windshield whippers on high. "You were saying Frannie was with child."

"She was in big trouble," he continued. "Her father demanded her to confess. She says, 'Yes, sir, I am, but let me explain.' She was ready to tell him that she was married. But her father was so mad he wouldn't let her finish the sentence. He just said, 'Who was it, by God! Tell me this minute or I'll beat you raw.' And she said, 'It was Hiram Frazier, Daddy, but let me explain.' She was trying to bring up the fact that our little baby was legal, you understand. But her father was so mad that he charged out of his house right then and there, grabbed up his hunting knife, and came to kill me."

"Jesus," I said before I thought better of it.

"Don't blaspheme," Hiram warned me casually, and went right on with his story. "So, anyway, her daddy ran off down the holler like a madman, with Frannie chasing after him yelling, 'Daddy, no, don't kill him!' But her father was filled with fire and it clogged up his ears. He'd never seen me, but he knew where our family lived. He went storming up to the Frazier household, didn't even knock on the door. My mom and dad weren't home. I was in the kitchen studying the schoolbooks. When I saw Frannie's father coming at me with a knife, I figured the old man had found out about the marriage and was mad about that. I lit off out the back door and into the woods. All the while, little Frannie was yelling, 'Wait, Daddy, wait!' Finally, by the side of Pistol Creek, body of water for which our town is named, the old man caught up with me and he was going to kill me sure. He spun me around so as not to stab me in the back, but just then, as he's about to stick me in the heart with his knife, he finally got a good look at my face. For the longest while—seemed like a year to me—the old man just stood there frozen, staring at me, knife held up high over my head."

"What was he doing?" I was lost in the story.

"Well, Frannie had the same question," Frazier went on, clearly enjoying the telling. "About that time she caught up with us, all out of breath on account of she's so close to having a baby, and she says, 'Daddy, what are you doing?' Well, the old man drops his knife, kind of stunned like, and turns around to Frannie. 'Lordy, girl,' he says to her, 'I have *never* in my life seen a boy this good-looking. He's too handsome to stick with a knife. I want to kill him, but I just can't!'"

I couldn't help laughing.

"And Frannie's sobbing by this time," Frazier went on, grinning. "'You didn't let me tell you that everything's all right because we got married last year and he's about to graduate from school and he's going to be a minister and it'll all be fine as long as you don't go putting a knife in him.'"

Hiram Frazier laughed so hard he began to cough. I was amazed at how the laughter changed his face. For a moment, he seemed like most other men.

"And her father was so happy," he managed between bouts of rasping his throat, "that he gave us money to buy a little house."

"Well, it's a great story," I concluded.

"I had happy times." Frazier sobered a little. "I have not always been as you see me now."

"You're still a preacher. You still do your work."

"How do you know I'm still a preacher?"

"You told me a moment ago, about your sermon in South Carolina."

"Two girls in a pumpkin," he whispered.

"Yes," I heard myself say. "That image may have been prophetic." I had no idea why I would say such a thing.

"Wouldn't be surprised." He closed his eyes. "When God wants to punish you, first He drives you mad. And you believe me when I say there's no greater madness than the gift of sight."

"You see things in your mind that later come true." I took him seriously.

"What do you think I saw in my vision?" he said, his voice hollow.

"Two girls in an orange Volkswagen were hit by a train a few nights ago here in this town," I said quickly, "or in the town outside of which I picked you up, I mean. You see how your images do sort of predict—"

"The gift of sight came to me when Frannie died," Hiram interrupted, absolutely emotionless. "It's a pestilence. I don't care to speak of it."

"I'm sorry."

"I don't want sympathy," he said softly. "I want a ride to the next town, and a contribution to my work if you can spare it."

"Have we met before?" I shot him a glance. "Your story sounds familiar."

"I meet so many people in my work."

"Speaking of your work, what was your congregation like, the one who heard you talk about the girls in the pumpkin?"

"Bums," he said instantly, "hoboes, drunkards, miscreants; wandering hulks: the cast out. The unhuddled masses yearning to breathe foul. America had a beautiful dream. I preach to the ones who were shaken awake, thrown from their beds, shunned by the dreamers. I teach them, tell them about their worth."

"It's good work, if I correctly understand what you're doing."

"You don't know." His voice returned to the sediment from which it had risen. He reverted to his previous mien, all lucidity dropping away. "I teach them about their contribution to this world: they are the dark part, the horror that balances light. They are God's counterweight. There is much work yet to be done in the world of Night. God saw the darkness and said let there be light, but He wasn't satisfied with that, so he divided the light from the darkness so that all people would know both. In the contrasting of opposites we see the world. How do we know good? By holding it up to evil. How do we know right? By seeing wrong, and recoiling. I am the envoy of darkness, the champion of the counterbalance. I bring back the deep Black to a world sick with pale eyes. I refresh the night with continual gifts, and then I bare my back to God's scourge. I am His favored punishment. I am the omega of God's lash, the final resting place of His whip. After me there will be no other. After me there will be a sufficiency of darkness upon the land, because my words are mighty, my message is cut from obsidian. This is my sermon, the final Revelation, and it is the Ending of the Light!"

His hands were shaking and his voice had risen to a deafening pitch in the cab of my truck.

"Yes, I understand your theory," I broke in, matching his volume. "But I disagree with it."

"Good!" he stormed back. "That only proves my point. You go ahead and be a creature of light. I'm your dark twin. I'm the shadow you never see. I'm the leaden stone that allows you to shine like gold. You owe me a debt, brother driver. And I want it now."

He turned my way, menacing and hot.

"What?" I tried to look at him and keep my eye on the road.

"Pay!" his voice stabbed.

Without warning his hand lashed out and I flinched, certain he would hit me. I shot a glance his way and saw the silver glint of a knife in his other hand.

I panicked. The truck swerved, and tires skidded across the wet blacktop. He was shuddered away from me, and the truck complained wildly. Thank God no one was coming at us from the opposite direction. We would have been killed. After a moment I was able to right the truck and slow down.

His hand was still out, palm up. His eyes were rimmed in coal red, burning into mine. He hadn't even noticed that we'd nearly crashed.

I pulled over to the side of the road, caught my breath.

"Pay!" he insisted.

I saw the vacant look in his eyes. He was not Hiram Frazier, he was the wandering creature, bereft of most of his humanity.

"Take back your hand," I told him evenly, "or I'll break every one of those fingers. It shouldn't be hard. Your bones are brittle."

"My bones are *hollow*," he snarled.

"All the easier for me to break," I returned, louder.

He sighed, pulled his hand back.

"I need a place to stay tonight," he said, his voice turned to pathos.

"You've mistaken my willingness to pick up a hitchhiker for a weakness you think you can exploit." I kept my voice firm, but lessened the threatening tone. "Your entire religious philosophy seems to be easily summed up by the cliché 'No good deed goes unpunished.' It probably seems like the devil's pretzel logic to most of the rubes you speak to, but I've seen masters of that kind of magic. I'm not your audience."

"Your parents were carnival people," he muttered slowly. "Mostly carny folk use that word *rube* in a case such as this."

"They were." No point explaining any more than that to him.

"Okay." He sighed. "Then here's the whole story: I need a drink. Take me to a place where I can get one, give me ten dollars."

"I'll set you out right here," I countered, "and then call the police to tell them where I left you. Happens the sheriff's a friend of mine."

"Don't do that." He shook his head.

"You're getting out of this truck now." I stared him down.

He considered his options, weighed my change of tone, and decided on the better part of valor. He took the door handle and opened his door. The rain had abated slightly. Only then did I see that he was not holding a knife in his right hand at all, though I had no idea what it was: only a flash of silver, then gone.

Confused, I started to speak, but he went first.

"You'll regret this," he said calmly as he slid out of the seat. "I'll remember you."

"No, you won't," I corrected. "You don't even remember where you were two nights ago."

"North Carolina!" he bellowed suddenly, rage burning his face. "Preaching!"

"Not really," I told him curtly, shifting into first. "I saw you two nights ago in my hometown."

I pulled the truck forward, the passenger-side door almost closed.

"I've never been to Georgia," he yelled as I pulled back onto the road.

I shifted into second, kept my eye on the road, and reached across the seat to shut the door completely. As I did, the stench of the man, still clinging to the seat, momentarily overwhelmed me.

I sat back behind the wheel, picked up speed, and rolled down my window. The rain splattered in, washed my face, a cold baptism.

I finally gave a glance to my rearview mirror. Hiram Frazier was nowhere to be found.

Clearly I'd seen a ghost. Theories concerning ghosts existed in abundance in the study of folklore, and I ran through most of them in my mind on the drive back to my cabin.

The primary thought has always been that revenants are spirits who cannot leave the earth because of unfinished business: murder victims looking for their killers, lovers separated too soon, wronged souls seeking retribution.

My own usual explanation for the supposed presence of ghosts was that they were merely a memory strong enough in the observer's mind as to manifest a physical form. Of course, my theory offered nothing in the way of explanation for Hiram Frazier.

By the time I finished reviewing these ghostly concepts in my mind, I had arrived home and the air had turned chillier.

I wanted hot espresso and apple pie.

My cabin was dull-cold. I hadn't bothered to turn on the heat, and it would take hours to really warm the house.

Instead I dashed upstairs for a glorious hot shower and a blessed change of clothing. Forty minutes later I was in my kitchen dressed in new black jeans, a black mock turtleneck, and my stockinged feet. I loaded the espresso machine with oily black coffee beans and stood silently while the symphony of machine noises clicked and hummed.

I even had one slice of apple tart left in my refrigerator from one of Lucinda's previous, extraordinary masterpieces. I set the oven at 350 to warm it.

There were many secrets to the dessert's success, including a crust that vanished on the tongue, and tree-fresh apples seared in butter and Calvados. I had watched her make the same dish perhaps a dozen times, but when I tried to duplicate the recipe in the sanctity of my own kitchen, the result was a sad excuse for anything culinary, so I was glad to have a leftover of the genuine article.

I set the last precious slice of tart on a square of aluminum foil, placed it in the oven, and set the timer. The espresso machine had done its work, and I sipped a demitasse staring out the window at wet leaves. I felt comforted for the first time in several days.

I had a sudden impulse, a lonely one, to call my friend Dr. Andrews in Atlanta. I thought I might convince him to help with the depressing work I had to do. He always lifted my spirits. I hadn't heard from him in a few weeks, so a call was in order no matter what the circumstances. But given that my greatest friend and ally on Blue Mountain, Sheriff Skidmore Needle, was absolutely disinterested in continuing our friendship, Andrews seemed essential to my well-being.

I turned down the oven, reached for the phone, and dialed.

He answered on the eleventh ring.

"Andrews," he mumbled.

"Devilin," I countered.

"Dev!" His voice sprang into high gear. "This is a startling coincidence. I was going to call you tonight. You'll never guess what great luck I've had. The Globe, the Globe Theatre in London—"

"I knew which Globe you meant," I interrupted.

"They've asked me to direct their next production of *The Winter's Tale*." He could barely contain himself.

"That's fantastic. When do you go?"

"Tomorrow!" He nearly leapt through the phone. "I'm leaving tomorrow. They only called this morning. I mean, I'm taking over for someone who dropped out, obviously, but I'm directing at the *Globe*!"

"No one deserves it more."

"Shut up," he said, dismissing the compliment immediately. "I was going to call you because you have to come with me. I've already seen to the extra ticket. You just have to drive down to Atlanta tonight, leave your truck at my place, and fly to London with me tomorrow."

"I can't," I stammered.

"You don't understand," he rushed in. "I'm not paying for your ticket. *They* are. The Globe. I told them you were my musical consultant, that you were a folklore expert and you had picked the perfect traditional English tunes from the period for the production. You can do that, can't you?"

"I could," I tried to tell him.

"It's settled then," he took off. "You're working. Isn't it amazing?"

I stared at the dial on the telephone. I was a single breath away from asking him when our flight was when the buzzer on the oven's timer went off. I glared at the oven for interrupting my vision of London. Then I smelled the apple pie and thought of the cook. In the next second I realized I wasn't going anywhere but over to Lucinda's house that night.

"Dev?" Andrews prodded. "Are you still there?"

"Sorry." I blew out a long breath. "Sorry, Winton. I can't go."

Obviously taken aback by my uncharacteristic use of his first name, Andrews fell silent.

"Something's happened here," I went on. "Lucinda's nieces have both been killed. They were hit by a train. She needs my help. In fact, that was why I was calling you. I wanted you to come up tonight and help me with my investigation."

"Investigation?" he said softly.

"Some people seem to believe they were murdered."

Silence again held sway.

"Dev," Andrews stuttered, "I mean, I can't pass up—"

"No, no, no," I interrupted quickly. "I don't intend for you to pass up this opportunity. But I'm needed here for the moment, so I can't leave for London tomorrow."

"I'm sorry, Fever." His voice was gentle.

"Look," I said, bucking up, "there's every possibility that the entire matter will be set to rest in a few days. If that's the case, does your invitation still hold?"

"Of course," he shot back immediately. "I won't even be cozied in for a week or so. I'll send you all the information tonight, the place where we're staying, the background on the play. The ticket you can change anytime. Incidentally, you have *read* the play?"

"I have. But it's been a while. There are songs?"

"Six, actually, sung by Autolycus. And later there's a dance of twelve satyrs."

"For which you will also need music," I guessed.

"Read it, refresh your memory," he instructed, "and pick fifteen or twenty good melodies."

"That many?"

"Choices."

"Right," I said.

"Dev? Is there any chance you'll actually do this? Come to England this fall, I mean?"

"Honestly, I don't know."

"Okay." He didn't bother to hide his disappointment. "Still, look at the songs, see what you think. I'd better nip off. Packing."

"Of course." I hesitated. "Have a good flight."

"Exactly," he mumbled, unsure how to get off the phone.

"I'm proud of you, Andrews. You'll do this splendidly."

"Thanks, Dev," he answered huskily.

"All right," I sighed. "Good-bye, then."

"All right."

We hung up. That was that.

I reached for the oven, quite depressed.

In a skull-splitting flash of recollection, like an instant migraine, I suddenly thought of a line from one of the songs in *A Winter's Tale*, perhaps prompted by Andrews's asking for my help on his project at the Globe. *Lawn as white as driven snow / Cypress black as e'er was crow.* I realized I knew it because I'd used it many times in one of my university lectures concerning how the concept of Taoist opposites (yin and yang, black and white) can be used as a tool for interpreting traditional American songs. The Appalachian variant from *Lonesome Dove* was an example: *The Crow is black you know my love / Although she may turn white.*

"Only by comparing radical opposites," my lecture generally concluded, "can we truly understand these songs, or, indeed, anything about the world in which we live."

It was exactly Hiram Frazier's apocalyptic vision of universal balance.

Eight

A quest for universality in life is laudable, and the recognition that there are more similarities than differences between seemingly disparate philosophies is the most important step toward a universal acceptance. I was, however, absolutely unwilling to pursue the way in which Hiram Frazier and I were alike.

To shake off the gloom, instead, I called Lucinda.

The phone rang almost as long as it had when I called Andrews.

"Hello?" she finally answered.

"I've had quite a day already," I said softly into the phone. "How are *you* doing?"

"Getting ready for the funeral. When are you coming?" There was a rustling sound. "No, you'll have to meet me there. We're about to be late."

She'd set herself to a kind of grim determination, her best way of handling a funeral for someone she loved. I'd seen the mood before, understood it, accepted it.

"I can be there if you want me to," I said, "but I'd prefer to take a nap."

"Come to the funeral," she complained. "You're not old enough to nap in the afternoon."

"Einstein napped in the afternoon," I offered lamely.

"Yes, well," she chided, "when you come up with your own unified field theory, you can take a nap. Until then, you have to be my date at the funeral."

"A funeral's not a date," I grumbled.

"What's the matter with you?" she rejoined in amazement. "In this town? Funerals and weddings are the best dates we've got. They'll have good food."

"Speaking of which," I said, "hold on."

I set down the phone, got a hot pad from the drawer by the stove, and took out the warmed slice of apple tart.

"Sorry," I told her, taking up the phone again. "I had the last bit of one of your apple tarts warming in the oven and I couldn't risk scorching it."

"Don't eat that now," she said sternly. "It'll spoil your appetite for funeral food."

Funeral food.

"But I just warmed it up," I told her, staring down at the perfect golden triangle, its heaven-scented steam rising to my face.

"Set it back in the fridge," she told me in no uncertain terms, "put on a sports coat, and meet me at the Methodist church."

"The Methodist?" I asked, surprised, considering what I knew to be the Dyson family religious disparity. "Not the Baptist or the Catholic?"

"It's a compromise." She sounded impatient. "Are you coming?"

"I suppose I have to."

"You do."

I knew she was right. Small-town code demanded that I attend. If I didn't, it would make my investigation more difficult afterward. It could even affect my future folk-material collecting in general. Missing a funeral of this import could have repercussions for years in Blue Mountain.

I could just hear June Cotage, for example: "I suppose when I die, you'll take a nap instead of coming to my funeral too."

I had no choice.

"See you there," I sighed.

"You're a good man, Fever," Lucy said sweetly, and hung up.

I gazed longingly at the apple tart, then began to fold the edges of the aluminum foil to put it back in the refrigerator.

"Paradise," I told it, "once nearly was mine. What's that from? *South Pacific?*"

The tart did not know; or if it did, kept its silent secret.

A funeral in Blue Mountain was always a social occasion as much as a memorial service. Folks dressed up, everyone brought food to the fellowship hall, a modicum of genuine sympathy and goodwill were in evidence. Of course, the dressing up was a declaration of economic status, the food a serious competition, and much of the sympathy never seemed to me to run overly deep.

The Methodist church was newly painted white from grounded cinder blocks to pointed high steeple, as it had been every six months since its original construction. The roof was also either retarred or replaced once a year. The building was nearly 150 years old, but it looked like a brand-new movie set.

Inside, the floors were polished gold, the pews were chocolate bronze, spotless and uncomfortable. The only stained glass was behind the altar, a lovely 1930s WPA project depiction of Jesus holding a lamb and smiling. The other windows were clear and looked out on one side at perfect green cedars and on the other at the manicured meeting grounds.

The place exemplified the cleanliness that was closest to godliness.

I was late, and the entire church was packed by the time I tiptoed in. Pastor Davis, regal in a black robe, was speaking about Tess in well-pronounced, round tones.

"I was thinking about the wrens in the spring of the year," he was saying, "and how the hours and the seasons turn like a wheel. Only yesterday these sweet girls were in a school play. Only last week they were riding bicycles and singing in the choir. But I believe that the soul occupies the body just the way the body occupies a house, or wrens nest in a tree."

I slipped in next to Lucinda, an ash-colored wool jacket over the rest of my black attire. Watertight, black construction boots had replaced my high-tops. Knowing I'd be tardy, she'd taken a place near the back and saved a spot for me beside her on the aisle.

"You'll be late to your *own* funeral, you know," she chided softly in my ear.

"Sh," I whispered, "I'm trying to listen to the funeral lecture."

She grinned.

Lucinda's smile made me think about her mother's funeral, years before. Lucinda had dressed in in black and stood somber-faced, but I knew she didn't really feel that. Everyone expected her to be sad, so she pretended to be, but she was actually quite happy.

"Mama always believed in a better home waiting in the sky," she'd told me confidentially. "When it was her time to go, I couldn't think of anything better than that. No more worry, no more trouble, no more pain in the body or in the mind. And she could see Daddy and Grandma."

"And Patsy Cline," I teased, "whom she always admired."

"Hush." She shook her head. "The point is, I have acted out my false sorrow, but my heart deep down is glad."

I smiled too. That sort of *acting* is a part of everyone's life. People say what they think they're supposed to say, or what they're told would be best.

"And as to Rory," Pastor Davis went on from his podium, "I recall how she thought a certain friendship ring had been stolen by her fifth-grade teacher, Mrs. Barksdale, the 'meanest woman' in the county."

Nearly everyone in the church laughed. We had all heard the story dozens of times.

"Rory and her best friend, Emma," the pastor told us again, "were caught talking in class, and Mrs. Barksdale said they were not allowed to talk to one another for the rest of the school year. It seemed a harsh punishment, but in our town the teacher is always right. So Emma gave Rory a silver ring the next day, a token of friendship, out on the playground. The ring would replace their conversations. Alas, Mrs. Barksdale saw this happen and took the ring away from Rory, saying it was forbidden. Mrs. Barksdale told the girls she would give the ring back at the end of the year. But at the end of that year, when Rory and Emma went together to ask for the ring back, Mrs. Barksdale told them she had no idea what they were talking about. The girls protested, and Mrs. Barksdale, in a rage, changed both of their final grades from A to B. That was the only year Rory ever got a B. Several years later, as you all know, Mrs. Barksdale succumbed to liver cancer. Rory, then in middle school, asked to sing at the funeral. She said it was her way of making peace with her old teacher. Church members may recall that Tess joined her sister in the loveliest version I personally have ever heard of one of our favorite hymns. The choir will now stand and sing for us the song that Rory sang at that funeral. We pray we may attempt, in the way Rory did, to make peace with our terrible loss."

The singers stood. The organ made a gentle nest of sound, and voices rose from it on invisible wings. The choir sang "Be Thou My Vision." Nearly everyone cried. Most remembered the girls' singing, angel voices in three-quarter time. We sang every verse in the book, and even I was sorry to hear us relinquish its final chord.

"And now," Pastor Davis said quietly at the conclusion of the hymn, "if you would all join us in the fellowship hall adjacent to this chapel, we'll share food with one another while the caskets are moved to the burial ground. Burial in one hour."

Five minutes later, the fellowship hall was packed. I strained my eyes to catch a glimpse of Judy, knowing she would be there, wondering if Orvid would be with her. Unfortunately I was immediately distracted by the folding tables laden with food.

A long line moved slowly past fifty or sixty choice items. People were laughing, talking, eating. I did not speak, preferring to concentrate on securing the best the buffet had to offer. Within ten minutes I had a paper plate packed to the edges, carefully selected and artfully arranged. I was trying to navigate to a wall where I could be safe from jostling. Precious cargo occupied every square millimeter of my plate: potato salad with bits of apple-smoked bacon, thumbnail-sized whole pickled beets, and a cassoulet of wild duck, black mushrooms, and white beans.

We boasted several prominent members of Ducks Unlimited in our county, and I fancied that the duck on my plate was fresh, and superbly prepared. I was wishing I'd had a proper steel fork instead of the white plastic monstrosity I felt irritating the fingers of my left hand.

I made it to a corner of the windowless cinder-block walls; breathed a sigh of relief. Just as I was about to settle against the concrete and address the duck, Lucinda called my name.

"Fever."

I searched for her face in the crowd, found it by the door.

I made it back through the fellowship hall to the door quickly, wearing a mask of patience.

"I'm trying to eat my duck," I explained to Lucinda as I approached.

"I see," she said distractedly. "You've got to come in the church fast. Skidmore's in there trying to stop the girls from being buried."

The fellowship hall was chaos. Robert Dyson had his Sunday coat off and was nose to nose with Skidmore. Mrs. Dyson was crying and, I noticed, surreptitiously fingering rosary beads. Everyone was talking or yelling. Pastor Davis was sheet white, standing firmly in the doorway that led back to the chapel.

"I have the order from Judge Hayes right here!" Skidmore was roaring, shaking a fistful of papers at his side.

"I don't care if you have orders from Jesus H. Christ on a cross!" Mr. Dyson matched Skid in volume and vehemence. "You're not taking my little girls!"

I turned to Lucinda. We were just inside the door.

"How did this start?" I asked her over the pandemonium.

"It was calm at first," she said, shaken by the scene. "I was standing with Robert and Sara. Skid came up and offered his condolences. He said he'd gotten some news from the coroner that made him want to have a few more tests done on the girls before they were buried."

"Your brother-in-law reacted badly," I surmised.

"You can't blame him, really. What's the matter with Skid?"

"Yes," I said slowly, "lately I'd like to know that too."

"Are you going to do something?" she demanded.

"I suppose," I sighed, handing her my plate of food.

I waded through a sea of distraught Christians, made it to Skid-more's side.

"Oh, great!" he exploded when he saw me. "You're *just* what I need right now."

"Skid," I responded gently. "Calm down. You're in your own church."

I turned to Mr. Dyson.

"I've been to this fellowship hall dozens of times since I've come back to Blue Mountain," I said calmly, "and it rarely gets this exciting. Is it like that in the Baptist church?"

"You tell your *buddy* he's not getting his hands on my daughters," Mr. Dyson shot back, in no mood for my pathetic attempt at placation.

"Well, strictly speaking," I told Mr. Dyson, "Skidmore is less my *buddy* than he is the county sheriff. The man who replaced Sheriff Maddox."

I'd pitched my voice so as to be heard by as many people as possible. The mention of our former sheriff's name produced the desired effect: a ripple of relative quiet around me.

"This man," I went on, indicating Skidmore, "is an officer of the court with a legal document in his hand. If you can take a deep breath and remember back to the horrific reign of Sheriff Maddox, I'm sure you'll see the difference between him and our new Sheriff Needle. Maddox would have drawn his pistol by now, arrested you, insulted your wife, and shown, in general, his patented brand of *anticompassion*. He wouldn't have argued with you, Mr. Dyson. He would have beaten you into the ground."

"Maddox," someone in the crowd growled. "He'd probably have shot somebody by now."

God bless him, whoever said it. I recalled many an encounter with

Sheriff Maddox when he was alive, not a single one of them pleasant. I was glad to know that others felt the way I did about him. He had died quite suddenly—dressed only in a red raincoat and saddle oxfords, in the arms of another man's wife. It seemed a fitting epitaphic image. Maddox died, leaving the post of county sheriff open for Skidmore to fill.

But the specter of the departed Maddox hovered over the crowd for a moment and produced an ashen calm.

"Now," I said to Skid, "exactly what's in the document that you're crumpling in your right hand?"

"I got the coroner's toxicology report an hour ago," he said, calming slightly. "The Dyson family was in such a hurry to get the girls ready for this service that they rushed the Deveroe boys over at the funeral parlor, which, in turn, truncated the coroner's work. But when I saw the initial finding, I rushed over to Judge Hayes to get this cease and desist. I mean, it's better to do it now than to exhume the bodies tomorrow, right?"

"Why?" was all Robert Dyson wanted to know.

"Do you really want me to tell you in front of all these people?" Skid's voice was distant and cold.

"What is it?" Sara Dyson chimed in, letting go of her rosary beads.

"All right," Skid sighed, still emotionless. "The initial toxicology report indicates that the girls might have been under the influence of hallucinogens."

The statement could have caused the room to erupt again, but instead it shut everything down. The fellowship hall fell silent as a tomb.

Only then did I finally see Judy. She was standing close to the hallway door, nodding, a grim look of determination on her face.

"But you don't believe," I pressed, trying to keep my voice down, "that the girls were taking illegal drugs."

I could still read Skid like a book. He had a wild look of determination in his eyes.

"Of course not," he answered me, his voice betraying a shaky underpinning. "I believe that they were poisoned with them, given drugs without their knowledge."

"What?" Mrs. Dyson whispered.

"And if that's true," Skid barreled forward, "then these drugs would most likely be the cause of the girls not getting off the railroad tracks."

"And that would change the coroner's report," I supplied, "to murder."

I followed Lucinda home shortly after that. No one wanted to stand around and watch as the bodies were loaded into hearses that should have carried them to their burial sites.

I pulled my truck up next to her car and got out, saw her to her front door.

"Listen," I said as gently as I could, "do you have some photos of the girls in your wallet? You know, school pictures or something?"

"What?" She glared at me.

"I have a few things to do." I locked eyes with her.

She nodded.

"You want to show the pictures to someone who might have seen them that night." She sighed.

"I'll give them back today."

She opened her purse, fiddled with her wallet, produced two yearbook-style portraits.

"You get enough to eat at the church?" she mumbled absently.

"Anyway," I said quickly, "I'll be back in a couple of hours. Will you be all right until then?"

"Uh-huh," she told me unsteadily, fishing in her purse for her house key. "Where are you going?"

"Over to the Palace in Pine City. I want to show these photos to someone. I might be able to discover if the girls had dates."

She stopped all motion for an instant.

"They might have," I said before she could form a sentence.

"I see." She opened her front door.

"Two hours."

She nodded and headed into her house.

I turned my truck around and headed for Pine City, trying to remember the name of the young man at the movie theater with whom I'd spoken, the usher-filmmaker. He'd said it wasn't a good name for a director.

What was it? I asked myself.

I spent the entire drive over the hill to Pine City failing to recall the boy's name and trying to ignore my stomach. As I pulled up to the Palace, I realized it was the middle of the afternoon and there probably wouldn't be anyone there.

I parked directly in front of the entrance. There were no lights inside.

The facade of the place was like its interior, a romantic amalgam of Moorish temples, Hollywood fantasy, and art deco glamour. The fired tiles had been cleaned to their former gold, and the marquee dazzled the entire town square with several thousand moving lights. The day's feature was *A Guy Named Joe,* a heartbreaking bit of World War II mysticism: a fighter pilot's ghost, Spencer Tracy, teaches the girl he loved in life to fall in love with another man, a man who was alive, his replacement, in fact. She fell in love with a younger pilot about to leave on a bombing mission, never knowing that the ghost of her dead lover had whispered in her ear. I stared up at the title feeling surrounded by ghosts.

I got out of the truck, stood on the sidewalk awhile trying to decide what to do. After a moment I thought I heard noise inside and stood at the glass doors peering in.

There seemed to be someone behind the popcorn machine.

I tapped on the glass and popcorn sprayed everywhere.

"What the hell!" A boy's face popped up from behind the counter.

"Hello," I called through the crack in the door. "It's Dr. Devilin here. I think I spoke to you on the phone."

"Christ." He leaned on the counter a moment. "You near scared the life out of me."

"Sorry," I said. "Can you talk for a second?"

"I'm not supposed to."

"It's about the girls I was telling you about." I rummaged in my coat pocket and found the snapshots I'd just gotten from Lucinda.

"Yeah," he said, heading my way. "People are talking about it now. I called around. Terrible."

I held up the photos even before he got to the door. He was a sandy-haired teenager, a touch on the hefty side even for our mountain community. He wore a button-down, white cotton shirt, thin, fifties-style maroon tie, black dress slacks, and white tennis shoes. The name badge said *Andy.*

He came to the door and opened it before he saw the pictures.

"Oh, yeah," he said quickly. "Damn. You don't forget those girls."

"Right." I stepped inside. "I was hoping."

"They came to the later show," he said, "last show of the night, you know? And they were all cute and stuff, but their boyfriends were kind of a pain in the ass."

"How so?" I asked, hoping I didn't look surprised that they *had* boyfriends.

"I know them from school," he sighed. "Jocks."

"Sports aficionados."

"They play football," he confirmed.

"I suppose it's not like when I was in school," I said, putting the photos away. "In those days, the sporting crowd lived in one universe and I seemed to live in another. *Smart* was exactly the last thing I wanted to be. When I was your age."

"The more things change," he sighed, "the more they stay the same, you know?"

"I know," I commiserated.

"Were you as big in high school as you are now?" he asked.

"About."

"Lucky," he said haplessly.

"Didn't help. I was often referred to as *Goliath* and several times as *Tiny,* an attempt at something of an ironic appellation."

"You were bigger though. You could have done something."

"Ever read *One Flew Over the Cuckoo's Nest?*"

"Saw the movie," he piped up. "Great stuff."

"What's the Chief's problem? Remember that character?"

"Ohhhh." He rolled out the sound. "He was a giant guy, but he thought he was too small to do anything about his problems."

"There you go."

"So you were, like, nuts?"

"What?" I scowled.

"The Chief was nuts. Wasn't everybody in an asylum in that movie?"

"Well, yes," I said quickly, "but I was making a point about being in high school."

"Look," he interrupted impatiently. "I really have to get the snack bar ready. And now I also have to clean up because you scared me and I decorated the place with popcorn."

"My fault. I'll help. So about these boys, the dates. Do you know their names?"

"Yeah." He headed back to the old glass counter. "One was Tony Riddick and the other one was Nickel Mathews."

I followed him in. ,

"Hang on," I said. "Is the Mathews boy related to Melissa Mathews of the sheriff's department, do you know?"

"Nickel is Melissa's cousin," he said wearily. "He's always going on about how he can get away with stuff because his cousin will fix it. But as far as I know, he never did anything, he just talked about it."

I'd followed him to the counter and begun to pick up popcorn kernels.

"Where do you want these?" I asked.

"Oh."

He went behind the counter and pulled out a large black plastic garbage bag.

"I'll get the vacuum," he said, "you don't really have to help. But thanks."

"Look, here's an uncomfortable question," I said, straightening up. "How much do you know about the drug culture in your high school?"

"Drug culture?" He laughed. "This isn't Atlanta. We don't have a

drug culture. If we want to destroy ourselves, we get drunk, as God intended."

"You're saying there are no drugs in your high school?" I asked him sternly.

He stopped what he was doing and looked me in the eye.

"If there were," he said soberly, "would I tell you?"

"You would if the two girls died from taking drugs," I told him, locked on his eyes.

"Oh." He looked down. "Damn. Those girls? I don't believe it."

"There are drugs in your high school," I pressed. I was sincerely hoping his answer would still be no.

"Yeah," he sighed. "Pretty much everything."

"So, what's popular?"

"Weed, of course," he said quickly. "I hate it. Makes me stupid. Meth is good. Good for work or studying. You know, like No-Doz."

"No hallucinogenics?"

"What year is this?" he chided. "Hendrix is dead, man—along with the acid culture."

"Nothing else? I read in *Time* magazine that ecstasy was making a comeback. As a party thing."

"I guess," he said softly, busying himself behind the popcorn machine. "That's *sort of* like a hallucinogen."

"Sometimes boys slip that into a Coke or something. Dose an unsuspecting person."

"No," he corrected. "You're thinking about the date-rape thing. X is just good clean fun."

"You actually seem to know a good bit about the subject," I said casually.

"Look," he exploded unexpectedly. "I'm trying to help you. And I know about the subject because I'm a worldly sort of person. I'm a filmmaker. See? An artist."

"And it's an artist's responsibility to know the world," I agreed, thinking it best to change the subject. "Who was your favorite? You were telling me on the phone. Lelouch?"

"Favorite, I don't know," he hedged, "but I like him. I like all the French new wave."

"I prefer Truffaut. He's got more of a humanist sensibility and a greater body of work. He often constructs a dynamic to make you think something terrible is going to happen, and then it turns out to be something wonderful instead."

No sense talking down to the boy.

"The opposite of real life," he sniped, "in other words."

"Well, you've been very helpful," I said, stepping back from the counter, "and I expect to be standing in line for one of your movies within the decade."

"Uh-huh." He shrugged.

"I'll see myself out."

I turned to leave.

"So, okay," he mumbled. "I hope you find out what happened to Tess and Rory, and stuff."

I stopped.

"I never told you their names." I turned.

He froze.

"Yes, you did." He stared hard at the countertop in front of him.

"You knew them," I said firmly, taking a step his direction. "You knew Tess and Rory. No point in lying about it, I can find out. That's an easy thing to check, you understand."

He fidgeted for a moment, then his shoulders sagged.

"Of course I knew them," he whined. "Damn."

"So why did you lead me to believe you didn't?"

"I don't know," he said defiantly, an imitation of a movie tough guy.

I took a quick step in his direction, growling, a generally threatening gesture coming from a large man with an expensive vocabulary.

"Listen, you little gob of spit," I snarled. "I've had a terrible day, I'm really hungry, and I don't care what I do to you. If you know something about Tess and Rory, tell me now. Do you understand?"

"Christ." He was startled, dropped the plastic garbage bag and took a dance backward. His breathing had increased and his eyes were wide.

"Why did you pretend not to know the girls?" I demanded.

"Because I thought I might get into trouble," he answered immediately, a high school kid again.

"Why would you get into trouble?" I moved another step in his direction.

"Because I sold some ecstasy to Nickel Mathews," he blurted out in a stage whisper, "on the night the girls died!"

Nine

All the way home I tried to calm down, wondering why I'd lost my temper so suddenly, why I'd used such a disgusting phrase to threaten Andy the drug-dealing filmmaker; and what to tell Skidmore about the boy. I'd simply left him standing in the lobby of the theater and lumbered away without any further conversation. I was so stunned by his revelation, I had no words. Cherubs were selling drugs in the local movie house. The war between the forces of light and the powers of darkness was over: the night had won.

As I drove, these thoughts gave way to a quiet desperation, a melancholy meditation on my own weltschmerz, which quickly moved to a great world-loathing, an existential nausea.

I generally loved to think of Blue Mountain as a world apart, a safe haven, a place where the reality I saw on the network news, in movies, or on television programs didn't really exist. I often convinced myself that I lived in Mayberry, or Brigadoon.

But twenty-first-century America would not covenant such places. I realized with a cold certainty that there were no places left in America untouched by dark matter. True innocence, like my *genuine* folklore, had turned to a quaint notion for addled academics. People like me were outdated archaeologists crawling over ancient tombs, lost souls who longed for a time that was, I concluded with great certainty, gone forever.

Autumn sun sank low behind blue pines on the ridges all around me. An aching amber light filled the road, the grass, the air rushing past my speeding truck. I saw in that light the twilight of our civilization, a pale fire burning out. I had an apocalyptic vision to match anything in Hiram Frazier's nightmares. I saw an angel standing in the sun. With a loud voice it called to all the birds, "Come! Gather for the great supper, to eat the flesh of kings, the flesh of captains, the flesh of mighty men." And all the birds were gorged with that flesh.

At least that's how I remembered the quote from Revelation. When in doubt, Revelation is the book of the Bible for harsh depression.

Alas, neither the image nor the contemplation did anything to assuage the pangs of my stomach. Appetite always belies the greater philosophical concerns, or mine does, at least. Since I wasn't certain how to proceed, food was obviously the answer.

I had a fleeting urge to drive to the Methodist church, see if any food was left there. I was still dressed for it, and I'd had some of the best meals in the world at family reunions in that church. Any church homecoming in our town was nothing more than an excuse to eat. Ordinarily all the good cooks in a family or the church or the entire county would indulge in a kind of friendly competition to see whose dish was the best.

For some reason I recalled a day from the previous April, the Carter family reunion, Girlinda's clan. Sky bluer than a china plate, air rich with honeysuckle, the yard at the side of the Methodist church was cluttered with table after table of unbelievable food. My eyes were desperate pirates after treasure, roving over those dishes with an abandon that might have been illegal.

Then I saw Melissa Mathews standing over one familiar-smelling dish, staring down at it.

"Is that rabbit stew?" I asked her.

She looked up.

"Uh-huh," she said, smiling. "Fresh. My cousin Nickel got this rabbit just yesterday out in back of my house. He didn't even have to shoot it. Got this rabbit by chunking rocks at it. So it don't have no shot-up taste. I cooked it myself. Have you some."

"I don't know." I peered at it dubiously. "What about that over there?"

I pointed to another big stew pot beside her elbow.

"That's the venison," she said, "which Uncle Hulitt got last year, but we froze it right after because didn't nobody want to eat it, you know, on account of Uncle Hulitt's funeral."

I nodded. Hulitt had accidentally shot himself after shooting the biggest deer of his hunting life. He'd been so excited about the kill that he'd dropped his rifle and it went off. He died before the deer did. I decided against the venison.

"I remember Hulitt's hunting accident," I said. "You didn't bring any of that pig foot this year, did you? You know you're famous for it."

"Shoot." She grinned. "I think you're the only one that eats them."

"I tried the first one last year because you told me it'd come from a pig that wore a lucky rabbit's foot around its neck. I thought it was a funny thing to say."

Melissa laughed then, and the sound of her laughter was like water over round rocks in a cold stream, music from nature, not a human sound at all.

"It worked for a good while too," she claimed, barely a smile on her face. "She was one lucky sow. We put off slaughtering that pig until the day she got caught rooting around in our corn patch. She rolled around so that the rabbit foot fell off from around her neck. I don't know how she got it around her neck in the first place. Pig ain't got no elbows, so I don't hardly see how she could reach way on around her back like that."

Melissa's chestnut hair always seemed just-washed, her eyes were shy but her posture was bold, and her lips were never far away from a smile. She was only a few years out of high school; dozens of men had courted her. But she was a self-confessed coward where men were concerned. She could be friendly with someone who had no interest in her, but she was terrified of any man who wanted her attention.

As a sheriff's deputy under the Maddox administration, she'd broken into a murderer's hotel room, jumped into the Nantahala River to save two elementary-school children, and fired her pistol more than a dozen times in the line of duty. But a halfhearted *hello* from a boy who was barely beginning to like, her, that would send her into paralysis.

I was clearly no threat, so she enjoyed her conversations with me, though there had only been three of them in the entire time I'd been back to Blue Mountain.

I could see why Skid might be attracted to her, though. And Skid's being married would make him an easy man for her to love.

I slowly withdrew my thoughts from the images of that lovely day and focused once again on the darkening road that lay before me.

But contained in my muddled Remembrance of Aprils Past was a nagging image, one that haunted. I saw Nickel Mathews, cousin to a law-enforcement officer. A boy who would throw a rock at a rabbit was someone who might feed drugs to a couple of sweet young girls.

When I finally pulled up in front of my house, I had decided what to do. I bounded up my front steps and through my front door, not even bothering to close it behind me. It would only take me a moment, I reasoned, to pick up the phone instead of heading to the refrigerator.

I dialed quickly.

"Sheriff's Office," Melissa said.

"Hello, Melissa. It's Dr. Devilin. Is Skid in?"

"No, sir," she said hesitantly, "but he said when you called to patch you through to his car. Can you hang on a minute?"

"Of course."

Before I could ask how Skid knew I'd be calling, a silence on the other end told me I was on hold.

A black wind took hold of the tops of trees, rattled them like snare drums. Dark clouds were rolling in once more, and it looked as if a heavy rain was imminent.

"Damn it, Fever!" Skid's voice jumped through the phone lines. "I told you to stay clear of all this mess with the Dyson sisters."

"I'm not sure what you're so mad about," I shot back, "especially after I helped you out at the church, but that's your business at the moment. I have some information."

"Mr. Dyson is very upset," he began.

"He's upset with *you*, Skid." I told him, voice several notes higher. "Now, listen: the usher at the Palace theater, his name is Andy something."

"Stop," he demanded. "I'm telling you as the *sheriff*, you have to quit looking into this business any further, or I'll take action."

"Shut up, Skidmore," I bellowed. "Andy sold ecstasy to Nickel Mathews, and Nickel Mathews was with the girls on the night the girls were killed. Ecstasy, Skid. A serotonin-raising chemical compound. Is that something you already knew, or am I, in fact, giving you important new information?"

My face was hot and I realized I was gripping the phone like a barbell.

I rarely found myself that angry more than once a decade, and my steam had risen twice in one hour that afternoon. I'd gotten almost that angry with Andy Newlander. What was the matter with me?

My ire did, however, have the desired effect. Skidmore was silent.

"Also did you know that someone besides you," I pressed on, "found Mr. Millroy and got the results of the coroner's investigation? The same toxicology report?"

Silence still reigned.

"Skid?"

"Andy Newlander sells drugs?" His voice was weak, absolutely exhausted.

"To Nickel Mathews," I answered, as gently as I could with my heart still thumping my sternum.

"Are you sure?" Skid's sails were windless.

"I asked him, and he admitted it."

"So the girls had taken ecstasy." Skid sighed heavily. "I guess that answers most of the questions."

"Well, we're not *certain* they took it. But Nickel could have slipped it in a drink at the movies."

"Seems a fair guess," Skid said, gaining strength again. "Nickel is a little piece of crap. Just the kind of boy who would do something like that."

"I don't believe I've ever heard you say anything that bad about anyone," I told him, covering up my amazement as best I could.

"I don't believe you ever told me to shut up before," he countered. "It's a brand-new day."

"Yes." I stared out the window at the gathering gray nimbus. "It certainly is that."

"I know I've been strange lately."

I could tell from his voice he'd mustered most of his energy simply to produce that one sentence. He fell silent after it.

"What's going on, Skid?"

"I can't tell you everything," he replied, stony. "But how about if you meet me over at Miss Etta's and we have a professional exchange of information."

"Gossip, you mean," I confirmed.

"Right," he agreed.

"Good," I said firmly, my mood already bolstering. "I'm starved."

"There's a surprise," Skid said expressionlessly.

He hung up before I had a chance to counter.

Miss Etta's was approaching nirvana to me as I drove the several miles from my house into town. I'd exchanged my dress jacket for the black leather one, but the rest of the ensemble remained: I was a patch of midnight.

Sense memory filled the air around my head with the steam of golden squash and onions, fried okra crisp as popcorn, cornbread more like cake than a bride would eat at her own wedding. I tried to remember what day it was. Tuesday lunch usually meant Crackling Catfish, a *Good Housekeeping* Prize recipe that Etta had invented when the world was young. She'd used the money to open her dining establishment, and without any further effort on her part, she had turned from twenty to seventy-two.

When the neon of her namesake sign appeared in the distance, I almost cried.

I parked fairly close to her door; the lunch crowd was long past and the weather would most likely keep latecomers away. Miss Etta closed at 3:00 P.M. anyway, so Skid and I were likely to be her last customers of the day. Generally her business was slow on funeral or church-meeting days anyway. I could see Skid through the window, he was already seated at a table by the door.

I pushed into the place, nodded once at Etta, and sat. Skid and I exchanged looks.

Etta herself arrived a moment later to deliver silverware wrapped in three paper napkins and two indestructible plastic plates big enough to hold an entire pumpkin.

Etta was dressed in her uniform: a black print, calf-length dress, blue slippers, a man's chocolate cardigan sweater; a wiry, gray bun. She retreated without a word.

Instead of going into the kitchen right away, we sat a moment in silence.

"So," I said finally. "How's your morning been?"

"I went over to visit Eppie Waldrup and impound the Volkswagen."

"You know that's not what I mean."

"Yeah, Fever, I'm really sorry for the way I've been acting lately."

"God, am I glad to hear you say that, Skid," I exhaled. "I've been very worried about you. Everyone has."

"Everyone has?" He seemed troubled.

"You know, Girlinda's called me several times," I admitted uncomfortably, "and Lucinda, you know, is concerned."

"My wife's called you?" He could barely say it.

"She didn't know what was the matter with you," I stammered. "She thought you might have said something to me. Of course, as it turned out, I was more in the dark than she."

He slumped in his seat.

"You know how we always used to make fun of Maddox," Skid said softly after a moment, "and talk about how mean he was?"

"Of course."

"I've been a short while on his job, and it doesn't seem so ridiculous to me now."

"What is it?" I wondered, staring.

"When you look at a beautiful garden," he answered hazily, "you don't think how many biting bugs, and poison spiders, and great big snakes can hide in there."

"And now your job in tending to the garden." I said, "is rooting out the reptiles."

"Exactly." He closed his eyes.

"After a while, you don't notice the dahlias anymore."

He took a breath, bit his lower lip. Then a slight flinch opened his eyes again.

"You went with dahlias?" he asked, a semblance of his old self creeping into the sound of his voice, if not a smile to his lips.

"Well," I played along, "a rose seemed too obvious, and I thought *cleome* would be a trifle obscure for a person of your sort."

"What the hell is cleome?"

"I rest my case." I smiled. "Sometimes they're called spider something-or-other, though, so you see why I thought of it."

"Right," he said, sitting up. "That would have been a good one."

Without further ado, he stood, scooped up his plate, and headed for the kitchen.

I followed.

We had the place to ourselves, surveying the vegetables simmering on the oversize stove. I knew better, but I loaded my plate with a few dabs of everything Miss Etta had cooked that day: sweet creamed corn, stewed-all-night beef, "white cloud" turnip-potato-butter mash. An unbelievable array of earthly delights winked their bubbles in my direction, and I forgot everything bad about the world in favor of inhaling those aromas.

God invented gastronomy, that much was certain to me.

A moment later and we were back at our table by the door, and I'd already finished two chicken wings, all the white cloud mash, most of the pickled beets, and half of the carrots with tarragon.

I glanced up to find Skid staring at me.

"What?" I managed around a mouthful of corn bread.

"You're eating like a condemned man." He laughed.

"You don't know the day I've had," I said, returning my attention to my plate.

I finished my meal in as much silence as fork scraping plate would permit and sat back.

"Damn," Skidmore admitted, "that was some powerful eating."

"I'm thinking about seconds," I said, casting a wistful eye in the direction of the kitchen.

"No, you're not," he insisted. "You sit right here for three minutes and let your stomach catch up with your mouth, you'll be complaining about how full you are."

"Not likely, but I'll take a break to talk for a second."

"Good." His face instantly lost its cheerful expression.

"After I heard about the toxicology report from Millroy, who is, by the way, a strange young man, I thought I should nip over to Pine City and check with this person at the movie house to see if the girls had had dates that night. And they had."

"Nickel Mathews," Skid said, eyes cold.

"And the Riddick boy."

"Tony's his first name."

"And Andy Newlander, this usher at the theater," I concluded, "told me that he'd sold the drug to Nickel. That's all. No one saw anyone give the drug to the girls, and the report from Millroy isn't remotely conclusive."

"Yes"—Skid nodded—"but there's more to the story. As I was saying on the phone, I can't tell you all of it, but I *can* tell you that there's a larger drug problem in our little hamlet than you would ever imagine. Melissa and I have been talking about this situation for quite some time now."

"You and Melissa seem to spend a lot of time together," I interrupted.

Skid's lips narrowed and his eyes burned.

"I said I can't tell you everything," he whispered through loosely clenched teeth. "You don't have any idea what all is involved."

"All right," I rejoined unsteadily, "for the moment let's just get on with your story."

"Nickel is messed up," Skid said plainly.

"Beginning with his name," I agreed, hoping to lighten the moment.

"Do you have any idea how he got it?" Skid challenged, still tense.

"It's a nickname, obviously."

"Not exactly." Skid leaned his elbows on the green Formica tabletop. "His father didn't name him anything when the boy was born. It just says 'Boy' on the birth certificate. And when Nickel was old enough to ask about it, he went to his father and wanted to know what his name was, instead of *boy*. And his father told him he wasn't anything that needed a name. Said he wasn't worth the trouble it would take to think one up. Told his own son he wasn't worth a dime."

"And then started calling him *Nickel*," I guessed.

"Exactly."

"Sounds like a good way to turn a child into a drug addict, the sort of boy who would throw rocks at a rabbit."

"Rocks at a rabbit?" Skid asked, scowling at me.

"Nothing," I hurried on. "So you and Melissa were talking about Nickel's problem."

"She's the one who got me onto this investigating drugs in the first place. She's got a personal stake in it, you understand, so we pursued it, and then we uncovered some incredible . . . I feel like the world I'm living in has no relationship whatsoever with the one I was in a year ago. I don't quite know what to do."

"You need peach cobbler," I said immediately. "I saw some in the kitchen."

"What the hell are you talking about?" He glared.

"Many people will tell you the sun is a lemon," I lectured, "or an orange, but I believe this is a less accurate metaphor than the peach. A peach is at once yellow and rosy, like a sunrise. And when it is peeled, a peach is the very image of sunlight at noon. When sliced and spiced and heated with the sort of witchery of which Miss Etta is capable, no one can argue with me that the result deserves its rightful place at the center of our culinary universe: the sun of all realities."

"You need help." He grinned.

"You need cobbler." I stood.

"Fever," he said, stopping me. "I just can't tell you everything that's going on."

"You keep saying that, Skid," I said quietly, frozen in my standing position by the table. "But it somehow involves Melissa, right?"

"We were together," he whispered, his voice hollow, "on the night the girls were killed."

No amount of prying or insisting after that would convince Skidmore to make any further confession—or get me any closer to peach cobbler.

I knew that his reticence was due partly to a natural, mountainbred obstinance. Something else was on his face, though, that affirmed my worst fear and the lowest town gossip. Skid and Melissa were having an affair.

The thought was barely in my head before my mind reeled at the prospect. Businessmen in Atlanta had affairs. Adults on Blue Mountain were single, courting, or married. No other category existed.

Sadly, that conceit was a product of my own mind, obviously a part of the fantasy I'd constructed about my hometown. It was a carefully crafted illusion to avoid facing more obvious realities, mundane and paltry.

No place on earth was untouched by dark matter.

Skid and I stood on the sidewalk in front of Miss Etta's, neither of us knowing what to say.

Finally I leaned on my truck, folded my arms, and reverted to the safety of my lecturer persona.

"Are you familiar with the concept of dark matter in astrophysics?"

"Honest to God, Fever," he said, shaking his head, "I don't know where in the world you come up with half the stuff you say."

"*Time* magazine, usually," I told him. "So when some group of astronomers tried to measure the rotational speed of certain galaxies, they came across something of a mystery. They discovered that most galaxies rotate more than twice as fast as they should be able to, and that creates a problem. The gravity around them shouldn't be able to hold them together. According to Einstein, they should be flying apart. But they weren't flying apart, something else besides gravity was keeping the galaxies together. One scientific explanation is that most galaxies are surrounded by some form of 'dark' matter, something that can't be observed by any method we know."

"Then why do they think it's there?" He sighed, his patience strained by my erudition.

"X-ray telescopes have discovered huge clouds of impossibly hot gases in clusters of galaxies." I folded my arms. "These hot gas clouds provide an independent measurement of dark matter. The measurement shows that there must be at least four times as much dark matter as all the stars and gas we observe, or the hot gas would escape the cluster."

"I see. There's more darkness all around us than there is light." He nodded. "You should really look into Girlinda's perennial suggestion to you and start seeing a therapist. I believe you might suffer from that clinical depression she's been reading about."

"I'm almost finished," I snapped. "One possible explanation for dark matter is the white dwarf."

Skidmore's head shot up so quickly it made his neck crack.

Which told me one of the things I wanted to know. Skidmore had met, or at least seen, Orvid Newcomb.

I kept my composure, feigning indifference to his surprise.

"A white dwarf," I continued easily, "is the final condensed state of a small star. White dwarfs are known to exist in abundance in the universe. They could explain the presence of dark matter if young galaxies produce white dwarfs that cool more rapidly than we think they do."

"Oh." He was clearly shaken.

"As you know, my studies in folklore and mythology have led me to believe that nearly everything we think and everything we observe is metaphorical. The practical science of dark matter is less important to me than the symbology involved. We do seem to be surrounded by more and more darkness. I make this observation because it seems to apply to the immediate, terrible reality of Tess and Rory."

"Yes." His face was drained of color. "I see that."

"And you see that no matter what you say, I can't really stop looking into it. I was doing it at first for Lucinda. But now I'm convinced that these boys gave Tess and Rory a drug that made them unable to recognize the danger they were in when they were sitting on the train tracks. I have to find out if it's true, and if it is, I have to make certain that you get those boys and readjust their lives. I'm telling you this because I want you to know that with or without your help or permission, I'm going to do this."

"Okay." He ran his hand over his hair and took in a deep breath. "I understand."

"I also want you to know that no matter what you've done or what you're doing," I offered more softly, "I'm your oldest and best friend. I won't let you go too far wrong before I start yelling at you to turn around."

"You mean in the investigation?" he asked uncertainly.

"Or anything else."

"Um," he stammered. "All right."

I was puzzled by his seeming lack of comprehension concerning the real meaning of my compassion, but before I could explore the matter further, we were both startled by Miss Etta.

She had shuffled to her door, swung it open, and called out:

"Devilin! That you?"

"Miss Etta?" I answered, a little surprised that she knew my name.

"Telephone for you," she grumbled.

"For me?" I thought she was mistaken. "In your place?"

"Well, do you want to get it or not?" She didn't wait for an answer. The door swung closed behind her.

"Who would even know I'm here?" I asked Skid.

"Better get it," he encouraged.

Still a little confused, I stepped onto the sidewalk and followed where Miss Etta had gone. She was back in her usual place behind the register, eyes closed. The phone was on the counter in front of her, receiver off the hook.

I picked it up carefully, trying not to disturb Etta any further.

"Hello?" I said gingerly into the phone.

"Dr. Devilin," the voice said quickly, "I'm glad you're still there. It's Melissa Mathews. I would have just come over there to Miss Etta's, but I'm not supposed to leave this desk while the sheriff is away. We've had a notice of disturbance at your house."

"What?"

"Well," she said, attempting to apply her official voice to the matter at hand, "Lucinda Foxe called us a while ago. She was looking for you and called your house and a strange man answered the phone!"

"What?" I demanded. "Are you sure?"

"That's what she said," Melissa confirmed.

"She just dialed the wrong number."

"No," Melissa said uncomfortably. "I asked her that. She was very upset. I'm sending a man up there right now."

"Did you know that Skidmore was here with me?"

"Oh my gosh," she sighed. "No, sir. Could you please let me talk to him, then?"

"God." I was barely comprehending what I was hearing.

Skid had come in and was staring at me, wanting answers.

"And then you call Ms. Foxe, hear? She's really worried," Melissa insisted.

"Yes," I managed into the phone. "Thank you, Melissa. I'll call Lucinda and go right home."

"Okay," she said cheerily. "You let us know if there's anything stolen or messed up, hear?"

I motioned for Skid to take the phone.

"Right," I told Melissa absently. "Here's Skid."

He took the phone from me.

"What?" Skid asked Melissa.

"An intruder was in my house," I told him, astonished, "and answered my phone when Lucinda called."

"Yes," Skid said, his lips tight, "you were right to call Dr. Devilin. I'll handle it now."

"I'm calling Lucinda this minute," I said to Skid.

He nodded.

"All right, Melissa," he said into the phone. "Damn."

He pushed the button on the phone, hanging up on Melissa, and handed me the receiver.

I dialed Lucinda's number. It barely rang once.

"Fever?" she said anxiously into the phone.

"How did you know it was me?"

"Thank God." She let out a long breath. "Where are you?"

"Miss Etta's. With Skid. Tell me what happened."

"I called to see what you were doing, if you'd found out anything, and a man answered your phone. He didn't even sound like a real person. I thought somehow it was the television or something."

"What do you mean?"

"His voice was unreal," she said, a little shaky.

"Well, one of Skid's deputies is going up there to chase him off," I assured her, sounding a little more confident than I felt. "Everything's fine. I'm going up there now to see if there's anything missing."

"Don't you go up there alone!" she insisted instantly. "And don't you let Skidmore send one of his sorry deputies for this. He has to go with you."

"I'll be all right."

"No," she said firmly, "either Skid goes up there with you or I'll meet you over there. Take your pick."

"Well, you're not meeting me over there."

"Let me talk to Skid," she said imperatively.

"Lucy," I tried.

"Fever," she rejoined. "I'll meet you at your house in twenty minutes, so help me God."

"Wait."

I held the phone to my chest.

"Look, do you have a second to convince Lucinda that I don't need you to hold my hand?" I said to Skid. "She wants you to go up with me up to my place."

"Give me the phone," he said, holding out his hand.

I acquiesced.

"Lucy," Skid said calmly into the phone, "it's Skidmore. What do you reckon Dr. Devilin would do without you and me?"

He smiled.

"That's right." He shot me a look. "I'll go up there with him. We'll make sure everything's all right, and then he'll come see you."

He looked me in the eye. I shook my head angrily.

"He agrees," Skid told Lucinda. "So we're going now. Okay. Bye."

He hung up.

"Each of those phone calls is going to run you boys a quarter," Miss Etta piped up, eyes still closed.

I dug a dollar bill out of my wallet and laid it on the counter.

"Keep the change."

"You're damned right," she agreed.

"I only have a few minutes," Skid said impatiently. "Let's go."

We took off out of the restaurant and were halfway up the side of the mountain before I allowed myself to reflect on Skid's reaction to the term *white dwarf* and the image of Orvid Newcomb it brought forth.

My reasoning followed this line: I knew that Orvid had been engaged in some sort of questionable activity on the night the girls died. I knew that Skidmore was uncomfortable telling me what he was doing that same night with Melissa. And I knew that Melissa's cousin Nickel had given drugs to the girls. My surmise was that Skid and Melissa had embarked upon some sort of shady date under the guise of keeping an eye on Nickel and his drug activities. In fact they had been too intent upon each other to stop the terrible events that had transpired.

Furthermore, I posited the likelihood that Orvid was the supplier of the drugs; he'd been waiting for a train delivery of some sort and witnessed the train wreck but was loath to relate too many incriminating details.

There it was: a very urban cancer in our idyllic hamlet. I felt queasy at the prospect, even a little light-headed. Could have been indigestion. God may have invented the gastronomic pleasures, but the devil took his due inside the many regrets of gluttony.

My cabin appeared over the rise, a dark gem in the misty air. Where the leaves had fallen on the roof, gold and rubies decked its crown. Where the rain had made black roof tiles slick, obsidian ruled. All around it the trees whispered, keeping secrets so ancient and so painful that they dared not speak aloud. I never failed to appreciate the beauty of my home even though, each time I saw it come into view, I felt a stab of the childhood melancholy that had driven me from it for so many years.

The front door was open.

When I'd first returned to the mountains several years before, I used to lock the door every time I went out. After a year had gone by, I only used the key if I was going to be gone for more than two or three days. The intruder hadn't broken in, he'd simply opened the front door.

I pulled up close to the porch and got out of the truck. Skidmore called out before his squad car had come to a halt.

"Wait," he said.

I didn't argue with his directive as I would normally have, because his concern felt pleasant, familiar; a return to what I wanted our friendship to be.

He climbed out of his cruiser, pistol pulled.

"Is that necessary?" I couldn't help asking.

"Didn't you just give me a lecture on how much evil has taken over the world?" he sighed. "Would you let me do the job the way you see it on the television just once?"

"Sorry." I grinned.

He walked loudly up the steps.

"Police!" he barked. "Out with your hands *straight* up over your head."

Silence answered.

Skid went into the house through the open door, stomping through the living room to frighten the intruder. I heard him yelling something else as he bounded up the stairs to the bedrooms. But after a moment it was obvious that our criminal had gone.

Skid appeared in the doorway.

"Come on in," he said at last from the doorway, a little relieved.

I leapt up the porch steps and into the front room. Oak beams that framed the large room downstairs seemed to give off a kind of golden light. To my right the little galley kitchen was undisturbed. The staircase in the far corner that led up to the three bedrooms sat silently.

"You checked upstairs?"

"Yup," Skid answered. "Take a look around and see if there's anything missing or broken."

Television, stereo, major items of furniture, and pieces of art on the walls were all undisturbed. The kitchen looked exactly as I'd left it.

"Nothing major," I reported. "In fact, nothing at all, that I can tell."

"Check upstairs."

I did. My bedroom was pristine, the other two hadn't been entered, in my opinion.

"Everything seems untouched," I reported, coming down the stairs.

Skid stood in the kitchen. In his hand, to my complete dismay, was the last bite of Lucinda's apple tart.

"This is *good*," he mumbled, wiping his lips with his index finger.

"I was saving that," I told him woefully.

"Well," he announced, brushing off his hands over the sink, "then you *have* to go to Lucinda's house, don't you? She'll make you another one if you tell her I ate your last piece."

"I would have gone over there anyway," I whined. "Damn. I was *saving* that."

"Call her," he said, ignoring my complaint.

He breezed past me toward the front door.

"I would have insisted on peach cobbler at Miss Etta's," I began, following him, "if I'd known someone would eat the last crumb of that tart."

He stopped moving, his back to me.

"Look," he said quietly, standing in the doorway, "even though I still have to tell you *officially* that you can't be messing around with my investigation, I can say that *personally* I couldn't be happier you're going to help. You know."

He looked down. It had been a difficult speech for him to make for some reason.

"Yes," I told him, confused. "I'll do what I can."

"I'll send someone up to get prints off the phone, that sort of thing" he said, sniffing. "Most likely won't do much good, but we'll give her a try. I don't think this was any big deal, do you? Kids, maybe."

"Where are you going now?"

"Back to the office," he sighed, "to see can I figure out a way to arrest Andy Newlander."

He left without another word. I stood in the door and watched him drive off, a clutch of apprehension in my chest.

The sound of his car had vanished down the mountain before I

123

realized I hadn't asked him the question we both wanted to know. Why had the intruder answered my phone?

I went to the phone, trying to decide how I could use it to call Lucinda without disturbing what could be fingerprint evidence on the receiver.

That's when my eye fell on something I hadn't noticed, the one thing that was different about the interior of my house.

A small black Bible was on the phone table, open. It wasn't mine.

I didn't want to touch it. I leaned in close to see that it had been opened to the book of Revelation, last chapter.

One sentence was underlined: *Behold I am coming soon, bringing my recompense, to repay every one for what he has done.*

I had been visited by Hiram Frazier.

Ten

The phone startled me, ringing jabbed my mind's vision of the wandering minister. I stared, trying to think how I might answer it without touching it. It rang again. I had an ice-white vision of Hiram Frazier on the other end, calling with his final judgment.

On the third ring I gave up and grabbed the receiver.

"Hello?" I tried to sound intimidating.

"Dr. Devilin?" the high-pitched voice asked.

"Yes, ma'am," I answered tentatively.

"God damn it, you little pissant," the voice grated, "it's Eppie Waldrup!"

He sounded like an eleven-year-old girl with the croup. As usual.

"Oh," I stammered quickly, "yes. Eppie. How are you?"

"How am I?" he snorted. "I'm terrible. You got to come down to my place right away."

"I do?" I said weakly.

Every effort I made to concentrate on what he was saying was usurped by the open Bible at which I stared.

"Somebody's been messing with that Volkswagen you were looking at the other day. And then the police came by and now they're accusing me of tampering with evidence. What evidence? It's a damned *Volkswagen*!"

"Calm down, Eppie," I said soothingly. "Who came by? Skidmore?"

"Yes," he answered hotly. "Earlier this morning. That's why you got to come over. You know me. You know I ain't tampering."

"Sheriff Needle," I said slowly, focusing, "actually accused you of evidence tampering?"

"Yes!"

I closed the Bible on the tabletop. I would not have it distract me one instant longer.

"And you didn't do *anything*," I said sternly, "to the car? You didn't think maybe you could salvage some parts from it?"

"Nothing," he insisted. "Damn."

He was silent a moment.

"Except, you know," he went on calmly, "that a certain part of the Volkswagen engine, the cylinder head, is a perfect C below middle C, so, of course, I have that hanging in the yard. You know. But that was *after* the other person messed with the car. After."

"Eppie," I told him, shaking my head, "what's the matter with you? Was there really somebody in your yard disturbing that car besides you, or are you trying to fool the sheriff? He's a very smart person."

"Someone else was here!" he swore. "And here's how I know it. When I first looked at the engine and the transmission and all, I seen that the car had definitely been shut off when it was hit by the train. Engine dead stopped."

"How could you tell that?"

"Oh, lots of ways," he answered, completely assured. "The cylinders was all shut down, the way the transmission locked, just certain things. It's also what kept the car from blowing up like you see in the movies. If there's gas all over everything and the spark plugs are still sparking, that sets off the gas and everything goes up. If the engine's off, it's just gas everywhere, no explosion, see?"

"Sort of."

"Well, take my word for it," he assured me. "So, what I'm saying is that when I came in this morning, someone had taken off the cylinder head. I thought it might be them kids that comes in here all the time, so I went to put it back. That's when I made my discovery about the perfect C below middle C."

"And then the police showed up," I guessed.

"About a hour later. Sheriff come to impound the car, but when he seen me with part of it hanging on the line, you know, he wanted me to explain what the hell I was doing. And he don't have the musical sense that you do, it was hard to tell him anything. He's mad."

"You have a lot of things hanging from that line," I said, hoping to hide my suspicion. "How did Skid know that one of those pieces of junk was from the girls' VW?"

"I don't know," Eppie stammered. "You got to help me, Doc."

"Okay," I sighed, "but why do I have to come over there right now?"

"Well," he said sheepishly, "there's one more thing that finally convinced me the engine was shut off when the car got hit."

"What is it?"

"A note from the person who was messing with the car last night," he confessed. "It was sitting on the engine block when I come in this morning. Got it right here. It says, 'This engine was turned off when this car was hit. Call Dr. Devilin and tell him that.'"

After a brief phone conversation checking in with Lucinda to assure her that I was all right and that nothing was missing from my home, I offered her my promise to be at her house for dinner. I told her I had a good deal of information for her, but that I'd rather tell it in person. It seemed too complicated, for one, trying to explain Hiram Frazier over the phone.

For the first time in a year, I locked my front door on the way out.

I sped toward Eppie's junkyard thinking about the note he'd read to me. Someone was shadowing my investigation; it seemed to me that Orvid Newcomb was the likely culprit. He'd gone to the coroner, Millroy, and somehow managed to get information about the girls. He'd taken the Volkswagen apart and ascertained or guessed something about it. The supposition that their car engine wasn't running when the girls were killed scarcely seemed important, except that it could be further verification of their drug-addled state.

I tried not to conjure images of the car sitting on the railroad tracks.

Instead I was again haunted by images of Tess and Rory in life. My mind veered to a summer not long past when Lucinda had showed me photographs of the girls' first road trip, going to the beach in their new VW. They were headed for Jekyll Island. Once a millionaires' playground, the island had long since been made a state-protected island, not too crowded most of the time, and at night bear and deer walked on the beach.

Apparently a tire had gone flat on the girls' Volkswagen less than halfway to the island, and the lug nuts were on the wheels tighter than they could turn. They had to flag down some help, and naturally, the help turned out to be college boys. The boys were going to Jekyll too because God will punish any parent who allows teenaged daughters to take a road trip on the first day of summer.

The girls spent most of their time at the beach with the tire-changing boys and reported to Lucinda that it was a good vacation. They played putt-putt and swam in the ocean; danced to the music on the jukeboxes and and drank Cokes; ate fried shrimp every night and felt grown-up.

The best photographs Lucinda had shown me were of the girls by the ocean. I could see into those bright images, to a reality where the girls splashed up salt water, collecting the summer in brown layers on their skin, in golden threads in their hair and salt droplets on their mouths. I had the notion that every time they blinked they were taking their own minute photographs, storing them in albums that made a library in the back of their minds.

That's the most important thing young people do, after all. They collect experiences for a book that is eventually supposed to become a life.

So I was again in a gray mood by the time I arrived in Pine City.

———

My truck pulled up to Eppie's junkyard emporium. He was waiting for me, engaged in his version of pacing back and forth: leaning forward in his chair and drumming his fingers on his knees.

His coveralls were dirtier than I'd ever seen them, smeared with a Jackson Pollock assemblage of dark colors and patterns. He managed to get himself out of his chair by the time I'd turned off my truck and gotten out the door.

"You made good time," he said absently.

"When was Skidmore here?" I asked instantly.

"Oh, sometime before lunch. He was here, then he got a call on his car radio from that dipsy deputy of his."

"Melissa," I guessed.

"Right." Eppie nodded. "And he was off."

"Did he tell you he was pressing charges or did he give you some kind of summons or paperwork?"

"No."

"Then what makes you think you're in trouble?"

"He's the sheriff," Eppie answered urgently. "He says I'm in trouble and I believe him."

"You're still thinking about Sheriff Maddox."

"Sheriff's a sheriff is my philosophy. Anyway, he took off when he got that phone message."

It only took a second to realize that the *message* had been me. That Skidmore had been at the junkyard when I talked to him on the phone. And he hadn't mentioned a thing about the car during lunch. That realization jarred me back to a chill where my old friend was concerned.

"You didn't show him the note you read me over the phone," I checked.

"Of course not," Eppie replied, his voice higher than ever. "It was for you. Damn. What do you think I am?"

"Sorry." I hid my expression.

He rummaged in his pocket a moment and produced a crumple of paper, held it out.

I took it, opened it as best I could.

The handwriting was rough, jagged.

"You found this note *on* the car engine?" I asked.

"Right."

"When?"

"This morning, early. Around six."

"So whoever left it was here during the night?"

"That's what's got me," Eppie confessed. "You know don't nobody come in here after dark on account of Bruno."

My eyes darted around the yard, suddenly straining to see Eppie's junkyard dog, the meanest animal in the United States. My fear of dogs in general was nothing compared to the concentrated terror that I felt whenever Bruno was near. He was a wolfhound, bigger than a Great Dane, loyal to Eppie and desperate to eat any other adult human being alive. Eppie had trained the dog personally, taking great care to teach it not to menace children and women over sixty. Every other pulsing creature was fair game. It was said that a bull had once wandered onto the property. Bruno dispatched it, eating half, leaving the rest for Eppie to barbecue.

A bull.

Eppie read the dread in my eyes.

"Not to worry, Doctor," he told me, only condescending a little. "The dog's chained up in back."

"So how did anyone get in here last night?" I marveled.

"That's one for the books all right." He grinned. "Look, you got to hear this."

He picked up a tire iron and went to his clothesline xylophone.

I followed, only mildly confused by Eppie's shift in concern. I knew him to be easily distracted, a man whose powers of concentration might be bested by a wandering toddler.

"You mean you haven't put the Volkswagen back together yet?" I asked, incredulous.

"Damage is already done," he said cavalierly, "and you will not believe this tone."

He came to a halt before a heavy gray mass hanging pendulously from the airplane wire that stretched between his office and a tele-phone pole, his bizarre array of metal car parts.

He raised the tire iron and hit the piece of metal delicately. It made a tone so deep and rich I felt it in my chest, it stopped up my ears. It was like a cathedral bell, the envy of Notre Dame.

"Beautiful," was all I could say.

"Yeah," he agreed proudly. "It completes the work. I got a full two octaves now. I'm done."

I roused myself from the hypnotic rapture of the sound, the over-tones still filling the air around me.

"No, you're not," I demanded. "You have to put that back in the girls' car."

"I know," he snapped. "I mean *eventually* I can get this, and then I'll have a complete set."

"You have to put it back today," I told him sternly, "and it still might not matter to Skid, because you did tamper with evidence in a homicide investigation."

"Homicide? I thought it was a train wreck."

I winced.

"It was," I answered hastily, "that's what I meant. That sound, it disoriented me. It's really something."

"Yeah," he said proudly. "C below middle C. Damn. I'm thinking of setting the whole thing up different now that I got two octaves, make it easier to play. You got any ideas about that?"

I only paused a moment to consider that if I were required to sit around a junkyard all day waiting for someone to come and buy something, I would have lost my mind long ago. I found it satisfying that Eppie had turned his lunacy toward music, however insane that music might be.

"I'd rather get back to this note that someone left last night," I told him, holding it out. "It says to call me."

"Yes."

"But you didn't. You waited until Skidmore was here and gone."

"I called you eventually."

"Why did you wait?"

"You heard the sound of this thing," he told me, turning his beaming expression in the direction of the Volkswagen engine part. "I had to set this up, you understand, and give it a listen."

"No, I mean, obviously your encounter with Skidmore made you call me."

Eppie's face changed, a cloud came over it. His shoulders sagged and his posture turned more solid. He looked at me with different eyes.

"Well, okay," he admitted, a little defiantly. "I thought it was this kind of a deal: I got a note that has your name on it, and it could get you into trouble. You're friends with the sheriff. So if I don't show this note to the sheriff, maybe you'll help me out and make him ease up on me about this evidence tampering, which I did not do."

"You're thinking about blackmailing me?" I looked him up and down, grinning. "Are you serious? In the first place, I don't care if you show that note to Skid. And in the second place, I don't have much influence of any kind with Skidmore these days. And in the third place, are you *serious*?"

"You said that."

"I mean it!" I stared at him. "Besides, I have the note in my hand."

I waved it at him.

He locked his eyes on me, and the menace in them was electric.

"Come on, Doc," he said gently, "I got a tire iron, and a mean dog twenty feet away. If I want that note back, I'll get it."

Eppie whistled once, low.

My head snapped around, my eyes once again desperately searching for any sign of Bruno.

"That's really why you called me?" I said softly, the wind knocked out of my confidence. "To get me to do you a favor with the law?"

"Look, I like you, Doc," he said, his eyes glued to mine, "and I always liked hearing my music on your tape recorder. But do you have any idea how many times a month I get hassled by the cops? This license and that fee and some other kind of rule about who you can sell what to. It's like they're *looking* for a reason to shut me down. I need you to tell Sheriff Needle to back off. I need my peace of mind."

I scoured the junkyard, the gnarled array of broken automobiles and heaps of metal, weedy brown remnants of Queen Anne's lace and goldenrod, red patches of clay, and the sad, sagging wire that held up Eppie Waldup's one redeeming social value. The landscape betrayed an almost complete lack of peace of mind. Eppie was not a delicate soul, despite the sound of his voice.

He was hiding something.

"All right," I sighed, attempting nonchalance. "I'll speak to Skidmore on your behalf. I do like your music, and it would be a shame not to hear it. I'll have to keep this note though. I want to study it."

"You give me your word you'll call off the sheriff," he said as sternly as he could.

"I'll try to speak with him about the subject today," I assured him. "Or tomorrow."

"Not good enough!" Eppie bellowed. "Bruno!"

The dog appeared out of nowhere, some black hell of shadows, and landed fifteen feet away from me, rattling his tether chain and snarling foam down his chin.

I sucked in a breath so suddenly that my heart stopped. My hands flew up and I stumbled backward, careening into jumbled lumps of metal.

"Good boy, Bruno," Eppie said menacingly. "Get a good smell of this man. You might need to find him later on."

The dog sniffed violently, creating a small tornado around its nose.

"God," I stammered, catching my breath.

"You see I'm serious. I take you at your word, but I got Bruno for insurance, you understand."

"You can have the note back," I gasped, throwing it to the ground.

"Don't need it," he answered casually.

I continued backing up, sipping short breaths, wheezing, until I got to my truck.

"This was unnecessary, Eppie," I assured him once my hand found the door handle. "You know how dogs affect me."

"Right," he said, his eyes burning holes in my head, "same way I feel about the police. And now I can trust you. Fear makes a man reliable."

I got into my truck. Bruno sat. Eppie dropped his tire iron.

My heart was thumping against the inside of my chest like an animal desperate to escape a cage.

How could anyone have gotten past that monster last night? I thought to myself as I started the truck, eyes glued to Bruno's slavering mien. *How would anyone survive that?*

Still shaking a little, I backed the truck away slowly, turned, and headed for the main road, uncertain where to go. The blood was still drumming in my temples, and I realized I hadn't exhaled.

I took a few deep breaths, staving off any memory of the event that had produced such a terror of dogs. Still, a snarling ground itself into my ears, and yellow teeth dripped with thick saliva just at the corner of my eye.

It was clear Eppie was concerned about something more than a few licensing violations. The most obvious explanation was that he was the hub of a stolen-car ring, his junkyard being a perfect place for such an enterprise. He thought I would be willing to convince Skidmore to look the other way. Eppie thought that Skidmore was as corrupt as our previous county sheriff, Maddox. I could barely tolerate the idea that Eppie Waldrup, with his strange musical talents, was, in the main, nothing more than a very common criminal.

In desperation I struggled to focus on the mystery at hand. What person could have come into Eppie's yard, spent time examining the Volkswagen engine, calmly penned a note, all with Bruno present.

By the time the answer came to me, I was nearly on the highway.

I turned toward Blue Mountain.

———

I pulled up in front of Judy's house fifteen minutes later, barely had the engine off before I was out of the truck and pounding on her front door.

"Orvid," I insisted, "are you in there? We have to talk *now*!"

The adrenaline from my encounter with Bruno gave the sound of my voice a higher pitch, a grate of strangeness.

Judy came to the door almost immediately. She was still dressed in her funeral attire: a sleek aubergine suit with an eggshell-white blouse.

"What do you think you're doing?" she asked, standing firm in her doorway. "You can't come storming up to my house on a day like this! And what makes you think Orvid is here?"

"If you don't let me in this minute, I'll come back with Sheriff Needle," I answered, stage whisper between clenched teeth. "He'll ask the questions instead of me."

"Orvid?" she said calmly, eyes locked on mine. "You feel like company?"

A voice from within spoke serenely, I couldn't hear exactly what he said. But after the briefest of hesitations, Judy stepped aside and I lunged into her living room.

Orvid was sitting on the sofa, cane in his hands. He was dressed all in black, linen pants perfectly tailored, black Italian loafers, and a midnight polo shirt.

A tea service was on the table in front of him, two perfect, bone-white china cups and a pale green pot in the image of a coiled dragon.

"Would you like some?" he asked me, smiling. "It's green tea, very beneficial."

"I got your note," I said harshly.

"Good," he responded sweetly, "I was hoping you'd understand."

"I understand that you've been shadowing my investigation every step of the way!"

"Your investigation," he repeated, as if the phrase made no sense. "Well, strictly speaking, it's not possible for me to shadow you since

I've been every place first. In the second place, I was under the impression that you weren't really offering much in the way of an investigation. And finally, I sort of asked you to come visit me, in a way, so you can relax, can't you, and have some tea? Judy-sweet, would you mind bringing another cup?"

Judy brushed past me and motored into the kitchen without a word.

"Why are you so upset?" Orvid's voice was honey.

I took a deep breath. I looked around the living room, trying to make some choices about Orvid and Judy. I knew I couldn't trust them completely, but compared to the other primary players in the events of the past days, they were almost kindly.

"Why am I so upset?" I said, as much to myself as to Orvid.

"You want to talk it out?" Orvid offered clinically.

I sat in the same sofa I had taken before, eyes glazed with thought.

"In no particular order," I sighed, "my girlfriend's in grief and she thinks I can help, but I can't. My best friend doesn't like me anymore. I've found out more terrible things about my home in the past three days than I have in the previous two years. And I was just menaced by the meanest dog on the planet. I can still smell its foul breath."

"Bruno's not so bad, to me," Orvid said, reaching for his teacup.

"That's because Bruno thinks you're a child," I said, eyelids lowered, "so he won't attack you."

"I was hoping that would be the case," Orvid admitted, "although the dog was trained by Eppie Waldrup, whose IQ has to be about the same as his waist size. I had a few tense moments."

"You're alive."

"The dog has a taste for raw beef. I brought him some treats."

"How did you get the new coroner to give you his information? He seems more the *barbecued* beef type."

"That was easier." Orvid smiled. "For Mr. Millroy, I was a college student, premed, on a scholarship and desperate to keep it. I mean, you have no idea how difficult a medical school can be for a person of my size, and if only I understood what he was doing a little better, I might make an impression on my professor."

"Shameless," I scolded, but there may have been a slight upward inclination at the corner of my mouth. "What else?"

"Well," he sighed, "I have to admit that you got to the kid at the movie house before I did."

His voice betrayed a certain irony that instantly made me realize there was something more to his admission.

"But you do know something about the boy, Andy Newlander," I said, sitting back in my sofa.

"I am primarily a creature of the night," Orvid said, primarily for effect, I assumed. "And in the dark, I see things other people don't see."

"I'm certain you do," I responded, not biting, "but I'm more curious about what you're doing at night than what you see other people doing."

"All right." He set down his cup.

Judy returned with a larger cup for me, poured tea into it without looking at me.

"Sugar?" she asked curtly.

"I wouldn't want to spoil the taste of the tea. Thank you, Judy."

"Did you hear?" Orvid asked Judy. "Dr. Devilin was menaced by Eppie Waldrup's junkyard dog."

Judy turned my way to hand me the cup.

"I have an inordinate fear of dogs," I said, trying to make light of my terror.

"Based, no doubt, on a childhood incident," Orvid said lazily. "Isn't that where these things usually come from?"

I took the cup from Judy. She still wouldn't look at me.

"As it happens," I told Orvid, "you're quite correct. I was attacked by a German shepherd when I was six or seven."

"There's more to it than that," Orvid objected amiably. "Something traumatic brought about a hatred for dogs so virulent that you'd refer to Bruno as *it* rather than *he*. I also notice your left knee is bouncing nervously and you are clenching your jaw. We're only *talking* about dogs, there's not a real one in sight."

I stopped my knee, hadn't even noticed I was doing it. And my jaw ached. I had been grinding my teeth since leaving Eppie's yard.

"You have a degree in psychology," I guessed.

"No." He smiled. "I'm flattered you would think so. Though I do find that academics generally think a degree is the only possible explanation for a good observation. The fact is that my work has encouraged me to be something of a student of human nature."

"Your work as a cutlery salesman," I said drily, looking at Judy. "Isn't that what you said?"

Orvid leaned forward. His pale eyes seemed to crack with an electric spark.

"I think we both know that's not entirely accurate," he said.

"Correct," I affirmed. "I believe I know what your business is. But I'm not certain how to proceed. I want to find out what happened to Tess and Rory, but I'm absolutely loath to delve too deeply into your affairs. Not because I'm afraid of you, though I probably ought to be, but because I've recently come to see there's enough darkness in my world without looking for any more."

"You don't know my business," he said, laughing. "But I would be interested to know what you think it is."

"And I'd be interested to know why you were tampering with the girls' engine last night. You realize that it looks as if you had something to do with their murder."

Judy's head snapped in my direction. The room was so quiet I could hear the steam from my teacup.

"So you're using that word," Orvid said calmly.

He was right. I'd gone from a conviction that the girls' death was accidental, to certain knowledge that they were murdered. In under forty-eight hours.

"They were killed," Judy rasped. "At least you know that now. But Orvid had nothing to do with it."

I simply stared.

In collecting stories or songs from a reluctant informant, silence is the greatest ally. It's always better to wait for the interview subject to fill in that silence than it is for the interviewer to keep talking.

"I'm going to tell you what I know," Orvid said finally. "And I hope you'll do the same. We really are in this together, for a number of reasons."

"I don't trust you," I said plainly, "but I can't think of anyone I do trust at the moment."

"Lucinda Foxe," Judy suggested, softening, a vaporous smile at her lips. "Your *girlfriend*. Don't usually hear a grown man use that word."

"Yes," I admitted, ignoring her mild taunting. "I do trust her."

"That's a start." Judy took a seat beside Orvid.

"Like Ariadne," I sighed.

"Sorry?" Judy inclined her ear my way.

"Nothing," I said, embarrassed.

"No," Orvid encouraged. "Who or what is Ariadne?"

"In ancient Greek folklore," I explained softly, "a young girl named Ariadne stood at the mouth of the Minotaur's labyrinth, holding a thread to help Theseus, the hero intent on slaying the Minotaur. Theseus took the other end, wandered deep into the cave, and found the monster, a man with the head of a bull. Down in the darkest part of the twisted stone corridors, Theseus killed the beast. No one had ever found their way out of the darkness of the Minotaur's maze, but since Ariadne stood waiting in the sun at the doorway, holding the thread, Theseus was able to retrace his steps and return to the world of light."

"Oh," Judy said, a quick glance to Orvid. "That's it."

"Poetry aside," Orvid said to me, shifting uncomfortably in his seat, "I believe you were about to say that you didn't trust me, but you would be willing to share information in our common cause, finding the person who killed the little girls."

Orvid cleared his throat, eyes closed.

"Yes," I conceded. "All right."

"Show of good faith," Orvid went on, wheezing a little, "I'll start. I'll try to finish telling you what I tried to say when you were here before. I believe I saw the murderer."

I was so stunned by his words that I was certain I'd heard incorrectly.

"You saw *what*?" I asked.

"I was in the abandoned train depot," he fired back, his voice rasping. "I was there for a good part of the night. It's a perfect vantage point, right at the bend in the tracks. You can see the crossing to your right and the trestle on the opposite side."

"You already told me you were there," I prompted him.

"I heard the crash," he admitted. "Horrendous. I didn't know what had happened, but since my business does not appreciate scrutiny, especially by the sort of person who would come to investigate a train wreck, I vanished almost instantly. When Judy told me the awful news, I realized I had been a witness of sorts to the events of the girls' demise."

"But," I whispered, "you didn't actually see the wreck?"

"No," he said slowly, "I was quite hidden in the train station, which, as you know from your examination of the scene, is around a bend toward the center of town. I did eventually see the train, it took a remarkably long time for it to come to a standstill."

He coughed.

"So," I said, taking a breath, "you were there, but you didn't actually see anything."

"Not exactly. I saw something that I think bears upon our work. I'm not quite sure how to relate it to you."

"Plainly," I insisted. "Honestly."

I had no idea what he wanted to tell me, but I could see the reluctance tensing his entire body.

He glanced at Judy, set down his teacup, breathing heavily. Judy touched his leg.

"Use your damned inhaler, sweetheart," she said gently. "Go on."

He complied sheepishly, an apologetic tilt of his head in my direction. He reached into the pocket of his linen pants and drew out a medicinal inhaler.

"I have monstrous asthma," he complained. "You would not believe the difficulty it causes me."

"It bothers him more when he's upset," Judy said, a look of complete adoration on her face as she stared at his profile.

"That's why I try to adopt a kind of Zen calm," he said ruefully. "It works about seventy percent of the time."

"The green tea usually helps," Judy said.

Orvid put the inhaler in his mouth and breathed in a shot of medicine big enough for a man my size. He winced, swallowed, and returned the inhaler to his pocket.

"Product of the albinism." He shrugged.

"What did you see?" I asked impatiently.

He nodded.

"I saw Sheriff Needle," Orvid complied, "and Deputy Mathews, his supposed paramour, out on the tracks."

"After the accident."

"No, that's just the point. I saw them at the trestle about a half an hour *before* the accident. And then they walked to the crossing, did something there, and went back to the trestle and disappeared into the wooded area there. I didn't see them again. They were not on the scene for the accident until later."

"What were they doing at the trestle? And how could you see them?"

"I see perfectly at night, as I said before," he told me a little wanly. "But I also had night-vision binoculars."

"You stayed out of sight from them," I suggested. "They didn't see you."

"Correct." He took in a deep breath.

"And you won't tell me what you were doing hiding in the abandoned train station with night-vision binoculars near midnight just before the train wreck?"

"It's not germane to the issue at hand," he said calmly. "The point is that I saw Skidmore and Melissa behaving very strangely around the railroad tracks, and then less than thirty minutes later the girls' Volkswagen got stuck on the tracks and a train hit it."

"And you examined the car," I went on hesitantly, "to see if you could determine what had gone wrong."

"And I believe that the engine was turned off when it was hit by the train. The car was not running."

"How you determined that is a mystery to me, but I admit to having absolutely no knowledge of automobiles. Did you realize that the keys were missing from the ignition?"

His head inclined in my direction.

"I assumed the police confiscated them," he began.

"But they did not," I assured him. "No one knows where the keys are. They weren't in the car, on either of the girls, and nowhere to be found at the scene. They're missing."

"They got knocked out of the car when the train hit, surely," Judy offered.

"Probably," Orvid said, clearly not convinced.

I could tell by his face that Orvid was reassessing his own internal assumptions.

"This is news to you," I said, "and it's changing your mind about something, I can see that. Something about Skidmore and Melissa? What did you think they were doing?"

"Please don't ask me why," he said, his voice grating once more, "but I thought they were doing something to the tracks, something to slow down or maybe even stop the train."

"At the trestle," I said.

"And at the crossing," he managed, reaching for his inhaler again.

I saw the look in his eye, a great sorrow.

"Christ!" I said suddenly, louder than I wanted to. "You think that what Skid and Melissa did to the tracks at the crossing is what stopped the girls' car!"

He nodded slowly.

"They didn't mean to," he said, his voice a garble, "but I think they may have been responsible for the girls' death."

Eleven

I left Judy's house in a daze. I would have stayed longer, challenged Orvid's hypothesis, but his asthma had really gotten the better of him, and he needed to rest. Judy insisted on ushering me out quickly, politely. I could tell she was worried.

With nowhere else to turn, I felt I had to confront Skid with the assertions Orvid had made. I took a gamble that he'd still be at the station and pressed on the accelerator. As the truck lurched toward Main Street, I realized how concerned I was about Skidmore. His voice, posture, even the lines in his face did not belong to the man I'd known all my life. He was changed; I didn't care for it.

The sun had gone beyond the western horizon. Still, some sort of light was scattered through a break in the charcoal clouds. The message was clear: beyond the bleak ceiling of this sky there lay something bright. Alas, such a revelation makes little difference to anyone who can look beyond the clouds but never fly there. In fact the light only taunted, seemed to cast longer shadows across the sloping face of Blue Mountain.

I rolled down Main Street moments later. All the rushing around had given me a headache and every muscle in my neck and shoulders was tense.

Some lights were on in the windows of the shops. A misting rain had begun to blur the edges of everything to the palest possible blue.

The sheriff's office was well lit. A lucky turn of events had kept

Skidmore there, his car was parked in front. I pulled my truck into the space next to his and got out quickly.

The front room of the Sheriff's Office was small, less intimidating than it had been during Sheriff Maddox's reign. Where wanted posters had once hung, there were now photos of the members of our entire police force, all five of them. Skid sporting his best haircut, several deputies who had been at their jobs for nearly twenty years, and a yearbook-style portrait of Melissa, hair pulled back, eyes sparkling. The fluorescent light was too bright, the furniture too old, but the walls were freshly painted and an enormous largemouth bass was mounted over the door to the left of the entrance, the one that led to the detention cells. It was a small lobby, barely enough space for five heavy wooden chairs and Melissa's desk.

She looked up when I came in.

"Dr. Devilin," she said, surprised.

"Hello, Melissa." I smiled quickly. "Is Skidmore in? I have something very important."

"Dev?" Skid called from in his office. "Is that you? I'm busy."

"Yes," I said back, "do you have five minutes? It's something you ought to hear."

I could hear him sigh.

"Five minutes," he said firmly. "No more. Melissa?"

"Yes, sir?" she piped up.

"Time him."

"Sir?"

"Look at your watch right now," Skid said impatiently, "and when five minutes is up, pull out your gun, come in here, and chase Dr. Devilin out of my office, you hear?"

"Uh-huh." She smiled, winked at me. "Should I put my bullet in the gun?"

"Five minutes!" Skid insisted.

I nodded to Melissa and moved immediately.

"Skid," I began before I could even see him, "I've heard something that I needed to ask you about right away."

"God," he said softly. "What now?"

I stepped past his threshold.

The office was a mess. Coffee cups and water bottles littered his desktop. Piles of papers covered every surface. Sticky notes were everywhere, at least twenty adhered to the phone. Even the chair across from his desk was filled with files. The overhead light was off, and the lamp on his desk gave the entire room a film noir ambience that I found amusing, even under the circumstances.

"Maid's day off?"

"Put those files on the floor, sit down in that chair, and tell me why you're here." His voice was firm.

I turned and closed the door to his office behind me, then did as he'd suggested, leaning into my side of the desk, my voice at a whisper.

"The hardest part is this, so I'm not beating around the bush about it," I began, eye to eye with Skidmore. "You and Melissa were in Pine City the night of the train accident. You did something to the tracks at the crossing and at the trestle, possibly something to slow down the train. Whatever it was that you did may have caused the girls to get stuck on the tracks."

I sat back in the chair.

All the color drained from Skid's face. His shoulders sagged and he bit his lower lip.

"Sometimes I forget," he said barely audibly, "that you're really good at finding things out."

"It's not just a natural talent. I work at it."

"Well, you're right," he sighed, "up to a point. I was there for a while that night, but it was before the accident. Me and Melissa, we were there for other reasons."

"No point in hiding what the gossip is," I said quickly, avoiding his eyes. "Were you and Melissa there for business or personal reasons?"

"Personal?" His voice was twice a loud as it had been. "God damn it, Fever, you *have* to know better than that. I mean, I know what the gossip is; little town like this, all you got to do is talk to a single woman over lunch, and by suppertime you're an item. But you got to realize that Melissa Mathews is a professional law enforcement officer and I treat her like Ned or any of these other deputies."

"Except that when Melissa tells you about her troubles, you spend your evenings with her, helping out. When's the last time you did that with Ned?"

"When's the last time *Ned* had the slightest notion that parking fines aren't our number one problem in this county?" He was nearly shouting. "Melissa did good detective work following her cousin Nickel, and when she had enough facts, she shared them with the sheriff. Then the sheriff and the deputy began an investigation about drug traffic in our town!"

I was about to up the stakes of the argument when I realized the actual point he was trying to make, though he wasn't expressing it in any coherent manner. He was chiding me for thinking of Melissa as an attractive woman first and a county servant second, the way everyone else in the town surely would have. My shame was the realization that he was correct in his assessment.

"You're right," I said firmly. "I'm wrong."

"Fever?" he said hesitantly, cocking his head to one side.

It was the only thing I could have said that would shock him that much, phrases so seldom in my mouth.

"I'm disappointed in myself for thinking the way I have. I owe you and Melissa an apology. I think you ought to speak to your wife exactly the way you did to me just now. I know I'm more of a feminist than she is, but Girlinda's her own person, and I think she'd be just as mortified as I am to realize how far her perception had strayed from the truth."

"Girlinda?"

"Remember, I told you that she called me a while back, in tears. Worried about you. I didn't know what to say to her. I certainly didn't help her. But you can. You've got to reassure her."

"What's the matter with everybody?" he moaned.

"You have to know that this sheriff job has changed you," I said, a little more defensively than I'd intended. "You're very strange lately."

He let out a breath so heavy it rustled the papers on his desk.

"I used to be one of them," he said softly, lifting his head in the direction of the outer room. "A deputy in the other room who thought that parking overtime and domestic fights was the worst of our troubles in Blue Mountain."

"Well," I said gently, "I refuse to let you wallow in the beauty of the days gone by, when you were a carefree deputy. You hated being a deputy under Maddox, and as to what your worst troubles were, I'll remind you that you solved two murders with me. Maddox was a horror, whereas you're the most brilliant sheriff this county has ever seen. The *good old days*? They haven't gotten here yet."

"Is that so?" he asked, a brief smile playing on his lips.

"Are you going to tell me what you were doing at the railroad crossing the other night?" I could feel my teeth grinding uncomfortably.

Skid stared at me, clearly trying to decide what to say.

"All right," he finally surrendered. "Deputy Mathews and I have been conducting an ongoing investigation concerning the drug traffic in our little corner of Eden. We believe that every now and again a certain railroad employee tosses a package off the train that goes through Pine City. We also believe that a local man recovers these packages and is the main distributor here in the county."

"What drugs?"

"A little weed"—he shrugged—"and recently, a lot of ecstasy."

"Really?" I didn't even bother to hide that I wasn't surprised.

"Melissa and me were on a stakeout. And before you make fun of me, I'm just as embarrassed to use the word *stakeout* as you are to hear it. But based on Melissa's observation of previous patterns, last Friday night was supposed to have been the next in this series of drop-offs. We were certain the man in question was hiding in the old train depot, waiting."

"You can just go ahead and use Orvid's name," I said, shifting in my seat. "I've already come to the conclusion that he's your so-called *man in question*."

He only stared a moment.

"How you come to know all this," Skidmore said, shaking his head, "is a mystery I don't care to solve."

"So you were staking out Orvid Newcomb."

"We were," he confirmed, "when there was a distraction down at the trestle."

"Wait," I interrupted. "*Did* you put something on the tracks?"

"Sensing foil," Skid said quietly. "One set at the crossing, one at the trestle, to see did the train slow down more than usual. It has to slow down for the curve, but we believed it slowed down more to drop off the packages. We'd taken a measurement of the same train every night for a week. We were trying to establish a predictable pattern."

"You're kidding," I said, mocking and amazed at the same time. "This really is like actual police work. You could have your own television show."

"I never liked you," he reported drily. "I pretended to 'cause I felt sorry for you, but now you're being such a pain in the butt, I can be honest about it now."

"Good to know," I said, grinning. "So you had some kind of official surveillance equipment with you?"

"All we needed was a laptop," he said, marveling a little at the technology. "It's really something, some of these programs they got."

"Anyway, I interrupted you. You saw something at the trestle."

"Well," he said, slumping a little in his seat, "we already knew that these rail riders hang out down there. Pine City's a good stop for them, because the train already has to slow down a little on account of the big curve coming into the city and the intersection, like I said, but these bums, they seemed to know that some nights it really goes slow. Slow enough to get on or get off."

"Because of the drug packages."

"That's what we think." His lips were thin, and he was staring at the top of his desk.

"I'll tell you what I hate about this more than anything," he said slowly. "I hate being a cliché. Small-town drug traffic. Is that weird, or, I don't know, cold or something?"

"No," I told him quietly. "I know what you mean. You thought we were immune. I did too."

"No place untouched by dark matter." He shook his head. "Is that what you said?"

"So you went to roust the hoboes."

"You remember May? That homeless woman who spoke French; lived at the county cemetery whenever she was up this way?"

"Of course."

"She's the one that told me about the slow train," Skid said, "good while back. I just filed it away in my head, another one of her strange observations, but when Melissa brought all this up about her cousin Nickel, I remembered it."

"You said you were distracted by the people at the trestle?" I said impatiently.

"Yes. There was some kind of disturbance, and we went to break it up. We had a while before the train was supposed to be by, and Orvid hadn't showed up yet."

"Think again," I said softly. "Orvid saw all this. He was already in the abandoned station."

Skid leaned forward quickly.

"Are you serious?" he growled.

"He told me about your going to the trestle."

"Okay." Skid sat back. "Damn."

"So what happened? With the disturbance?"

"Oh, it was just a little fight. Happens a lot. They're all zombie drunk and most of them have some kind of mental situation."

"You went to break up the fight."

"We did." He grinned. "You should have seen this one old guy, a real character. Said he was a preacher and was trying to save the rest of them. Genuine hellfire-and-brimstone type."

"He was the cause of the fight," I whispered, my pulse quickening. Skid stared at me.

"Fever?" he asked. "Your face is all drained. You're white as a sheet. What the hell?"

"That man, the preacher, is named Hiram Frazier." I swallowed. "He's the one who broke into my house. He's insane."

Twelve

It took some doing, but I managed to tell Skidmore all I knew about Hiram Frazier. I hadn't realized until I had to talk about him how inexplicably frightened he made me feel. I was having a little difficulty breathing. I had no idea why talking about the man gave me such discomfort, but I was nearly shaking by the time I finished talking about him.

"And after you were gone from my house," I concluded my brief tale, "I found a Bible open to a certain passage in Revelation right by the phone."

"Your Bible?"

"Never saw it before."

"What was the passage?"

" 'Behold I am coming soon, bringing my recompense, to repay every one for what he has done.' " My voice sounded as if it were coming from inside a cave.

"Jesus," Skid breathed. "Why didn't you tell me about this before?"

"I thought it was just a weird encounter. Nothing to tell, really. But now I think there's something much more to him than meets the eye."

I didn't want to confess to Skidmore or to anyone that I had considered it a real possibility that the man was a ghost.

"Name's Hiram Frazier?" Skid typed something into his desktop computer. "I'll check, see what we got."

"You ran him off from the rest of the people at the trestle that night," I suggested, my words slurring slightly.

"Yes. He was clearly the instigator. We moved him along."

"I saw him that night, out on the highway closer to home."

"What time?"

"No idea." I rubbed my forehead. "Look, I know this sounds strange, but I did a research article about a year ago concerning train hopping that included a statistical report of accidents that happen, like at the crossing the other night. I was just telling Lucinda about it. I got most of the information from the Federal Railroad Administration, but of course I interviewed a number of men. When Frazier was in my car, he told me a story that I thought maybe I'd heard before. Now there's something buzzing in the back of my head. I have to have a look at those interviews. I think they may have mentioned this Hiram Frazier character."

The lamp on Skid's desk was surrounded by a vague halo, and the rest of the room was dimming.

"You seem kind of shook up," Skidmore said skeptically. "Are you positive they talked about *this* man?"

"No." I closed my eyes, trying to hear the interviews in my mind. "But there's something I can't quite remember that's ringing a lot of subconscious bells."

"Okay." Skidmore's voice was completely in earnest. "Find the interviews."

He had had a sufficient number of experiences with me during our lifelong friendship to know when to ignore me, and when to take me seriously.

"They're on tape, you know," I said.

"I figured. I'll do a little follow-up on this computer search for Frazier, and you call me or come back here if you've got something you want me to know."

"Yes." I stood absently.

"You okay to drive?" he asked sternly, seeing my unsteadiness. "You look funny."

"I feel strange," I mumbled.

"You having a spell?" He stood too. "You haven't had one of those in a good while."

"I feel strange," I repeated. "Light-headed. And my heart's trying to crack a rib."

"You're breathing funny too," he said suddenly, moving around his desk. "Melissa!"

She appeared in the doorway instantly.

"Call J.J. and get an ambulance here *now!*" Skid barked.

"Wait," I protested. "I'm okay."

"Call!" Skid insisted.

"I'm having an anxiety attack," I managed, barely able to breathe. Melissa paused.

"You sure?" Skid demanded to know.

"I've had enough of them," I assured him. "Something's wrong, but it's mostly in my head, not my body."

"Should I call?" Melissa asked weakly.

"I just need some water," I told her, "and to catch my breath."

Every time I closed my eyes, images of snarling dogs and the dead-man stare of Hiram Frazier's eyes swam in my mind.

"What the hell is it, Fever?" Skid said, searching my eyes.

"I'm having a minor episode because something I know subconsciously is trying to swim up to my consciousness. And whatever it is that's buried is bothering me enough to engender this little attack. It's probably causing some sort of ambivalent state of which I'm unaware. That ambivalence is the root of my distress."

"I barely know what you're talking about," Skid said wearily, "but I know it means something to you."

"I know something important," I said, trying to clarify, "that I don't know I know."

"Yeah." Skid nodded curtly. "Stop trying to explain it. You just sound crazier."

"Right." I got my bearings. "I think the best thing I can do is go home and dig up those notes and tapes. I'll call you when I do."

"If that homeless man is wandering around up there," Melissa interrupted, her brow furrowed, "and he's already broke into Dr. Devilin's house once, should he go up there by himself? I'm sorry, but I overheard what you said about the Bible quote and all."

"Good point," Skid allowed.

"I don't need someone to walk me to my door," I answered, irritated. "The state I'm in, I'm a serious threat to anyone who comes close to me."

Melissa looked up into my eyes. I stood nearly a foot taller. She let out a little laugh.

"Well, I wouldn't want to mess with you right now," she said lightly.

I looked at Skid.

"There you are," I told him. "Professional assessment from an officer of the law."

"Uh-huh," he said wryly, "but if you get your ass kicked, don't come running to me."

"You know," I said, regaining a little composure, moving out of Skid's office, "you never used to apply that sort of language to your daily affairs. I've noticed a decline in your vocabulary since you became sheriff."

"I'm sorry," he said contritely.

"Good."

"All kinds of damn sorry," he went on. "Sorry as hell."

"God." I looked at Melissa imploringly.

"It's the job," she said, mock concern. "Won't be long before he's kicking stray dogs and arresting little children."

I headed for the exit, hand in the air waving to them, not looking back.

"I'll call."

I drove back home with the windows down, the fresh air reviving me. Night drew a quick shade over the sky, it always does in autumn in the mountains. Sunset never happens slowly. My headlights were on before I was up the mountain.

I sat in the truck a moment, headlights shining directly onto the porch. My front door was solidly closed. No shadows moved. Still, I revved the engine to let lurking strangers know I was there. For some reason I even blinked the lights on and off several times, a bizarre attempt at aggressive behavior.

Partially satisfied, after a time, that no one was around the house, I turned off the truck and headed in.

The wind brushed a scattering of silver rain that brushed my face, the ground, the roof of the house. The moon was invisible behind dull nimbostratus. Thunder in the distance presaged an oncoming downpour. Jagged flickers of lightning shocked the clouds.

I stomped loudly up the steps of the porch, continuing my efforts to frighten, and found that my front door was still locked. Good.

Key in, the lock clicked, and I instantly turned on the living room lights. I went right to the kitchen and turned on those lights too, then locked the front door behind me.

The chill in the air did nothing to soothe the tingling hot edge of my hairline. I felt a flu coming on. I pulled off my jacket. Lightning flashed again outside, closely followed by thunder and an infinitesimal brownout. The storm was coming closer.

I checked everywhere a man might hide: closets, dark corners, behind the sofa. Then I grabbed a stout umbrella and charged upstairs, waving the umbrella before me as if it were a saber, making harsh exhalations of breath partly to sound mean, partly out of fear.

Upstairs rooms were as vacant of intruders as those downstairs had been. I relaxed a little.

Back downstairs, umbrella returned to its place, I rummaged in the credenza where I kept my Wollensak tape recorder. Beside the recorder, I found several spiral notebooks in which I had written quick reference keys to the tapes. Arcane as it was, my system was familiar to me, and I could find anything I was looking for instantaneously.

The reference notebook led me to Tape 174, "Rail Hoppers incident 6, at three-quarters of an inch in." I wanted to try that one first because it was underlined and asterisked in my notes.

I pulled out the tape recorder, the box marked 174, and found a pencil just in case I wanted to jot down something. I plugged in the machine, flipped the notebook to a blank page, sat on the sofa, threaded the tape. I turned on the Wollensak, fast-forwarded it to about the right place, and hit *play*.

"... at about suppertime." A scratchy voice leapt from the machine in the middle of a sentence. "He was crazier than most. Told all manner of holy-holy. I didn't pay much attention."

"But you say he was a preacher?" I heard my own voice interrupt.

"That's what *he* said," the voice corrected. "Who knows. Half these boys in the yard, they tell you near about anything if they think it'll get 'em somewheres. I only started listening to him when he told us about his good trick."

"Yes." My voice on tape sounded tinny to me. "Some of the others told me about a man with a trick. He has a certain way of getting money from people."

"It's a good one," the voice cackled, "if you can pull it off."

"But they say that man isn't here anymore."

"Nope," the man on the tape confirmed, "gone-gone. Ain't seed him in a month or more. He was crazier than most. Said he was the Lord's whipping boy."

"Did he say why?"

"Some crap about his wife dead in the bed," the voice mumbled. "I didn't pay much attention."

"Until he told you about his trick."

"It was a good one," the voice said, sprightly again. "If you can pull it off."

"Can you describe it to me?"

"Let me hear myself on the tape again," the man asked.

"Tell me about the trick, and I will."

"Okay," the man said quickly. "Well, he had to be waiting at a stoplight, and he'd have to catch a car with the driver's window down, or get the driver to roll down the window, which is harder. If the car got caught by the red light, he would step up quick, shove his arm in the car, turn off the engine, and take the key!"

He howled with laughter. Even on the tape it was a haunted, hollow sound.

"What they hell can they do?" the voice went on after a moment.

"They can't drive the car till you give 'em the key. And you don't do that till they give you the money. It's perfect. If you can make it work."

"You keep saying that," I said on the tape. "Have you tried it?"

"Yes." His voice was different. "Once. I don't do it no more. I should have chose an old woman driver, or a kid. Somebody that gets scared. I had a man driver, and as soon as I put my hand in the car, he stepped on the gas and took off. Ran a red light. I almost lost my arm. Nearly got drug through the entire intersection."

"So it's dangerous. This man's trick."

"I ain't never heard of nobody that can make it work except him."

"You don't know his name."

"He said he was from Tennessee. My name's Georgie."

"Well, thank you, Georgie, for telling me about this."

"Did the others tell you too?"

"Yes. I have about five versions of this. They're almost exactly the same."

"So you see I ain't lying. Let me hear my voice now. You got five dollars?"

"I'll just rewind the tape."

The machine went silent. It had been at that moment that I had rewound it so that the informant could hear himself.

I stopped the tape. My hand was shaking. I was certain I heard strange noises outside. When I stood up, my head was light. I may actually have staggered a little trying to get to the phone. All the while the thing that had struggled in the back of my mind was surfacing, a huge flesh-eating monster.

No one had found the keys to the Volkswagen. The engine might have been off when the train hit it. Buried somewhere in my subconscious I had known the answer to those two riddles almost when I had heard about them. But I would not allow myself to remember, I'd kept insisting that the wreck had been an accident.

I made it to the phone, dialed Skid's number.

"Hello, Melissa," I said after a moment. "Let me speak to Skid, please."

"Dr. Devilin? Is that you? You don't sound like yourself. You still having that spell?"

"Please, Melissa," I said softly. "Just let me talk to Skid."

"Okay." She sounded worried.

The line was silent a moment. Then:

"Fever?" Skid's voice was rich with concern.

"I found what I was looking for. I know what happened."

"Sorry?"

"The *girls*." I sat on the arm of the sofa. "It didn't have anything to do with drugs. We were wrong about that."

"What are you talking about?"

"Hiram Frazier," I began.

But before I could say anything more, lightning and thunder exploded simultaneously and the house was plunged into darkness.

The phone was dead.

My breathing quickened, and I could feel the pulse at my temples.

I hung up, a little numb.

Brief power outages were so common on the mountain that I kept several oil lamps, matches, and a flashlight in the kitchen pantry.

I stood up just as another bolt of lightning snapped, attendant thunder shaking the windows.

I moved quickly to the kitchen, fetched the lamps, lit them, and pulled out the flash light.

I checked the front door again, even though I knew it was locked. I went to each window, made certain the locks were tight.

Outside, black as pitch, the rain began to pummel the roof. I pulled all the curtains, went back to the kitchen.

Hot tea seemed the right idea. It was for just such occasions that I had kept my old gas stove.

I struck a match, turned on the gas, and instantly flame leapt into a comfortable circle barely smaller than my silver kettle. I thought peppermint tea would be best, nothing with caffeine. I was jangled enough. The oil lamps made the kitchen butter-bright, and I felt better. I had gotten the tea, pulled a mug out of the cupboard, and found the honey before I realized that I was retreating.

I knew I had to go immediately into town to tell Skidmore my revelation. I couldn't hang about the darkened house, afraid to go out, seriously attempting to avoid the thoughts in my mind. The impulse to light the lamps and have tea was a boyhood regression, a retreat to all the times I'd been alone in the house when I was seven, and ten, and fourteen, with no idea where my parents were, or when they would return. I was stunned at how instantaneously I had fallen into the pattern, as quickly as the thunder had followed lightning. I was disappointed that the pattern was so ingrained, down to the peppermint tea I'd drunk as a boy.

I turned off the flame under the kettle, blew out both lamps. A thin ghost rose up from each and quickly dissipated, my mother and father, leaving the house once again.

I grabbed the flashlight, scooped up my jacket, and headed for the door, keys in hand. The rain was pounding harder and I thought about the umbrella I'd left by the door, but I didn't want to be hampered by it. I could just make a dash for the truck, stay dry enough.

Out on the porch, flashlight under my arm, I locked my front door, checked it twice, struggled to get my jacket on.

I ran the flashlight's beam over my truck and around it. Everything seemed fine. I twirled my keys absently on their ring.

Rain pierced the air with a thousand silver spears. I drew in a breath and stepped off the porch, lurching the ten or twelve steps to where I'd left the truck.

Another lightning bolt momentarily turned the pitch sky to pale day. Before I completely realized that I had seen the man's shadow move around the side of the porch, he was upon me.

I was plunged backward into the black lake of night, dead to the world.

Thirteen

I came to on the front porch with Eppie Waldrup standing over me, a fistful of my jacket in his right hand.

"Sorry to scare you, Doc," he said in his eerie high voice. "But I got to know what you're doing."

"Doing?" I could barely breathe.

Clearly he had wrestled me to the ground; I had passed out. I was certain that my neck had a railroad spike somewhere in it.

"I know you went to talk to Sheriff Needle," he said, his face like a red pumpkin, close to mine. "I got eyes and ears everywhere. I need to know what did you say to him."

"About you?" I managed. "Nothing."

"Yeah, I heard that too." He pulled on my coat and I sat up, my nose touching his. "See, that's a problem. Remember our deal? You was to explain to Sheriff Needle that I need my space. I thought me and Bruno made that clear. Need my *space,* you hear me? Now I have to whup your ass, you understand?"

He tightened his grip on my jacket and cocked his other arm back. A fist the size of a ham hovered over my face.

"No!" I said, coming more conscious. "I don't understand!"

My right hand flew up and grabbed his thumb, snapped it backward as hard as I could.

He dropped me, squealing.

I scuttled back, out from under him, and got to my feet before he stood up straight.

I kicked his kneecap, like kicking a soccer ball.

He brought his leg up involuntarily, a bad move.

Eppie tumbled away from me, down the porch steps, his head thudding in the wet ground of my yard.

I looked around for anything I could use as a weapon.

But Eppie was down and couldn't quite manage his way anywhere else. Breath knocked out of him, he was momentarily immobilized. His legs rested on my steps, his left hand held his right thumb, and he was moaning like a sick cat.

"Here's my decision, Eppie," I snarled. "I'm going to get in my truck now and run over your head as many times as it takes to pop it like a tomato."

I jangled my keys, which were, amazingly, still in my hand. I'd had my index finger through the key ring, and the keys had stayed with me.

"What?" he said in disbelief.

"You just lie right there," I told him.

I took a few quick steps and jumped over him, landing on the ground close enough to his head to scare him significantly. He covered his face with his arms and sucked in a breath.

I turned and squatted down.

"You understand what a strange person I am, right, Eppie?" I began persuasively.

"Uh-huh," he croaked, face still obscured.

"You ought to know better than to threaten me twice in one day. I'm used to being picked on by all sorts of bullies; I take as much as I can and then I snap. Like a dry twig. And when that happens, I have no idea what I'll do. Sometimes I black out and people have to tell me what I did. I'm not proud of it, but I have no control, you understand. If I run over your head right now with my truck, for example, I wouldn't be held responsible. In the first place, you attacked me and I was defending myself. And in the second place, I'm not mentally competent. Everyone knows that, just like you do. So I'm going to start my truck now."

Eppie's hands were trembling. He started thrashing from side to side, trying to get himself up.

"Christ Almighty, Doc," he sobbed, "you got to come to your senses. You love my music. You remember that? My music? I don't deserve to get my head run over. *Damn!*"

I stood.

"You have to get this, Eppie: I'm not going to do a thing for you. If you send your dog after me, I'll kill it. If you mess with me again, I'll kill you. I'm in the middle of something that's disturbing my entire cognitive field, and I'm *not* in the mood for any more crap from you."

I heard a car. I was hoping it was Skid, coming to see if I was all right. Headlights momentarily illuminated the surreal scene at the bottom of my steps.

"Somebody's coming," Eppie said, hysteria electrifying his words. "You *can't* do anything to me now."

"It's probably the Sheriff," I told him. "I was talking to him on the phone when my power went out. Good. I don't have to run over you, I can just have you arrested. Trespassing, assault, what else?"

"Ohhh," Eppie whined, "everything happens to me."

The car pulled up behind my truck. It was as far away from a police cruiser as an automobile could get: a spotless white Mercedes two-seater, lower to the ground than most sports cars, looking fast even when it came to a stop.

Lights still on, the driver threw open his door and jumped out.

"Are you all right, Dr. Devilin?"

I was momentarily disoriented by the size and sound of the man; it took me a second to respond.

"Yes, Mr. Newcomb," I said, stepping back from Eppie. "Thank you for asking. And how strange to see you here."

"Who's your friend?" Orvid said, standing behind his car door.

"Eppie," I said to the man at my feet, "do you know Orvid Newcomb?"

Eppie held up his uninjured hand.

"Help me up, would you, Doc? I ain't about to cause you no more trouble. I'm happy that ain't the sheriff."

I exhaled, planted my feet, and offered Eppie my hand. It took some doing, but the big man came to his feet. He turned in the direction of the headlights.

"I don't believe I've had the pleasure," he said, wiping his forehead.

"Orvid," I called, "this is Eppie Waldrup, owns the auto junkyard near Pine City with which you are passingly familiar."

"I've met your dog," Orvid said, amused.

"What?" Eppie was completely confused.

It appeared to me that he had never seen Orvid.

"He's met your dog," I repeated to Eppie.

"Is that a little boy?" Eppie asked me under his breath, squinting, trying to make out the form behind the door.

"No," I said. "Mr. Newcomb is—what? A figment of your imagination."

On cue, as I'd hoped he would, Orvid stepped from behind his car door and into the illumination of his lights. He made a striking figure, slightly backlit, hair matted to his head from the rain, a primal image. Without warning he drew the long blade from his cane and held it high over his head, with attendant mad expression and a low growl.

"Jesus Katy!" Eppie shrieked, staggering away from the vision.

I stepped close to Eppie, whispering.

"Your idea is that fear is motivational," I said through clenched teeth. "Makes a person do what you want, right?

"Yes," was all he could say, eyes wide and white.

"Well, it doesn't work quite that way with me. Fear makes me mad. Fear makes me want to hurt the person who's frightened me, any way I can. That's my story, and you know I mean it."

"I do." I could barely hear him.

"Where did you park?"

"I saw his truck back there," Orvid called. "It's the tow truck?"

"Tow truck," Eppie affirmed, nodding, unable to look at Orvid. "Up the road."

"Haul yourself up to it, then," I concluded, "and get the hell away from me, permanently, or Mr. Newcomb and I will pay you a visit in your sleep. Understand?"

"Yes," Eppie shot back, moving sideways away from me, putting my truck between himself and Orvid, and eventually waddling past the crest of the road into the night.

Still, I'm certain he was not out of earshot by the time Orvid and I had begun to howl with laughter.

Moments later Orvid and I were standing in my kitchen, oil lamps lit, tea kettle ready. We'd used half a roll of paper towels to dry ourselves. We'd heard Eppie's truck thunder away, and I'd invited Orvid inside.

"I was talking to Skidmore on the phone," I said, lighting the eye under the kettle once again, "when I lost power and the phone went dead."

"That must happen a lot up here," Orvid said patiently.

"It'll be back on in a while." I got out the tea. "I was going to have peppermint tea, then I thought better of it and decided to talk to Skid in person."

Orvid grinned. It was an eerie expression in the light of the oil lamps. It made his face more innocent.

"Peppermint tea." He sighed. "I used to drink that when I was a kid."

"Yes," I said, avoiding our similarity. "But I realized I needed to get down the mountain to Skid, finish our conversation. It was important. I'm going to do that in a second, but I have to know why you're here."

"It was important?" he said, leaning on his cane. "What you were going to tell him?"

"I know what happened to the girls," I blurted out.

I realized I'd been bursting to say that sentence to someone. I didn't quite know why I'd said it to Orvid Newcomb, but it suddenly seemed it would be a great relief to be able to express my theory out loud.

"Do you mind if I sit down?" he said, heading for the kitchen table.

"Of course," I stammered, "I'll be telling Skidmore everything in a moment, you realize."

I got out a second teacup and then followed him to the table.

"What do you think happened?" he said before we sat.

"I believe that a man named Hiram Frazier waited at the railroad crossing, stopped the girls' car, asked them for money, and when they didn't give him any, he reached in and took the keys out of the car."

"Oh, my God." Orvid looked down, staring at the red Formica of my tabletop. My brief speech had startled him, but I had the impression he might have somehow heard the theory or thought of it himself.

"What?"

"Please go on," he said, obviously shaken.

"He kept the keys," I continued a little hesitantly, "and said he wouldn't give them back until the girls gave him money. Tess was driving; Rory was wearing headphones at the time of the accident, listening to a CD."

"I may have seen this man." Orvid's face was stone.

That was it.

"You saw Hiram Frazier?"

"Of course I didn't know who he was that night," Orvid said, his eyes far away. "All in black, a scarecrow. Nearly transparent in the moonlight. He did something to the car?"

"No, I'm saying he took the keys," I said again. "The girls were laughing, trying to figure out what to do. It wouldn't have occurred to them to be frightened or angry, at least that's the portrait I have of them from Lucinda. Tess was dealing with Hiram Frazier, Rory had music blasting in her ears. By the time they realized a train was bearing down, they didn't have any hope of getting out of the car."

"Or they were so disoriented by the strangeness of the situation," Orvid added, "that they didn't even quite realize the danger they were in."

"Very possible," I said, an involuntary shiver icing up my spine. "I've been in close proximity to the man, and it's hard to pay attention to anything else when he's nearby."

"I see," Orvid said slowly.

His eyes appeared to be taking assessments. I felt he must be trying to decide if I had a fear of wandering vagrants to match my terror of dogs.

"If you don't believe me," I said, "I can take time to lay out my reasoning, but if you think I'm right, that would be a waste of time at the moment."

He locked eyes with me, staring past the pupils.

"I believe you," he said after a moment. "Do you mind if I call Judy just for a moment?"

The kettle responded by whistling.

"Go right ahead." I got up to answer the kettle.

Orvid pulled out a cell phone, hit speed dial, and murmured into the speaker.

"Hey," he said softly, "I'm with Dr. Devilin, and what do you suppose he told me? The man who caused the train wreck is named Hiram Frazier. . . . Yes. I thought so too. I love you."

He closed his cell phone.

I tried to pretend I hadn't heard his conversation, attempting to give him the illusion of privacy.

"I have to tell Skidmore about this, as I was saying," I told Orvid, my back to him.

"Want to borrow my phone?"

"I'd rather speak to him in person, considering his state of mind. It's my impression that you'd just as soon *not* go along with me."

"Correct," he agreed. "But before you decide what to do next, wouldn't you like to know why I'm here?"

"I would."

"Incidentally," he said, clearing his throat. "What the hell was going on between you and Eppie Waldrup? It would seem to me that it takes a lot to make a man that size get up off his ass and pay anybody a visit."

I folded my arms and leaned on the counter.

"Eppie is involved in something illegal," I said coldly, "and he was hoping I would convince Skidmore to turn a blind eye."

"Illegal?" Orvid said, strangely arch.

"That's my surmise. He says it has to do with permits and licenses, but I'm assuming it has to do with stolen cars. Wouldn't you think that was a good bet at an auto junkyard?"

"Could be." Orvid nodded slowly.

"At any rate, that's why he menaced me with your friend Bruno just before I came to visit you at Judy's, and why he came here tonight. He'd already been informed by someone that I'd spoken to Skidmore and I hadn't mentioned Eppie."

"Who?" Orvid sat up a little. "Do you know who Eppie's contact might be?"

"Not the slightest idea," I admitted, "but I don't want to be distracted by him at the moment. Partly because I think it clouds my ability to concentrate on pursuing Hiram Frazier and bringing him to Skidmore, and partly because I'm embarrassed that I lost my temper when Eppie attacked me. In fact I threatened him."

"You threatened Eppie Waldrup?" Orvid didn't bother to hide his glee. "How?"

"Well," I stammered, "I may have suggested that I'd run over his head with my truck."

"What?" Orvid said, laughing out loud.

"Until it popped like a tomato."

Orvid couldn't contain himself. He almost fell off the chair.

"That's fantastic," he finally managed.

"I don't see why," I said, chagrin growing.

"Okay," Orvid said, composing himself. "I'll tell you why. Because I love to see a bully put in his place. I've been the butt of that kind of behavior most of my life. I like to see the tables turned."

From the sound of his voice I could tell Orvid wasn't being completely honest. Clearly, he *lived* to see the tables turned.

"Ignoring that for the moment as well," I breezed on, "you now have to tell me why you're here."

"Yes." Orvid's demeanor changed almost instantly. He looked

down. "I could tell, when you left Judy's house, that you were upset. I thought at first it was just your concern about your friend Skidmore, and the possibility that he might have been responsible for the girls' death."

"It was nothing more than sensing foil, by the way," I interrupted, "that sent information to a laptop computer. That's all Skid and Melissa were doing to the tracks. A glorified speed trap. It couldn't have had anything to do with the car stopping. I know what made the car stop."

"This Hiram Frazier." Orvid's voice betrayed a skepticism that his face told me he wanted to keep hidden.

"But we're talking at cross-purposes," I said, unaccountably tensing. "I wanted to tell you my story and you have to tell me yours. I suggest we stop for a second and gather our thoughts."

"I see." He nodded ruefully. "You still have to decide how much to tell me."

"Yes, but that's not what I'm saying. I hate a conversation where both people are so intent on saying what they want to say that neither listens, especially in an attempt to share information."

"Most people aren't ever listening anyway," he said, eyes bright. "They're just waiting quietly until the other person stops talking so they can say what they want to say."

"Exactly." I leaned back on the counter. "I want to give my full attention to listening to you for a moment."

"This is part of your field research technique, I'd imagine. Collecting your folk stories and that sort of thing, you *listen*. With everything you've got."

"And it's not always an easy thing to do."

"For most people, I'd agree." He sat back. "So, I'll proceed. Sitting in Judy's living room, I thought that you were mostly upset about Skidmore's hand in the girls' accident. But I got to thinking about the other things you said and I wanted to reiterate my suggestion that we join forces in finding the truth about this matter."

"To what *other things* do you refer?" I asked drily.

"You feel you have to help your friend Lucinda but you can't. You think Skidmore Needle doesn't care for you anymore, and worst of all, you're having an attack of good old-fashioned existential fear and loathing because you've found out some things about your little mountain home that you don't particularly care to know."

I exhaled laboriously.

"Well," I agreed, "that about sums it up."

"Alas," he continued, "I know the feeling."

"You do?" I instantly wished my voice hadn't sounded like a child's.

"Well, for one thing, Judy says she wants me to find out what happened to the girls, but what she's really hoping I can do, in the back of her mind, is bring them back to life. I have a plethora of talents, but I'm afraid Lazarus-raising isn't among them."

I couldn't help smiling, even in the presence of such a macabre suggestion.

"For another thing, Sheriff Needle never liked me," Orvid went on, "and finally, I discover that a kind of sickness unto death is present in my spirit most of the time."

"You insist on emphasizing our similarities. But what is it that gives you existential nausea?"

"It's probably associated with my work."

"About which you'll still tell me nothing," I assumed.

He took a moment, tapping his finger idly on the tabletop.

"I will say," he answered, "that I was waiting in the abandoned train station that night for a delivery of sorts. The train that passes through Pine City shortly before midnight slows down considerably because of the big turns, the blind crossing, and the trestle. It's an ideal place for someone to throw a package off the train."

"A package which you retrieve." I nodded. "I already know something about that."

I stopped short of telling Orvid that Skidmore had been at the railroad tracks that night to keep an eye on Orvid. Or that I knew the packages he waited for contained drugs.

"You don't really know anything about it," Orvid said matter-of-factly. "The point is, I actually do kind of understand your current dark mood. I think that you and I should team up, attack some very small portion of the darkness, and make things a little better. That's why I'm here."

"Laudable. Why didn't you just call me?"

"I'm more persuasive in person," he said, smiling. "And I don't trust telephones."

Because they might be tapped or bugged or whatever word is the current police jargon, I thought.

"Now you," Orvid prompted. "I'm done with the speaking portion of my program. Ready to listen."

"Really," I said, sounding a little snide, I thought. "What would you like to hear?"

"How you know about this man, Hiram Frazier," Orvid said immediately.

"As I was saying," I sighed, reaching for the tea bags, "I met him. Picked him up in my truck and gave him a ride. He asked me for money, which I did not give to him, and he was angry about that. He later broke into this house and left me a foreboding Bible message."

"Explain," Orvid said slowly.

"I believe he broke into my house to scare me and left his Bible open to a certain passage in Revelation concerning revenge. Presumably because I didn't give him money."

"So he really is out of his mind," Orvid concluded.

"Yes."

"But what makes you think," Orvid asked evenly, "that he took the keys out of the Volkswagen at the train crossing?"

His face was a mask of patience, one I might wear if I were collecting stories from a mental patient.

I put tea bags into the cups I'd laid out, poured water, slid Orvid's cup toward him.

"If the electricity were on," I told him, "I'd play you a tape I have, something I collected a year ago or more that seems fairly conclusive. It's a good description of the person I know as Hiram Frazier and the unique manner in which he sometimes acquires money."

"You have this on tape?" Orvid's entire mien had shifted.

"I came directly from Skidmore's office in order to find the tape. I knew there was something in my mind, I just couldn't make it surface. When Skidmore told me about the train hoppers at the trestle that night, something ignited."

"You're a very strange man," Orvid said, picking up his teacup.

"I believe 'Look who's talking' is the correct response," I told him.

"Tell me exactly what's on the tape."

"I wish you could hear it for yourself. The informant's voice, when he's talking about Frazier, is very revealing."

"But until your power is restored . . ." he prompted.

"He kept referring to a wandering preacher that caused trouble among the other train hoppers. The description fit Frazier, though that name was never mentioned. Then the informant told me about Frazier's trick, even said he'd tried it himself once, but couldn't make it work."

"And you're convinced Frazier did this." Orvid's gaze was suddenly overwhelming.

"I'm not sure what you mean," I said, unsteadied by his intensity.

"I trust my instincts," he said precisely. "It's my impression that you're the same."

"Yes, I see what you're saying. And the conclusion of my intuition as well as these facts is that Hiram Frazier did this terrible thing. I have to find him, now, and make him realize what he's done. I feel an almost overwhelming need to see that he knows what he took away from us. Lucinda doted on the girls, and as I believe I said earlier, I trust Lucinda. Her assessment is that we've lost a significant light in the passing of those two, and I think she's correct. I can barely tolerate seeing the pain in her eyes."

"Exactly the same with Judy," Orvid said quietly.

In that moment, with those words, a barrier broke between us, at least in my mind. I saw that, in fact, Orvid Newcomb and I were not a great deal different. I could see from his expression that he was making new assessments of his own, coming to new conclusions.

"We have to work together," he said, his intensity growing, "to find this man."

"I obviously agree that he needs to be found," I hedged, "and held accountable for his deed. But I'm more inclined to let Skidmore take the lead in pursuing him, and leaving his chastisement to the law."

"The law." Orvid's voice was colored more with ridicule than contempt. "You have to believe me when I say that I'm all too familiar with how often the law goes awry; how little justice actually comes out of our judicial system."

"I certainly believe that is your perception. But I don't share your views."

"Spoken like a man who's never had a true experience of American jurisprudence."

"Be that as it may," I responded, "I'd have to say that the urge to help Skidmore in his investigation is, apparently, irresistible to me. So I'm at something of a loss as to how to proceed."

"Tell your sheriff friend what you've discovered," Orvid argued reasonably, "see what information he has, then help me catch the man responsible for the deaths of Tess and Rory Dyson."

Any decision in life is situational. On another day, in spring, say, when the garden was budding and Skidmore and I were on better terms, I might not have made a bargain with Orvid Newcomb.

But somewhere close to us, out in the dark, there was a hulk of a human being, a husk, a madman prowling where stalks of corn turned brown. It was November, the house was dark and cold, and too many things were dead.

Fourteen

"All right." I reached for one of the oil lamps. "How should we proceed?"

Orvid downed his tea and managed his way off the chair.

"If you wouldn't mind," he said, "I'd like to have a look around your house and the yard, see if I can scare up anything of this Hiram Frazier. It seems the appropriate place to start. How long ago do you think he was in your house?"

"Within the last several hours."

"So I might see something you overlooked." Orvid squinted. "You found no evidence of his break-in?"

"Except for the Bible," I told him. "I'll show you."

Orvid followed me into the living room. I held the oil lamp low, pointing to the closed Revised Standard Version by the phone.

"And it was open to Revelation?" he asked.

I turned to the passage. It wasn't hard to find, the spine of the book had deliberately been bent back at the exact page, and the intimidating passage was underlined.

Orvid leaned close and read.

"'Behold I am coming soon,'" Orvid quoted, "'bringing my recompense, to repay every one for what he has done.' Very impressive."

"It would be more so if you'd met the man," I assured him.

"Why don't you head on into town," he suggested. "Talk to Sheriff Needle about your ideas, and meet me at the railroad crossing in, say, an hour? Will that be enough time?"

"Depending on what Skid's found, and how much he wants to know."

"I know you've realized that I'm a silent partner," Orvid said, smiling, "in our pursuit."

"If he brings your name up," I warned, "I won't lie. But I see no reason to reveal anything that's not immediately salient."

"I'll trust your judgment," Orvid said easily.

I looked down at his face, so intent on the Bible verse. He didn't seem to care what I told Skidmore.

I realized in that moment, in the liquid light from the lamp, that here was a man completely devoid of fear. Either he had made great efforts to rid himself of his demons, or they had been burned out of him by experience, but the result was clear: nothing on this earth could frighten Orvid Newcomb.

I also realized that I envied that phenomenon—nearly as much as I found it unattainable.

"I don't need the flashlight to get to my truck," I said, setting the oil lamp beside the Bible on the table. "Or you can use this lamp."

"Fine," Orvid murmured absently.

His face was transfixed, staring at the Bible, as if to absorb something of the man who'd left it in my house.

"I'll see you in an hour or so at the railroad crossing," I said, heading for the door. "If the power happens to come back on while you're still here, leave the kitchen light on, would you?"

"Yes." He still didn't move.

"All right, then."

I was off, closing the front door quietly behind me.

The rain had nearly stopped, the cloud carrying it almost blown from the mountaintop. Here and there, through the net of night, I could see pinpoints of white, stars straining to offer a remote hope of illumination.

I barreled into my truck, gunned the engine, and spun the tires in mud before I backed up onto the road.

Fifteen minutes later I was down the mountain and onto our main street. All the lights in town were out. Everything was closed anyway. The only light came from emergency lamps around the police station.

I pulled up in front. I could see Skid's face in the window.

He opened the door for me, cup of coffee in his hand.

"I expected you'd be down here when our power went out in the middle of your call."

"Mine went out too," I told him. "A little unusual that you'd lose power at the same time I would. How often does that happen?"

"Big storm, I guess," Skid said, heading for his office. "I found out a few things about your boy."

The station was lit by big battery torches, no candles or oil lamps for official police business.

I was surprised to see Skid's computer still on. The light from its monitor was eerie, like a window to another world.

"How is your computer still on?" I asked, following him.

"Backup battery surge protector. Absolutely invaluable. I'm about to turn it off, though. Got what I need."

"What did you get?" I took a seat in front of his desk.

"Hiram Frazier," he began with no preliminaries, "has three outstanding warrants. One from Atlanta, one from Clarksville. Also a very old one from Tennessee, which is the worst one."

"What are they for?" I leaned forward onto the desk.

Skid sat, sighing. His face, painted with gray light from the monitor, looked easily ten years older than his age.

"Atlanta's for a strange incident involving a car stopped at lights near midtown at the downtown connector," he told me, staring at the screen.

"I know what he did. Save that. What about the other two?"

"Clarksville wants him for breaking and entering." Skid shrugged. "Busted the back door of a church and slept on top of the altar. Nothing. But the Tennessee warrant, the old one, is for murder."

"What?" I sat up.

"It's down as an unsolved murder in Pistol Creek."

"His wife."

Skid looked up slowly, eyes on mine.

"How the hell did you know *that?*"

"I guessed," I admitted, "but he did tell me that the reason for his wandering was the death of his wife. He said he woke up one morning and she was dead in the bed beside him."

"There aren't many details," Skid said, reading the screen, "but his wife was discovered dead in their bed. Heart attack."

"Then why was he suspected of murder?"

"Her entire body was covered with bruises. And Frazier did not report the death; the body was found by a church member several days after the death."

"He was arrested?"

"No, he'd taken off. Never found. Nothing was ever proved. Fugitive ever since."

"How long ago?"

"Seventeen years," Skid said softly. "They stopped looking over ten years ago. Listed the event as an unsolved, possible homicide."

"My God." I slumped down in the chair.

"Now tell me what you think he did in Atlanta," Skid said, shutting down his computer.

"I know what he did." I bit my upper lip a moment. "He stood at a traffic light; when it turned red, he came up to the driver's side of a car with its windows down, reached into the car, turned off the engine, took the keys, and refused to give them back until the driver gave him money."

I grinned just as the light from the monitor blinked off and Skid's expression was obscured by darkness.

"Okay." The sound of his voice told me I was right. "You *have* to tell me how you found that one out."

"The reason I called you from home," I said, my eyes adjusting to the low light of his office, "when we were cut off, is that I found the tapes I was looking for. Several of the train hoppers described a wild preacher whose trick was to perform just such a feat. He seemed to have perfected it."

"He was standing at that exit off the southbound downtown connector that goes to Fourteenth Street." Skid was stalling, for some reason. There was no value in telling me where the man had been standing.

"You understand what I'm telling you," I said, a little edgy.

"Say it out loud."

"Hiram Frazier took the keys out of Tess and Rory's Volkswagen," I shot back, "and that's why they got hit by the train."

"Yes." The word was made entirely out of lead. "That was my conclusion. Damn. I just had to hear someone else say it. Somehow I knew that's why you called."

I had thought myself the only one capable of coming to such a far-fetched conclusion. Had that been my opinion because the idea was so outrageous, or was it because I considered myself the only person strange enough to arrive at such an insight? Either way, it was oddly comforting to have the deduction affirmed.

"So you agree the girls' death was not exactly accidental," I said, "and, as it turns out, had nothing to do with drugs."

"I do."

"You're still going to arrest Andy Newlander."

"If I possibly can," he assured me. "And I just might kick Nickel Mathews's ass. But I reckon that'll have to wait a while."

"Because you'd like to get Hiram Frazier first."

"Yes."

"What do you want me to do?"

"What do I *want* you to do?" he sighed. "Go home, write an article, get drunk, call Lucinda, and shut up."

"In that order."

"Exactly."

"But what I'm *going* to do," I went on, "is find Hiram Frazier. And I'll tell you why. Your way of working is a good way, the police way. My way gets results too, and you know it, though it's a completely different approach. If we apply both methods at the same time, it tremendously increases the odds of our actually finding the man. You have to agree."

"I don't have to," he sighed. "But I'm afraid I do. And I want to get him. Real bad."

"So do I," I said quietly.

"Our first step may be the same one," he warned. "I'm going to come up to your house and see what kind of evidence he may have left there. If we're lucky, we might have a trail."

"It rained really hard on the mountain. I can't imagine you'd find anything outside."

"We'll dust the Bible for prints," Skid went on, "check the rest of the place. You can be there if you want."

"I actually have another idea," I hedged. "I think I'll go over to Pine City, check the crossing one more time, have a look at the trestle, that sort of thing."

"We've gone over and over all that," Skid said, eyebrows raised. "But if that's your choice, go on."

"Neither seems to yield much hope of accomplishing our task at the moment, I agree, but twenty-four hours ago, we wouldn't have ever come up with the bizarre notion of what Hiram Frazier did."

"I guess that's true."

His voice betrayed a fear that I found in my mind as well: the police had been looking for the man for seventeen years. We barely had a prayer of catching Hiram Frazier.

I had a moment of worry about Orvid as I left the police station, wondering if I ought to fly up to my house and warn him that the police were on their way. But I quickly realized that Orvid was the sort of person who could take care of himself; might even be offended if I thought otherwise. So I aimed my truck for Pine City, hoping Orvid might be there, instead, when I arrived.

The night was clearing slightly. A blackberry sky, rough and rounded, seemed to spin above the mountains. Moonlight, soft and clear, edged the horizon and would be high within the hour, ladling silver light into the valley, leading night onward toward morning.

The road was a mirror of that sky, black painted here and there with alabaster, a dark river that drew me onward toward an absolutely unknown destination.

But the first stop on that journey was the railroad crossing at Pine City. I was surprised how quickly it appeared before me, preoccupied with my thoughts as I was.

Orvid was nowhere to be seen. I parked my truck where I had before, reached for the flashlight I kept in the glove compartment.

I stepped out onto a mat of tall, wet grass. The rhododendrons were heavy with rain. As I rounded my truck and clicked on the flashlight, I tried to remember why the road was called Bee's Crossing. I'd been told when I was young, I just couldn't remember. Maybe I'd even collected the story and had it on tape, a thought that sent me into my usual reflection on the value of my tapes. Hidden in the magnetic arrangement of molecules along a thin strip of acetate, I had in my possession the final words of the last real ladder-back chairmaker in Georgia. I had a horde of words and music from long-dead storytellers, fiddlers who could no longer play, grandmothers who remembered the day their grandfathers came home from the Civil War. And on several, possible evidence of a man responsible for the deaths of two young girls.

Every shred of doubt I may have had in my mind about Hiram Frazier had been removed when Skid had confirmed my guess about his roadside activity in Atlanta. There was no doubt that he was the strange man with the key trick.

In my mind, like a flash of lightning, I saw an image of Hiram Frazier, and the thought that accompanied it made me drop my flashlight. This morning when I'd thrown him out of my truck, he'd grabbed what I mistook for a knife. It turned out to be a set of keys. He'd almost held them up for me to see, but I'd been too agitated to focus on them. Now my mind had reconstructed the image. Had I actually seen Tess and Rory's keys in his hand?

The language of his strange "vision," two girls in a pumpkin, came back to me. The rambling words were clearly a recollection, through what was surely his alcoholic haze, of the girls' death.

I bent to pick up the flashlight and was startled by a voice from behind the rhododendrons.

"Stop throwing that light around," Orvid whispered. "We're kind of trying to do this in secret, aren't we?"

"Orvid," I whispered back. "Where are you?"

He stepped out from behind the tall hedge. He'd donned a black rain poncho that would have made him invisible in the night, but for the white glow of his face.

"You talked to Skidmore?" he said calmly.

"Yes," I said, straightening and keeping the flashlight pointed to the ground. "He told me Hiram Frazier has three outstanding warrants. One of them involves an incident in Atlanta exactly like the scenario I described to you about taking the girls' car keys."

"Seriously?" Orvid asked, stepping closer to me.

"Absolutely," I confirmed. "And one of the warrants is for murder."

"Murder?" Orvid seemed more amused than surprised.

"His wife," I said quickly, "it's a cold warrant. The case is closed as unsolved."

"Well," Orvid told me heartily, "let's solve it."

He turned and headed toward the railroad tracks.

"Where are you going?" I said aloud, following him a step or two.

"To the trestle," he said without slowing. "I see some people down there."

I followed, though I could see no one. He seemed to be certain of what he was doing, which was more than I could say.

We were fifty feet closer before I could make out human forms. Seven ragged coats tattered in the wind.

A few spots underneath the trestle seemed relatively dry, and the people there had started a fire in what looked like a rusted barbecue grill.

They saw us coming. One nudged another and several stood, but none of them moved—or seemed overly concerned. They might even have taken us for kindred spirits. We certainly wouldn't have been mistaken for any sort of authority figures. They were huddled around the fire, several shivering, all with the same vacant look. These men had learned that, for them, all sensation was bad. Physical, emotional, and spiritual awareness were only doorways to disappointment and pain. The extent to which they could keep from feeling anything was the extent to which they might make it through another night until morning.

"Evening," Orvid called out when we drew near.

One or two men nodded; no one spoke.

"Can we get next to your fire?" Orvid went on.

No one moved.

I brushed my wet hair backward across the top of my head.

"Or get under there out of the rain?" I ventured.

One of the men sniffed.

"We saw your truck," he said defiantly.

They knew we weren't in their tribe.

"I just want to ask you some questions," I began, still walking toward them, pasting a smile to my face. "I'm a folklorist, and I collect stories. I was wondering if I could talk with you, and later, if you agree, I'd like to tape-record what you say."

"How much?" the man said.

It was hard to tell his age. His face had been cleaned by the rain but his hair was filthy, ratted to the side of his head, and one of his eyes was milky and swollen.

"What do you mean, 'how much'?" I asked amiably.

"How much you pay for the stories?" His good eye burned into mine.

I stopped walking. Orvid took my cue.

"There's no pay involved," I said, dropping the smile. "I want to know about the preacher."

Another of the men jumped up.

"See!" he said, his voice a harsh gargle. "I told you that crazy dickweed would get us in trouble. Always gets us in trouble."

"So you do know him," I continued to the man with one good eye.

"No idea what you're talking about," he said, dead cold. "Clear on away from here."

He took a step my direction, and the rest of the men stood up. The rough-throated man suddenly had a two-by-four in his hand, several nail points sticking out one side. Another drew a bicycle chain out of some hidden place beside him and began swinging it slowly.

I sighed.

"You know the preacher," I said, as emotionlessly as I could manage. "He's the one that's in trouble, not you."

"Don't know a preacher," the milk-eyed man told me with a crackling laugh. "Do we look like we know a preacher?"

Orvid turned to me, utterly at peace.

"You can wait in the truck if you want to," he said, his voice a motionless, clear pond.

"What?" I didn't know what he meant.

Before he could explain, the man with the two-by-four took several steps in my direction, raising the board high above his head. I stumbled backward quickly.

In a single fluid move, Orvid somehow managed to place his cane between the man's ankles, tripping him. The man tumbled to the ground. Orvid backhanded the man's skull with the thick top of the cane, and the man lay still, facedown in wet grass.

The others at the trestle were momentarily frozen.

"No one else will get hurt," I said quickly, "if any of you can tell us where the preacher's gone."

"What if we don't know?" the one-eyed man said, still fiery and ready to fight.

I shook my head and looked down at his fallen comrade.

"You think this one's voice sounds bad now?" I said, staring at the fallen man with the two-by-four still loosely in his hands. "Wait until he wakes up after sleeping all night in the cold, wet grass."

"If he wakes up at all," Orvid added amiably.

"Preacher headed west," the man with the bicycle chain said quickly. "Adairsville. That's what we heard."

"No, I heard he went back home," the one-eyed man sneered. "So I guess we don't really know nothing."

"Adairsville is on the way to Chattanooga," I said steadily, "and his home is in Tennessee."

The one-eyed man looked down, cursed something I couldn't quite hear.

"Could I come get Georgie?" the man with the bicycle chain said, nodding his head in the direction of the body at my feet. "We're buddies. He does have an awful sore throat."

"Georgie?" I looked down.

"Come on," Orvid said wearily. "If we pick the right route, we might see Frazier on the road."

"The road?"

"To Adairsville," Orvid said, turning his back on the men under the trestle and heading for my truck.

The highway west was a two-lane blacktop; the twists and turns made a sane driver slow down under the best of conditions, but wet asphalt in the middle of the night slowed my truck to a crawl.

Orvid had been talkative. He'd kept a steady stream of words going from the time we got into my truck until an hour later as we slowly descended a long, dark slope. I thought it was just idle chatter.

"What's the last thing you remember about Tess and Rory?" he asked me. "I mean an actual experience with the girls. Judy talks about them all the time, but I don't know how anyone else sees them."

"I don't know," I answered, not quite comprehending his question. "Why are you asking me that?"

"Go on. Try to think of one."

His demeanor was so compelling, I somehow felt it necessary to respond the way he wanted me to. I did my best to scan my ravaged mind for images of those sweet faces.

"Maybe a couple of years ago at Halloween," I told him slowly, trying to reconstruct my memory, "when Skidmore and I were at the old abandoned Newcomb house. You know the one."

"I do. It was empty long before I was born, but the family occasionally talks about taking it back and renovating."

"You know it's where we do our haunted house for Halloween sometimes."

"I know. Tell me about it," Orvid said, a gentle psychologist.

"It's perfect for that," I said, steering the truck onto blacktop. "How it clings to the side of the hill, House of Usher, all the rooms have been ransacked. It's gray, all semblance of paint long gone. The roof keeps water out in some places, but a tree caved in the porch a long time ago. The whole place was crawling with toads and bugs and field mice."

"It used to be the greatest mansion in the county," Orvid said quietly.

"Well, it looked great for our purposes, of course. All the walls were weather-beaten, and the lawn was nothing but weeds. From the outside, standing a way off, all you could see was the fallen-down porch, the broken windows, and the holes in the roof. Once you got up close, there was even more damage, and weeds were just as comfortable in the kitchen as in the yard."

"Still, there's a semblance of a road left in front of it," Orvid ventured. "At one time somebody thought enough of the place to put in a road up to it."

"But it doesn't go anywhere," I reminded him.

"Go on with your story," he sighed.

"Skid and I got to the place just a little before sundown with the intent of getting set up for this haunted house. Several school groups were due shortly after sunset. I felt a little foolish, a grown man actually planning how to scare the life out of a couple of truckloads of children. But Skidmore was having the time of his life. I think he took it more seriously than the children did.

"Tess and Rory had helped organize it all, that's the point," I went on. "That's the reason Lucinda encouraged me to do my part. The plan was that the girls would bring the truckloads of kids to the house; Skidmore and I would be the ghosts. Skid brought the sheets."

"Sheets?" Orvid protested. "Were you the lamest ghosts in the state?"

"We were harmless ghosts. There we sat, Skidmore and I, just before sundown, trying on his wife's good bed linen. I don't mind admitting that I had a little something to help me get in the spirit of the thing, a nip or two of apple brandy. So by the time the sun set behind the bare pecan trees, it was a wonderful night indeed. Crickets started up, there was an owl in the house, which made just the right sound for our adventure. Light was fading fast from the sky, and the two of us took our places in the living room, squatted down out of sight, with our sheets wrapped around us. Breeze came up and brought a chill. I looked at my watch; it was the very witching time of night."

"What kind of parents," Orvid objected, "would let their little seven-year-olds be taken way back off the road by two teenaged girls to be scared to death by two odd, full-grown men?"

"When it was announced at several of the churches that there would be a haunted house on Halloween night," I answered, mock-offended, "we had more than twenty families sign up."

"Yet another reason for me to move somewhere else," Orvid said, grinning.

"After a little while," I continued my story, ignoring his taunting, "the moon was completely hidden by clouds. I'd just come back to Blue Mountain and I'd forgotten the real meaning of *dark*. It was nothing like night in Atlanta. There didn't seem to be a speck of light in the universe. The moon was hidden, the stars; I could barely see my hand in front of my face. Have you ever heard a peacock cry?"

"What? No, I don't think so."

"Sounds just like a woman screaming," I said.

"What are you talking about?" he asked.

"You didn't know that your crazy relatives had peacocks on that property? There must be dozens of them still wandering around."

"After all this time?"

"They mate," I assured him.

"There were peacocks?" He shook his head.

"They sound like a woman screaming," I said again, Karloff-like. "Perfect for our play. About that time we heard a truck coming up the road. The kids were singing something, but I couldn't make out what it was. When they pulled up to the front of the house, the singing stopped. We could hear Tess announcing, in her scary voice, 'Here it is: the haunted house.' All the kids let out an *oooh* and Rory spoke up. 'It was ten years ago tonight,' she began, her head poked out the rider's side so we could all hear her. 'There was a young couple out riding in the dark. The boy wanted to go to the abandoned farm, but the girl had more sense than that and just wanted to go on home.' Tess took up again. 'But the boy wouldn't hear of it. He took the girl to this very spot.' At that second, they turned off the headlights and the kids were plunged into darkness. Got a fair scream out of the crowd."

"I can just imagine the lawsuits," Orvid chided.

" 'The couple's car was parked right here, just like we are,' Rory told the kids. 'And the boy was laughing and joking about how scared the girl was, when all of a sudden, there was a noise from inside the farmhouse.' Which was our cue, of course, and Skid and I knocked around the loose boards and generally caused a commotion, which made one of the damned peacocks call out. That got an even bigger scream than before. Tess said, 'What was that?' and Rory said, 'I don't know.' Skid and I let out a howl, and several of the kids blew out a lung yelling. I could hear Tess over the noise: 'I was afraid this might happen! We shouldn't have come here on the anniversary of the night those two went into that house ten years ago.' Rory said, 'They never did come back out. And I hear that on Halloween night, after sunset, you can see their ghosts wandering through the ruins.' "

"Your hint to get up and menace," Orvid guessed.

"Right. We popped up and started our ghostly impersonations with our sheets slung over our heads. I thought the kids would die. They were all screaming and crying; calling for their mothers. The problem was that Skid and I had never had practiced this thing, which was a mistake. The girls seemed to think it would be a good idea, since it was so dark, that they turn on their headlights and shine them into the house so the kids could see the ghosts better. Our eyes had adjusted to the dark, and when we were hit with the light, we couldn't see a thing."

"Like someone suddenly shining a flashlight in your eyes," Orvid accused.

"Exactly," I said, belittling his accusation. "We were yelling and making scary sounds as best we could, but we were blind. Skid bumped into me. I tried to get out of his way and tripped over an old board in the floor and fell down against what had been the wall between the kitchen and the living room. The old wall just crumbled, collapsed completely. Made a hell of a noise. So did I. Skid, meantime, had hit his head on something, which caused him to cuss, a rare occasion for him. The kids were still screaming and the lights were still on, and Skid and I assumed we were destroying the entire spooky gestalt, so we thought it best to just disappear like a good ghost should. I made my way crashing through the wall where I had knocked it in and tried to get out the kitchen door. Skid tried to jump out the back window of the living room. Alas, since the lights had crippled us, neither one of us made it. I ended up facedown in the kitchen flailing away at the sheet in which I was tangled, and Skid caught his sheet on the window, ripped it, and he slapped down on the sill hard enough to make him cuss again."

"The Three Stooges make a haunted house," Orvid said, shaking his head.

"By this time, of course, we could hear Tess laughing, and Rory was yelling at the kids that the ghosts were mad and they were coming to get everybody, so the kids were still screaming their heads off. Skid called out to me, rubbing his head, 'I think that went pretty well.' The girls drove off, and that was that."

I fell silent, and the noise of the truck engine took over.

I didn't quite know how to communicate to Orvid how much I had enjoyed that night with Skid, the spooky feeling of the place. I was certain that no one was genuinely frightened, but a part of us all liked imagining the ghostly couple. It wasn't frightening as much as it was comforting. Movies where people are sliced up and worse in a sea of blood and guts, *that's* genuinely frightening, mostly because it comes from headlines, happens every day on the streets of New York and Chicago; Atlanta, Miami. I was in favor of *The Wolf Man, Dracula*—movies in black and white. *Bride of Frankenstein,* with her white hair and the cobwebs in the corner of the castle. There was no reality to those threats. Nothing about them was believable. They were just for fun. Like a couple of grown men in bedroom sheets jumping around and making noises in an old house.

And just as I was about to say something to Orvid along those lines, the moon came out from behind the clouds and, small as it was, lit the countryside around us.

"I don't believe I've ever seen a crescent moon this bright, have you?" Orvid mused. "Look at how pretty it makes everything."

The breeze picked up, rustled the trees; sent another hundred thousand leaves downward.

"You enjoyed the haunted house," Orvid went on.

"It was good." I nodded.

"So that's a pretty nice memory of the girls," he said softly. "And fairly significant, what with you playing a ghost and all. Considering."

"Yes," I realized, "it is."

"That's a better way to remember them than anything else I can think of. And P.S.: maybe it pays you to think a little bit about what a good friend Sheriff Skidmore Needle has been to you most of your life. Since the memory you've just chosen about the girls was actually more a memory about him than anything else."

I let out a long, slow breath. With it a great number of minuscule, black ghosts, roughly the size of musical notes, left my body to join the night sky above.

"Are we absolutely certain that you don't have a degree in psychology?" I asked Orvid.

"Only the one experience has provided."

"Well, Dr. Newcomb," I said formally, "thanks for the session."

I finally realized that he was talking to keep my mind occupied.

"How far do you want to go?" I asked suddenly, interrupting his commentary on the difference between cold rain and summer rain.

"Yes." He fell silent.

"*Yes* is not a distance."

"You've had time to assess," he sighed. "Good, I was running out of one-sided conversation."

"You mean you've just been chattering on so I could gather my thoughts."

"More or less. You *have* been preoccupied."

"All right, I have," I agreed, "but some of that has to do with Georgie."

"Who?"

"Georgie is the man with the nail-studded two-by-four whom you dispatched about a half an hour ago."

"Really? You think you know his name?" Orvid shifted in his seat so that he could see me better. "You were worried about him? I didn't hit him hard enough to do much damage. I'm very precise about that sort of thing."

"I'd imagine you would be," I sniffed, "but as it happens, I had him in my mind because I believe he was the informant who originally told me about Hiram Frazier, the man on the tape I was telling you about."

"What?" Orvid's voice bordered on the shrill. "Stop the truck."

I shot him a glance. His face was in dead earnest.

I let off the gas, tapped the brakes several times, my truck slowed. We were coming to a wide paved shoulder, a place where the big trucks could pull to one side and let cars pass. I came to a stop, windshield wipers still slapping back and forth. I tapped the emergency button on the dash, and my lights began to flash.

"Yes?" I turned to him.

"You knew the man I knocked out?"

"No," I said patiently, "but I think he might be the person I talked to a year ago who told me about Frazier's little key trick."

"Because his name is Georgie?"

"And he looked a little familiar."

"That's what you've been thinking about," Orvid said, not blinking.

"I believe that all coincidence has meaning," I answered slowly. "An event of this sort is significant in the fabric of reality."

"I agree. That's why I asked you to stop the truck. But there's more to your introspection. I can tell."

"You're absolutely certain you don't have a degree in psychology?" I said, slumping a little in my seat.

"What is it that you're worried about?" he pressed.

"I'm afraid of Hiram Frazier," I blurted out. "I admit it. Something about him absolutely terrifies me. He's like something out of my worst dreams: a body without a soul, eyes without content or context, lost."

"A ghost," Orvid said simply. "Only real."

"I have a friend, June Cotage, who sometimes tells a story that ends with 'I don't believe in ghosts, but this is different. This really happened.'"

"That's right." Orvid smiled.

"I can barely stand to think about him," I said, softer.

"Then you have to find out why you're afraid of the man. You have to learn what about him frightens you."

"I suppose."

"And you believe that this most recent coincidence is a road sign, an indication from something in the universe." Orvid looked out the window. "Which it might be, who's to say? I'm not a big believer in that sort of thing, but Judy is."

"So how far are you expecting me to drive tonight? That's what I was asking a moment ago."

"As far as it takes to find the man we're looking for." Orvid let out a breath.

"And why am I driving, anyway?" I complained.

"Do you actually think you could fit into my Mercedes sports coupe?" He laughed. "You'd look like a Shriner in a parade, a big man in a toy car."

"Good point."

"Anyway, my car wasn't back there. I drove by Judy's on the way to the train crossing and got her to drop me off. I don't like to leave my nice car just sitting around a place like that."

"I see you didn't spend much time at my house investigating," I said to him, heavy-lidded. "But the point is, I don't think we're going to find Hiram Frazier on the road tonight. Maybe not at all. It's pouring down rain, it's getting late, and I'm hungry."

"What's the next town?"

"If we stay on this road, there's nothing until Rabun Gap, but if we hurry, we might make dinner at the Dillard House."

"The fabled Dillard House," Orvid said, sitting back. "My cousin Tristan took me there once when I was very young, but I still remember the biscuits and honey."

"So you wouldn't mind a bite."

I turned off my emergency lights, checked an empty road in both directions, and pressed the gas pedal.

"I could eat." He looked out the window. "But you know we're not far from New Hope Primitive Baptist Church."

How Orvid knew about that church would remain a mystery because I was so startled that he knew it at all. And I was taken by my sudden memories of the place.

I pictured the interior of the building perfectly, plain rough boards, polished floors, backless wooden pews. Exposed rafters hung low over the congregation. There was a single, white door at one end of the long building, a simple altar table at the other. The walls were lined with glass windows painted black, glass and all. The only light in the place were the oil lamps on the altar; there was no electricity in the building.

New Hope was a snake-handling church, a place where the minister drank lye and ate rat poison to prove the power of his faith. He'd been bitten by cottonmouth, copperhead, and rattlesnake without so much as a blink of his eye. He'd never been to a hospital, never looked at an aspirin, never missed a day in church.

There were still a few other churches like it in the mountains, but they were growing rare. My minister friend on Blue Mountain, Hek

Cotage, had stopped his snake services in favor of wife June's more sedate explanations of faith. Hek was still capable of a trance when he was preaching, and there was no telling what might come out of his mouth, but he had not taken up serpents in over a year. Which made New Hope unique at least in our area.

I had spoken to the minister there many times, a humorless bachelor who called himself Levi. He lived in a trailer close to the church. His congregation had dwindled over the years, but he had never once wavered in his dedication to the faith.

I once told him that his penchant for reptiles, based on the biblical injunction to "take up serpents," was the Western equivalent to an ancient Taoist notion.

"Allowing Tao to come into you," I'd told him, "makes you like an innocent child. Poisonous insects will not bite, wild animals attack; no weapon can harm you."

"That's it," he'd affirmed with a curt nod of his head. "Like a child."

He never asked me what the Tao was, or anything about it. His eyes never met mine.

I found the power of his belief awe-inspiring, even though he was clearly a disturbed man.

I wrenched myself from my thoughts, shot a glance to Orvid.

"It is just the sort of place Hiram Frazier might know about," I said. "Good call. I'm going to ignore the nagging questions in my mind about your knowledge of the place."

"I assume you know the minister there," Orvid said, glossing over my suspicions. "I remember that you wrote some sort of article or monograph concerning a serpent bowl. Am I remembering that correctly?"

"You have not ceased to astonish me since the second we met."

"I said that Tristan talked about you a good bit," Orvid reminded me. "And I read a lot."

I could tell from the sound of his voice there was more to his interest in me than idle curiosity. Perhaps I had misread him. Perhaps he did, after all, believe we might be related. I never dwelled on such possibilities. My mother's propensities toward a dazzling array of paramours could have made me related to anyone in the state of Georgia. Or Tennessee.

"I do, in fact, know the minister at New Hope," I said, eyes deliberately on the road. "But he'll be asleep by now. He's a sunup-to-sundown sort of person."

"Still," Orvid suggested, "we could swing by the church."

"I didn't tell you that one of the current warrants for Frazier," I said, my pulse quickening, "is for breaking into a church in Clarksville and sleeping on the altar."

Orvid's breathing increased noticeably.

"So really, let's shoot by the church before we eat," he encouraged.

"Agreed."

I pressed the accelerator harder, the wheels skidded on wet pavement, and we shot forward toward New Hope.

Fifteen

The church sat close to a bend in the mud road. Water washed off its roof in torrents, and the black windows made the building appear to be a dead hulk.

Rain pounded like rubber mallets on the roof and hood of my truck, a deafening din. I pulled up close to the front door of New Hope.

"Why are the windows blacked out?" Orvid asked over the noise.

"People are curious about what goes on inside," I told him, shifting into park, "and Preacher Levi does not care for the idle eye. He would prefer to have a visitor brave the confines of the building."

"Where said visitor might fall under Preacher Levi's hypnotic sway," Orvid added, a slight grin touching his lips.

"Exactly," I confirmed. "But also, the members of this church need concentration. It would not do well for anyone to be holding a rattlesnake in one hand and suddenly be distracted from the trance state by leering neighbors, or a nice view. That's just an invitation to a poisonous bite."

"Yes," Orvid said more seriously, "concentration on the task at hand. I understand that."

Once again I had the impression that Orvid was employing a bit of judicious understatement. The concept of *concentration* was more than a casual element of his regimen. It was an imperative.

The moonless sky dipped low to the earth, helped to hide the trailer behind the church. I tried to peer through the darkness, past the distraction of the windshield wipers, but everything was black beyond the back of the church.

"It doesn't look like anyone's broken into the church," Orvid ventured, staring at the front door. "Is there a back way in?"

"No."

We both sat, trying to decide how to proceed.

"I have an umbrella under my seat," I said absently.

"I don't think it would help both of us at the same time. If you hold it, it'll be too high for me, and if I hold it, you'd have to walk on all fours."

"You can have it. I'm already as wet as I can get."

"No." He took hold of the door handle. "I like to have both hands free."

He shoved the door open and got out of the truck.

Not one to be outdone in the category of manly deportment, I too eschewed the umbrella. I turned off the headlights and shut down the truck.

The air around us plummeted into darkness. It took a moment for my eyes to adjust. I could barely make out Orvid's back as he moved toward the church.

He checked the front door.

"Locked," he reported.

I started around the church.

"The preacher's trailer is back here," I told Orvid.

He followed.

Night air was polished, wet obsidian, a slick black jewel set in the emptiness above the earth. Rain battered it constantly, a vain attempt to split the diamond. But the darkness would not be broken.

The soaked grass seemed to grasp at my ankles, hands of the buried souls beneath the earth around the church, hoping for help out of their drenched resting place.

The hushing static of the rain and the wet rustle of the last leaves on the trees all around us filled my ears, made sound a part of the absence of light.

The smell of sodden earth, decayed leaves, mildew and rust, filled the air around me.

All senses were stopped.

By the time I saw the trailer, I felt I had walked a mile in the rain.

"There." I pointed.

But Orvid was ahead of me. He'd seen something.

He turned and held his finger to his lips. I fell silent.

Although the curtains of the trailer were pulled tight, it was obvious a light was on inside. And as I took a step or two closer, I could tell that the curtains closest to the door were parted just enough for a single eyeball to be seen peering at us from inside.

"He's seen us," Orvid whispered. "No good trying to pretend he hasn't. Go to the door."

I nodded.

"Preacher Levi?" I called, loud enough to startle both Orvid and the man at the window.

The curtains shut immediately.

"It's Dr. Devilin," I went on. "Sorry to disturb you so late, but I have some rather urgent business."

There was no reply, but I could hear the preacher moving around inside the trailer, even through the masking noise of the sheets of rain.

Orvid slowly positioned himself by the door to one side of the hinges, so that if the door opened, he would be hidden behind it.

I took my cue and moved toward the other side of the door, clearly visible to Levi when he opened up.

After a moment the door cracked and his muffled voice shot through.

"Who is it?"

"It's Fever Devilin," I said.

I waved.

"Oh." He sniffed. "You."

"Look, I would never bother you if it weren't important, but there's a man wanted for murder running around loose up here, and I have reason to believe he might try to break into your church. He did just that in Clarksville not too along ago."

"Break into the church?" he grunted. "Why'd he want to do that?"

"He's something of a preacher himself," I explained. "He had a congregation in Tennessee, until he murdered his wife."

"Murdered?" Preacher Levi opened the door wide. "Is that true?"

Orvid was nearly pinned to the side of the trailer behind the door.

"You know me," I said deliberately. "You know the kind of person I am. I don't lie. And maybe you remember that the county sheriff is a friend of mine. And Hek Cotage too."

"Hek's a good'n," Levi muttered, something almost like a smile beginning at one corner of his mouth.

"He is that." I grinned back.

"Don't know about that wife of his," Levi grumbled, any hint of a smile gone.

"The point is," I said hurriedly, "that there's a man possibly headed this way who just may try to break into your church."

"Uh," Levi began, "yeah. About that. Maybe you'd better come on in."

"Into your trailer?"

He'd never invited me into his home before.

"Yeah." He bumped Orvid with the door several times. "And tell your little friend he can come in too."

Orvid appeared, somewhat chagrined.

"So much for stealth," Orvid said to no one in particular.

"Let's have us some coffee," Levi said, disappearing into the recesses of the trailer.

Orvid looked at me, I politely indicated that he might go in ahead of me.

He did; I followed.

The trailer was Spartan. It was only one open room. A sink and a gas stove were in one corner, a wooden kitchen table close to them, four solid chairs. At the far end of the rectangular space there was a cot and an oil lamp. Above the cot was a large wooden cross with a serpent coiling up it. At the foot of the cot there was a wooden trunk, lid open. Nothing else adorned the walls or floor. There was no other furniture. The front of the trailer had two windows, one on either side of the door, and a third window over the sink looked out the back, into the woods.

On the kitchen table there were two candles in nice crystal candlestick holders, Levi's ever-present Bible, and, to my astonishment, a silver and glass Bodum French-press coffeemaker, nearly empty.

Beside it sat an ancient stone mortar-and-pestle set that had obviously been used to grind whole coffee beans by hand.

"I'll make fresh," Levi told us, his back to the door.

He grabbed the French press, pulled out the plunger, opened the window above his sink, and tossed out the old coffee and grounds. He washed out the press for what seemed like five minutes, not speaking, not turning to look at us.

Orvid and I stood silent, watching him, wondering what we were doing. I knew better than to speak before Levi was ready. I'd made the mistake of prompting him in one of our early meetings years before, and he'd stopped talking altogether. Patience was a necessary ally in the house of Levi. Luckily, Orvid followed my lead and contented himself with taking in every detail of the interior of the trailer.

Finally Levi turned.

"There." He shook the press. "Sit you down."

He nodded toward his kitchen table.

"We're kind of wet," I ventured.

"I don't care about that," Levi responded in a monotone.

I shot a quick glance to Orvid and we took seats.

Levi spent another ten agonizing minutes grinding more coffee beans while the gas eye under his old tin kettle did its best to boil water and I did my best to keep quiet. Orvid seemed perfectly at peace. All the while the rain made a constant drumming rhythm on the roof of the trailer.

At long last Levi stood and poured the contents of the mortar into the bottom of the French press. He reached for the kettle, poured in the steaming water, and rested the plunger of the press at the top of the glass cylinder.

"Let it sit," he said with a nod.

He replaced the kettle on the stove, sat down, folded his hands as if he might pray, and looked down at the open Bible on the tabletop.

"Now," he began, his voice taking on the diction and demeanor of his sermons. "The man you seek has been by this way."

Orvid almost fell out of his seat, and I made some sort of surprised noise that didn't sound human.

"He said he was a wandering preacher," Levi continued, apparently oblivious to our response. "Used to happen a lot in the old days. My daddy and granddaddy was preachers in this same church, New Hope, and when I was a sprite, they'd come by this way all the time. Great men of God, burned by hot sun; shivered to the bone by hellish ice on the mountaintops. They would tell of a wide world, a terrifying place filled with devilment and decay. And one by one that world gobbled up those men, and they were gone. I missed them, near as much as I missed my kin when they passed. But this man tonight, I could see the vapor in his eyes. He was not a creature of this earth. I made myself invisible to him, and the demon passed though this place without doing harm."

Orvid looked over at me, helpless.

I did my best to nod reassuringly, then turned my full attention to Preacher Levi.

"A man visited you tonight." I chose my words and tone of voice carefully.

"Did." Levi didn't look up.

"He was dressed in black," I continued, almost in monotone, "white hair, grizzled, early sixties."

"That's him."

"What did he want," I said quietly, "do you mind my asking?"

"Said he wanted shelter from the storm," Levi answered grimly. "But you could see he was a creature untouched by wind nor rain. His eyes was blank. No soul in him. A wandering sheaf."

"You were lucky to get rid of it." I leaned in a little closer.

"I was that," he agreed, a little more heartily than he had been speaking.

"How did you do it?"

"I vanished," Levi repeated simply. "I was gone from this place. And the demon passed through without doing harm."

"Where did you go when you vanished?" I was careful not to sound overly interested.

"Beulah Land," he said, as if it should have been obvious. "Where all my words come from. All my silence goes."

"Yes," I said, quickly agreeing. "And when you came back, when you appeared again, the other preacher was gone."

"Was."

"Do you know how long it all took?" I ventured.

"A thousand years are but the blinking of His eye," Levi muttered.

"I understand." I looked at the French press. "That's a very nice coffeemaker."

Orvid's head twitched. He could not believe I was changing the subject.

"Makes good coffee," Levi agreed.

"Where did you get it?"

"It was a gift," he said uncomfortably.

"I understand," I assured him. "Is the coffee ready?"

Levi looked up, gave the press a perfunctory examination, and pushed the plunger down without another word.

He stood, fetched three spotless white coffee mugs. He poured Orvid's first, turned the mug around three times, and slid it across the wooden tabletop toward Orvid, handle directly toward him. I got the same treatment. Then Levi poured his own cup last.

"Don't keep sugar," Levi told us, "but I got some sourwood honey that's good."

"I'd love some," I said.

Orvid merely shook his head.

Levi went to the trunk at the foot of his bed, reached in, came back with an unopened mason jar filled with dark amber honey. He pulled a teaspoon from the dish drainer beside his sink and handed the honey and spoon to me.

"Honey's a present too," he explained. "I ain't had none."

"Thank you."

We sat for a moment. I mixed the honey into my coffee, Orvid sipped his, Levi stared blankly.

"I know it's late for you," I said to Levi, setting my spoon down on the table.

"It is."

Levi stood, took my spoon away, fetched a dish towel, wiped the place where I'd laid the spoon, examined the spot, wiped again.

"But I won't sleep this night," he continued once he was satisfied with his cleaning work.

"I understand. I've met the man who was here tonight. He frightens me too."

Levi laughed, but it was not a pleasant sound. It was a noise filled with rebuke.

"I have no fear of the demon," Levi said, his voice rising. "I shun sleep tonight in case of his return. I cannot have him soil this place, the home and place of worship of my congregation and my family. I stand a sentinel."

"And we're disturbing you," I said hurriedly.

I gulped my coffee, burned my tongue, and urged Orvid to do the same. Orvid's eyes were filled with questions, but I admired his trust in my instincts.

Levi stood, ready to see us out.

"I believe that the man will not return," I said, taking my cup to Levi's sink. "You sent him away. He's gone."

"When he come in my door, the sun was just set." Levi's voice had calmed. "When he left, it was dark like now."

"Thank you," I said, not looking at him.

Levi went to the door, opened it, looked down. Orvid got out quickly. I lingered in front of Levi a moment.

"Will I see you again?" I asked.

It was a ritual parting, I'd done it with Levi several times before. I wasn't prepared for what happened.

His head shot up and his eyes pierced mine. His gaze locked me into my place as surely as if I had been bound by iron. He probed every corner of my being with an overwhelming stare, and I felt a sting of electric shock across my face and down my arms.

"Yes," he pronounced finally. "But time will pass, and we will be older."

He looked down again, and I took a small step backward unsteadily.

"Good-bye, Preacher Levi," I managed.

"Doctor," he whispered.

As soon as I got out, the door closed silently behind me.

Rain washed my face.

Orvid couldn't contain himself long enough to make it to my truck.

"What the hell was that?" he whispered under his breath, more amused than anything else.

"You mean his prediction when I left?" I whispered back. "Wasn't that something?"

"I mean the whole thing," Orvid answered. "What is that guy?"

"Get in the truck," I insisted.

We climbed into my truck, soaked.

I was backing out onto the road that led to the highway before Orvid tried again.

"All right," he declared, "let's start with the basics. What's wrong with the man?"

"There's nothing wrong with him," I explained as we drove out onto the highway. "He's a fourth- or fifth-generation preacher in the same church as his father and grandfather, he's never touched a woman, and he regularly drinks poison and handles rattlesnakes. These are things that are bound to make a person colorful, but other than that, he's perfectly normal."

"Like you or me."

"Exactly."

"Your definition of the word *normal* is so broad, I see now," he accused, "as to render the word meaningless when you say it. I therefore reject his normalcy in favor of my opinion: that he is a loon."

"Really," I shot back. "The guy's been bitten a hundred times by snakes that would kill you or me."

"That makes it worse," Orvid insisted. "He's seriously abnormal."

"And he lives in that sparse trailer because all the money he gets in his collection plate is given away to people in this community who need it, sick people, old, hungry children. I'd say we could use a few more abnormal citizens of his type. I mean in the world."

"Well," Orvid responded, somewhat meeker, "I'll give you that."

"And P.S.," I pressed, "he saw Hiram Frazier and recognized him for what he was."

"He thought Hiram Frazier was a *demon*," Orvid said, back to his incredulity.

"Do you think that's incorrect?" I asked, pulse increasing. "Let me tell you that most folk motifs are based on hyperbolic observation. I would say that a phrase like *demonic possession* is just another way of saying *irresistible compulsion* or *dissociative behavior*. Since language is only a system of symbols trying to explain observations, I'd say that calling Hiram Frazier a demon is more accurate than calling him schizophrenic. I know you agree with me to some extent because when I first met you, your choice was to make a very theatrical entrance based on the folklore of your stature. A little person is just a little person until hyperbole makes him supernatural, with extrahuman attributes. Unless you actually do live under a hill and forge miraculous iron."

Rain pelted the truck as we headed west.

"Are you finished?" Orvid said after a moment.

"I think so," I told him, pulse slowing.

"Don't you think it's a little odd that we decide to visit Preacher Levi and, mirabile dictu, the man we're after has been to visit only a few minutes or hours earlier?"

"I have a theory," I announced.

"I can't wait."

"I believe that Hiram Frazier wants to be caught. I think he's deliberately leaving us a trail."

Orvid sighed.

"That old chestnut," he said, shaking his head. "Cheap police psychology. The criminal always wants to be apprehended."

"No, I think it's deeper than that with Frazier. I think he wants something more than apprehension. He wants release, and he's somehow gotten the idea that I can give it to him."

"Wait," Orvid said, deliberately taking in a deep breath. "What on earth makes you think that?"

"He thinks we're kindred spirits," I offered uncomfortably. "Brothers."

"Why?" Orvid was clearly baffled.

"He's the dark matter, I'm the light matter. Equal opposites."

"No idea what you're talking about."

"Frazier's looking for something. And he's looking everywhere. Didn't it occur to you that Frazier and Preacher Levi are potentially kindred? With one or two shifts in the hazard of life's events, one could be the other."

"There but for fortune." Orvid nodded.

"Right."

"Let's start over." Orvid's voice changed again, this time all business. "Several things about Preacher Levi, do you mind?"

"Of course not."

"First, then. He had a cross with a snake on it. Isn't that a satanic symbol?"

"Absolutely not," I said firmly. "Jesus tells us in John three:fourteen. 'As Moses lifted up the serpent in the wilderness, even so must the Son of man be lifted up.' The goldsmith Hieronymus Magdeburger created a series of coins in the sixteenth century called the Serpent Lifted Up with Jesus crucified on one side, and a serpent twining the cross on the other. And in a fifteenth-century painting by Piero di Cosimo called *St. John the Evangelist,* St. John is blessing a Communion cup that holds a coiled snake. This kind of iconography abounds."

"Fine. Dr. Know-it-all." Orvid cleared his throat. "What about the fact that you insisted on leaving just as Preacher Levi began revealing that our quarry had been in his trailer?"

"Preacher Levi was in the middle of a trance-prayer when we barged in on him. I've seen it before. That's the reason he seemed sullen, or vague. He was barely conscious. He was really anxious to get back to his altered state. It was hard for him to move, talk to us, wash a spoon."

"All right, I give up." Orvid was doing his best to take it all in. "So explain the fact that the man doesn't seem to have electricity but *does* possess a very chic coffee press."

"Most of the *things* that Levi has," I said, smiling, "are gifts from parishioners. Some of them are things he can give away, but some are given to him in such a way as to make him obliged to use them. I don't understand his rules concerning which is which, but I've observed in previous meetings with him that some of these things, though they embarrass or inconvenience him, absolutely *must* be used in the course of his daily life. The French press was obviously one of those things. He does have electricity in the trailer, by the way. He just doesn't like to use it."

Orvid stared out the window for a moment, watching a landscape drenched in black and green fly by.

"And you somehow have the idea that Frazier is leaving us a trail?" he finally asked. "You're pretty sure?"

I looked at him for a second, admiring the way he had obviously assimilated the information I'd given him, made judgments, and arrived at conclusions.

"I am."

"Then we're on the right path, I suppose." Orvid laid his head back. "Do you still want to stop at the Dillard House?"

"I'm still hungry, but I think it would be best to stay on the road now. Hiram Frazier's in Adairsville."

Orvid laughed.

"Already?" he asked. "Did he fly?"

"I'm serious." I stared at the black highway. "I have a feeling about it. He's there now."

I didn't want to tell Orvid about the visceral tug in my chest, a part of my solar plexus that seemed drawn to something darker than night. I didn't want to admit to myself that it might have been Hiram Frazier calling me.

I don't know if Orvid thought that the sound of my voice was convincing enough, or if he finally decided that I was out of my mind.

Either way, he didn't say another word.

I drove fast. He closed his eyes, appeared to sleep until we were all the way to the outskirts of Adairsville, and the moon was at the top of a gray, gravel sky.

Sixteen

The streets leading to the historic downtown section of Adairsville were empty; everyone was asleep. Though the moon was barely visible behind charcoal clouds, light rain laid a shroud over everything, obscuring light and softening shadows. I had no desire to look at my watch; I thought it must be past one o'clock in the morning.

"Frazier seems to follow the rail lines," I said sleepily, hoping to rouse Orvid. "I believe he's been a train hopper for some time, so he would know that the tracks lead to Adairsville. It's a famous station, the beginning site of a great Civil War train chase. In some ways it's the mother of Georgia train stations, especially to old-timers. And it's on the way to Chattanooga, which would send Frazier toward Pistol Creek, his home."

"He's not *really* going home," Orvid said to me, stirring.

"No," I countered a little impatiently, "he's headed in that direction so it will be easy to follow. Easy for me."

"Oh, for Christ sake," Orvid muttered.

"Somewhere in what's left of Frazier's mind is a realization of what he's done. Maybe there's enough *preacher* still left in him to force him to stand up to what he's done."

"I reject that. There's nothing human left in the guy. I know these people. They've burned out anything worthwhile with a careless combination of drugs, alcohol, and a complete lack of accountability."

"I see." I made my voice as cold as I could. "Well, if I were in their shoes, I would hope for a more charitable assessment of my situation."

"Not every wandering spirit is a romantic figure, Doctor," Orvid said, his voice hissing. "Mostly they're criminals and mental patients, you understand that."

I slowed the truck.

"I understand that we disagree about this." I shot him a look. "But you and I both believe that he's here, or headed this way. It was your idea to come here in the first place, remember?"

"Frazier would follow the rails." Orvid shrugged. "And the fact is that he probably did tell the guys at the trestle in Pine City that he was going to Adairsville. We didn't give them time to think up a good lie, these guys are always slow on the uptake."

"Then why are you arguing with me about his being here?"

"I just don't see how he would have gotten here this quickly."

"He was ahead of us at New Hope," I insisted. "How do you think that happened? He presents a pathetic figure in the rain. I picked him up hitchhiking; others would do the same."

"Maybe. Or could he have hopped a train?" Orvid suggested. "A train would have gotten here faster than we could, given the rainy conditions."

"And the fact that the roads I took curve around very strangely, but the rails are a straighter shot here."

"So maybe it is possible that he's already here." Orvid seemed to be waking up. "Where do we start?"

"The old train depot downtown was turned into a welcome center or something," I said, thinking, "but it seems to me there's an abandoned textile mill, further down the tracks, that some of the old-timers told me about on one of my collecting tapes. It would be the perfect place to get out of the storm until morning. It's secluded, and its very close to the tracks."

"Great place to wait for the next train, in other words. You're sure you know where this mill is?"

"Not exactly"—I peered into the night—"but I can find the historic depot. It's right downtown and Adairsville's old main street is only a block long or so. We can follow the tracks north from there."

"Worth a try."

I headed for the old center of town. The first thing we saw was the station house. It had been nicely restored, painted yellow, and it was the only thing lit up. No one was there, of course, but it was cheery. A sign told us that we had arrived at the town welcome center, a tourist bureau, and start place for the reenactment of "the Great Chase" involving the General, a Civil War train.

I had a moment of odd reflection. I thought of how the centers of most towns in the mountains were occupied by Civil War memorials. The vanquished always feel the sting of war more than the victors. And when Grant was in the White House, a Southern sense of hopelessness was exceeded only by a dark, righteous-seeming rage. That president had been commander of the conquerors, a Union general who had approved of Sherman's burning scar in the land where our homes and lives had once dwelled. Still, I wondered if replacing the brooding sense of loss with a bright, shiny tourist center wasn't somehow eroding a bit of the character of the South.

As luck would have it, I was roused from such ridiculous flights of pensivity by a bright, shiny tourist sign: *Old Mill.* There was even an arrow.

"I'm guessing it's that way," Orvid said, deadpan, pointing the same direction as the arrow.

"Could be," I allowed, turning the truck.

As the lights of the tourist center faded behind us and the road turned into shadow, I was surprised to let out a sigh of relief. I was actually more comfortable in the dark. Why that would be I couldn't guess, but the answer would soon become all too obvious.

The old mill loomed ahead of us like the bones of a huge dead animal. A rusted Parthenon, moonlight shot through it exactly the way beams of light broke holes in the high November clouds.

High, black weeds made a nest for the carcass, and wind shook the trees around it, a harsh, warning whisper in the rustle of the leaves. Here and there a shadow darted. I was glad I wasn't alone.

"Nice place," Orvid said softly. "Perfect for the man we're after, don't you think?"

"I do."

I turned off the truck engine and my headlights. The landscape around us took on a dusted gloom in the pale moonlight.

We sat for a moment, surveying the weird desolation. All four walls were partially standing, the roof was gone. No window had glass in it, no door was closed. The hulk was made mostly of brick, some wood, the occasional stone. Some sort of vine had taken over the better part of the back of the building. It was impossible to tell what the vine was in the dark, but it looked like poison ivy to me. Most of the recesses of the place were pitch-black, impenetrable. The glaze of white moonbeams across the tops of bricks only made the dark places darker.

"In some ways," Orvid said, barely above a whisper, "this is beautiful."

"You see where the entrance used to be," I said, ignoring his sad aesthetic judgment, "over there by the big oak?"

Next to a leafless black trunk, the ruin of a doorway seemed the best spot to enter, a double-wide space relatively free of debris and vegetation.

"Let's go," he answered, nodding.

We both got out quickly. For my part, I was trying not to think too much about what we might find in the place, fearing what that thinking might do to my resolve. Orvid, on the other hand, seemed eager to forage.

As we moved toward the entrance, small sounds distracted us: night birds, or bats, stirred up the air high above our heads; something moved in the denser woods beyond the entrance door.

"What was that?" I whispered.

"Possum?" Orvid said without thinking. "Come on."

He plunged forward, taking the last few steps faster than I did, and hopped through the door.

"Wait," I called, still whispering.

I followed where he had gone.

Orvid stood in the middle of bits of brick and dried-out weeds. A pool of moonlight lay just beyond where he stood, his silhouette etched against it. Before I could say anything, he grabbed the top of his cane and drew out a vicious silver blade; it looked three feet long.

"What the hell are you doing?" I stammered, stumbling toward him.

"Sh!" Orvid answered, electric eyes glancing my way.

"No, seriously," I demanded, "what do you think you're going to do with that?"

"Do?" he responded, lowering the blade a little. "I'm going to kill Hiram Frazier."

"Kill him?" I froze.

"Yes," Orvid shot back, irritated. "What were you going to do?"

"Take him to Skidmore," I answered, my face clearly stunned by his revelation.

Orvid rested the tip of his weapon gently on the ground.

"How were you going to do that?" he asked, amused.

"I was going to, that's all."

"You don't think he might disagree with your suggestion?"

"Yes, but I'd convince him."

"This man is not someone you can reason with," Orvid objected. "He doesn't have those faculties any longer. Surely you must realize that."

"I'm much bigger than he is."

"Eppie Waldrup is bigger than you are, and you dropped him down your front porch like a sack of wet cement. And P.S.: everyone's bigger than I am."

All I needed was an image of Georgie, the man at the train trestle laid out on the ground, to apprehend his point.

"Fine," I said quickly, "but no matter what, I didn't chase him to kill him."

"Why not, exactly?"

"Because that's not something you *do*!" I exploded. "You don't chase down a derelict and cut his head off because you're pretty sure he was involved in an accident."

"I wasn't going to cut his head off," Orvid began. "But now that you mention it, that would be fairly decisive."

"That's hardly the key issue. You want to kill him!"

"I'm *going* to kill him."

I could see the look in Orvid's eye, even in the dim light. There was no doubt, no hesitation there. His intention was clear. If we found Frazier, Orvid would dispatch him instantly. I knew it.

"Orvid," I said, starting over, "let's discuss this."

"Nothing to discuss," he said firmly.

"Well," I said, folding my arms, "I really can't stand by while you murder someone. Would you kill me too?"

"Of course not," he said. "All I'd have to do is disable you for a moment."

Reminding myself again that I'd recently seen him disable a man with no effort whatsoever, I took a different tack.

"Skidmore knows I'm looking for Frazier. At the very least, he'll eventually ask me if I found anything. I won't lie to him, I've already told you that. I'd have to tell him what you did."

"Judy and I are moving after this," Orvid said, a smile on his lips. "Somewhere in Europe, I think. The main thing that was keeping her in Georgia was the Dyson girls, so that's done with. She's ready to move. We'd disappear. You and Deputy Dogg would never even find Frazier's body, let alone Judy and me. There'd simply be no case."

"Orvid," I fumed, "we can't actually be having an argument about killing a human being, can we? I mean, I just can't let that happen. I'd do everything I could to stop you. I mean it."

"Why?" he exploded. "Isn't Lucinda in torment because Tess and Rory are dead? Isn't she wondering how and why a thing like that can happen? Wouldn't you do anything to give her some respite from that?"

"Yes," I said, taking a step toward him, "but her solution would never be to murder the man responsible!"

"Well," he answered, calming. "There's where Lucinda and Judy are different. Hunting down Hiram Frazier and killing him, that was more or less Judy's idea."

"Judy wants you to kill him?" I couldn't believe it.

"She does," he said, breathing deeply to calm himself. "In fact, she hasn't let up on me since we came to the conclusion that Frazier was responsible for the accident."

"No," I insisted, "we haven't come to any conclusion about that, we're just speculating. That's another good reason not to hack off his head, we're just *guessing*!"

"I'm not going to hack off his head," Orvid snarled. "Why do you keep saying that?"

"Well, what else would you do with that scythe?"

"Plenty," Orvid answered. "Nick the jugular, cut the hamstrings, come up under the sternum for the heart, slip in at the back of his head, base of the medulla oblongata."

I stopped breathing. It was suddenly clear to me that Orvid had done that sort of thing before.

"We're absolutely at cross-purposes," I said quietly, steeling my voice. "I can't be a party to this. I'm going home."

I turned my back on the man with the sword and headed toward the doorway.

"Stop," Orvid commanded.

I kept walking.

"Fever, wait," he said, his voice softening.

I slowed.

"I don't have any desire to do you harm," Orvid began. "How about if we keep looking for Frazier, and I hold off on my mission at least until we see him and you have a chance to talk him into coming with us to face the sheriff?"

I turned.

Orvid replaced his blade, and he was once again holding a stylish walking cane.

"I wouldn't have expected you to be this reasonable," I said suspiciously, "after that look in your eye a moment ago."

"And I didn't think you'd object so strongly to my plan. I had no idea. I thought you'd endorse it. It's simple and direct and solves everyone's problems."

"It's morally reprehensible."

"According to whose plan?" Orvid said, resting on his cane.

I was certain that he had not given up on his plan to kill Frazier. He was clearly humoring me. But at least he'd put away his blade. What I didn't tell Orvid was how difficult it had been for me to argue against the murder, a confession I was barely able to make to myself. A part of me would be happy to see Hiram Frazier die.

I looked around, burying such thoughts. Instead I let my eyes run over the geography of the ruined mill. It offered almost no place to hide. All the walls were crumbled.

"Well," I said to Orvid, managing a wan smile, "we've done everything we can to warn Frazier, if he's here."

"Yelling and threatening to kill him," he agreed, "yes, you're probably right."

"If he was here at all," I said, softer.

"We should still have a look around." Orvid surveyed the place.

"I think it might be worth a quick look in the back. There were most likely train tracks close by at one time, usually the case with a mill this size. We could see if the tracks were there."

"Are you sure they're still operable?" Orvid said, a spark of excitement in his voice.

"Absolutely," I said, moving toward the back of the building. "That would be the way freights get to Chattanooga."

"Indeed." He nodded. "Then let's go have a look."

We moved through the rubble and weeds to the back of the mill through wide-open expanses in what was left of the building. No one could have been hiding there.

Not fifty feet from the back of the building I could see railroad tracks.

"There." I pointed.

"I see them," Orvid said, moving faster.

The tracks seemed recently worn. The top of the rail was steel gray, not a trace of rust red.

"Which way is town?" Orvid said, trying to get his bearings.

"South, and a little east." I inclined my head slightly. "That way."

The tracks ran straight toward the town in that direction, probably right to the tourist center. The opposite way, down the mostly westward run, they disappeared into a thick cover of evergreens.

"I think I'm just going to see where the tracks go," Orvid said, peering into the evergreens. "It looks like they might bend a little more northward up there, and there's a clearing, can you see?"

I strained.

"No," I reported, "but we know your eyes are better than mine in the dark."

"Well, if they do bend, it would be a lot like the turn in the tracks at Pine City, a place where the train has to slow down."

"A perfect place to hop on."

"I'm checking it out." Orvid started down the tracks. "Are you coming?"

"Wait," I told him. "I've got a flashlight in my truck. It looks kind of dark in the woody part."

"Good. Go get it, then catch up. I'll follow straight down the tracks."

He took off and I turned back the other way, loping toward my truck. A minute later I rummaged under the driver's seat and came out with my trusty flashlight.

I snapped it on; the beam shattered shadows in the mill. I dashed through the mill once again, toward the woods where Orvid had gone.

I was almost to the the back of the building, my light glancing off the steel beams of the tracks, when I heard a deep voice directly behind me whisper a curse.

Seventeen

I spun around.

Hiram Frazier stood framed by brick and moonlight, a rusted iron bar in his right hand. His black suit was soaked, and his shoes frayed at the soles. Hair was wild about his head, face a mask of gnarled pain. The eyes were red blisters, burning holes in the air around the face

My flashlight was blinding him.

"Put down that damned torch!" He raised his iron bar and took a step toward me.

I stumbled back, clicking off the flashlight.

"You waiting for the train?" Frazier said, his voice like a hollow stone tunnel.

I started to speak before I realized he didn't know who I was.

"Yes," I said, my voice low. "It slows down around the bend in the woods."

"I know that," he snapped. "I been ride these rails for a hundred years, you don't think I know that?"

His words were slurred, and he swayed unsteadily. He was full of liquor, full to the brim. The smell of it poured out his mouth, oozed from his skin, his scars. Rage and bone were all that kept him standing. It was clear that he might explode at any moment.

I took another step back from him, deciding on something of a risky course of action.

"Are you Hiram Frazier?"

"What?" he roused, trying to focus his eyes. "That's my name."
He peered all around me, trying to see me in the dark through a
drunken fog.

"Everyone knows the preacher from Pistol Creek," I continued,
my voice steady.

"Stop!" He dropped the iron bar and put his hands to his ears.
"No one knows who I am. No one knows what I am."

"You're Hiram Frazier, wandering preacher," I said, stronger,
"and the Lord's whipping boy."

"Oh," he moaned low. "I am."

"You have a trick. You know how to get money whenever you
want it. You stick close to the rail crossings and red lights and you
reach into the cars and take their keys."

"What are you?" he whispered, looking down at the ground.

I took a deep breath. My heart was pounding.

"You were at a train crossing a few nights ago. You stood there in
the rain until an orange Volkswagen came by. A pumpkin car."

"Pumpkin car," he repeated softly.

"Two young girls were in the car, and you took their keys."

"I did?" he asked helplessly. "It sounds like me."

"Only there was a train coming."

"The Lord's recompense," Frazier rattled hypnotically, "come to
repay every one for what he has done."

"No," I hedged, careful not to break the spell he was under, "it
was a train, a train coming around the bend. You didn't give the keys
back, and the girls didn't have time to get out of the car. They were
killed."

"I don't remember," he howled.

"It was just two nights ago," I coaxed.

"I had a church in Pistol Creek, Tennessee," he mumbled, "many
years back. Good congregation: sober, plain, and mean. But the Lord
took me as his testing scourge. I awoke one morning to find my wife,
my jewel, she was stone-cold dead in the bed beside me. No warning,
no word of farewell. We all come to death, one way or another. Some

come to it slow. This is my punishment: to be a traveling creature, a beacon to woman and man. If you would shun the burning hell, you'd take a warning by me."

"And two nights ago you tried to get two girls to give you money," I prompted.

"Two virgins in a pumpkin carriage," he said, his voice growing louder. "Laughing. God smote them. For no good reason. Just took them, sent them a black snake belching smoke which roared over them like an iron thunder. They were gone before the noise of it left the air. Gone."

He held his hands wide, a poisoned imitation of the crucifixion.

"When God wants to purge this earth," Frazier went on, gaining strength, "he sends a dark angel. No creature of light can help this pustule globe. There is no salvation, there is only cleansing. Those who are pure are washed clean, those who are weak are washed away. There are Two Rivers in God's wilderness, the one that rides a body to sweet fields arrayed in living green and pastures of delight, the other that turns molten and purges skin from bone, in a place no human tongue can tell."

He thumped his chest hard, it made a hollow drumming sound.

"God chose me!" he shouted. "I am a soldier in the army of darkness, God's purging river. But it's hard. It's hard to do."

"Why?" I asked, hoping to steer his thinking back to Tess and Rory.

"Because God's Ways are impossible to comprehend." Frazier heaved a sigh, a lifetime of desperation in a single breath. "He's taken my mind. It's gone. My mind is dead. But this body keeps doing things, things I can't even recall on the morrow of the next day."

"What things?"

"I drink," he confessed, suddenly weeping, his entire demeanor collapsed into begging for pity. "No other way to bear the pain. The demon of alcohol chases all other demons away. I concentrate all my efforts on that one demon, and God keeps the rest at bay."

"The demon of memory."

223

"Gone," he said with a flourish of his wrist.

"Guilt."

"Swallowed up," he said, his voice shifting again. "I know you?" His eyes were clearing a little. His head stilled and his breathing steadied.

"We've met. You told me before that you saw the accident the other night at the rail crossing in Pine City."

"Pine City," he said, closing his eyes, "is the one with the nice rhododendrons."

That was the moment I was convinced something of the human was still left inside the blasted body of Hiram Frazier.

"Yes," I sighed.

"Two girls," he mumbled, eyes still closed. "The one driving was laughing, fishing around in her purse, looking for money for me. The other was laughing too, with little earmuffs on. Nobody heard the train."

"You remember now." The *earmuffs* were Rory's headphones.

"I do," he answered, his voice quavering.

His eyes flashed open.

"Why you to make me recall that?" he growled. "What *are* you?"

"You remember taking their keys?" I demanded.

He blinked hard, squeezing his eyes shut for a long moment. In the meantime his hand rummaged in a torn coat pocket.

Seconds later he produced a set of three keys. They were held together by a key ring with a silver *VW* on it.

"You didn't mean for it to happen," I said softly. "You didn't mean for them to be hit by the train."

"It was not my doing," he said, still holding out the keys. "God brought the train."

"But you took the keys," I insisted.

"God brought the train," he said, slipping back into incoherence.

"You have to go with me," I told him firmly. "You have to come back to Pine City."

"What?" His eyes had gone blurry again, and he searched around my head, trying to pinpoint my face. "Go where?"

I took a quick step in his direction. The confidence I'd gained from my recent meeting with Eppie, not to mention the age differential between Frazier and me, made me bold.

"I have to take you with me," I said sternly, "back to Pine City where it happened, to the sheriff. You'll explain what you did, it was an accident."

"No," he whined, "I'm going home to Pistol Creek."

"Not tonight," I insisted, reaching for his arm.

He staggered sideways, about to topple.

"Why'd I have to go with you?" His words were so run together they were barely comprehensible.

"Because you were responsible for the deaths of two people!" I told him, my voice booming.

"God brought a train!" he shouted back, spitting.

Without warning, Frazier swung his arm like an opening door and it connected with my shoulder.

I staggered sideways, stunned; instantly pumped with adrenaline.

Frazier reached down and grabbed the iron bar he'd dropped, cocked it back like a baseball bat, and took a swing at my head.

I blew out a breath and snapped my head back. The bar only missed me by inches. I looked around for anything to use against him, moving away from Frazier and pumping my lungs.

He was growling, a low sound that leaked from his head. His face was lowered and his dead eyes glared at me from the tops of their sockets. A weak strand of drool soiled his lower lip, and I could see how many of his teeth were missing. There was nothing in that body but the desecrated passion for preservation, an insect compulsion.

I took a few more steps backward and planted myself, readying for an attack.

He stood staring.

"Hiram," I began, hoping to rouse the human being inside the husk.

"God!" he exploded. "How do you know my name?"

He swung the iron bar back and forth in front of him like a scythe, coming at me. He was moving faster than I would have imagined he could.

Without thinking, I did what I'd seen my friend Andrews do a dozen times in rugby matches: I dove toward Frazier's legs; toppled him like a bowling pin.

He went down hard, pounding the ground with an organ-churning thud.

"Hellfire!" he howled.

I leapt to my feet, panic breath forcing strangled sounds from my throat. I pulled a solid brick from the crumbling wall beside me, the only weapon I could think of.

Frazier was on his feet, unsteady but filled with a power past exhaustion. He started toward me again and I threw the brick with all my strength, underhanded, hoping to catch his chin. Instead the brick hit the arm holding the rod and he dropped it once more.

Without skipping a beat he ignored his fallen weapon; charged me.

I sidestepped easily, but I could feel a slow terror growing in the pit of my stomach. I had no idea how to stop this man, and he would never stop himself.

Frazier stumbled past me, but he swung his hand backward, grabbing my leg. I fell onto my back, instantly kicking and flailing my arms, hoping to fend him off that way.

But Frazier was on top of me instantly, his thumbs pressed into my Adam's apple, his palms tight on my jugular. Within seconds I could feel myself blacking out.

Eyes wide, I pounded both sides of his head over and over, battering his ears, his temples, to no avail. My fists were wind.

In absolute desperation I shot my thumbs into his eyes, ground them into his sockets. I imagined his eyeballs bursting like grapes.

They did not.

But Frazier roared and pulled back long enough for me to kick my way out from under him. I skittered backward, crab walking, until I was several feet away from where he lay on his side, cursing, words I could not understand, hands over his eyes.

I scoured the dark weeds around me and found the iron bar.

I hefted it and had every intention of bashing Frazier's skull. I moved slowly his way, the bar in both hands, slightly over my right shoulder.

He heard me coming, lowered his hands. Through his red, dimmed eyes he could see me and began to moan.

"Stop. Stop!" His voice rose like a train whistle in the distance.

I was still light-headed; the red imprint of his vise grip still lingered in burning on my neck.

"I'll go," he whimpered. "Take me where you want. I'll go along quiet."

He rocked a little, back and forth in the wet grass and muddy ground. I raised the iron bar above my head, already seeing his skull cave in.

"What are you doing?" he whimpered.

I froze. What *was* I doing?

I dropped the iron instantly, my senses flooding back. A sudden realization that I had been about to kill a man shocked my body, and I began to tremble. The adrenaline and sweat mixed with November chill, and I was freezing to the bone, unable to stop shivering.

"Where do I have to go?" Frazier said weakly, dead still.

"Pine," was all I could manage before sucking in painful breath.

"Okay, then," he said, rolling slowly to a sitting posture.

He put his hands out beside him and tried three times to stand while I stared at him. He rocked in my direction, but could not get up, and I could not help him.

Slowly I became aware of tree frogs and night birds, bats and crickets, grinding pieces of the night sky into black sounds. The moon broke free of its cloud-gray prison long enough to spill milky light on the bricks around me, the dead grass, here and there a sedate spray of wild ageratum, mauve in the moonlight.

My breathing became more regular and my throat seemed to open wider, taking in pins of cold air. I trembled less violently and folded my arms in front of me to keep from an obvious appearance of shaking.

Frazier still sat on the ground, trying to stand.

"You think you beat me," he sneered, defiant. "You can't hold back the night. Look around you. Half of every life on this miserable world is spent in nighttime. It's God's counterweight. There is much work yet to be done in the world of night. God divided the light from the darkness, He did not put an end to the night. He saw that all nations, all people, must know both. This contrast of opposites is God's way, and I am the envoy of darkness, the angel of the counterbalance. I bring the deep Black to a world sick with pale eyes. I refresh the night with continual gifts."

"Right," I said, my normal voice returned, a little weakened. "You'll have to get some new material, you know. You've said all this to me before."

"I have?" He looked up at me suspiciously.

"Get up," I urged him, sounding exactly as exhausted as I was.

"Your face does not come to me," he said slowly.

"I gave you a ride yesterday morning, and then, as it happens, you visited my house."

"How would I visit your house?" he snapped. "Ain't been inside a human dwelling in ten years."

"You were just in Preacher Levi's trailer. Couldn't have been much more than three or four hours ago."

"There!" he shouted, leaping to his feet. "How you to know a thing like that? Proof!"

What he meant was a mystery, but what he had done was diabolically ingenious.

Frazier had managed to keep me off guard long enough for him to inch his way toward the iron bar on the ground, grab it, and jump to his feet wielding it.

"Now," he bellowed, "I smite you back to hell whence you come!"

The bar caught my upper arm at about the biceps, and I thought I could feel the bone crack. White pain shot outward from the blow in every direction. My heart exploded, pumping so hard I thought it might shoot through my ribs and into the night, a red comet.

Too stunned to move, I watched in wonder as he circled me.

"You cannot die," Frazier muttered, his words a mush in his mouth, "but that body you took can be beat to a pile."

He swung the bar wildly, barely missing my head.

I lumbered sideways, still dumbfounded by the surprise of his attack.

He readied another blow.

I concentrated hard, balanced my weight, kicked horizontally with my right leg directly into his lower abdomen. I felt the connection; the give in his gut sickened me.

He flew backward, skidding on his backside, but was up and swinging with preternatural agility before I could get my leg back on the ground. I hopped away from him.

Not fast enough.

He flew at me, caught the side of my head with a glancing crash. It shook my teeth, but didn't connect strongly enough to do the damage it had intended.

I burst, running. I thought to make it over the brick wall next to me, try a desperate dash for the truck.

If I could get in, lock the doors, I might live.

I was vaguely aware of a train whistle knifing white through the black air, but I took it for another sound from Frazier, high whine or a yelp.

I stumbled over the brick edges of the low wall and miraculously managed to retain my footing, kept running. I could hear Frazier behind me, snarling.

The sound brought a sudden image to my mind: a drooling Bruno, Eppie's junkyard dog. I was propelled faster toward the haven of my truck.

Before I had taken two more leaping steps, I felt Frazier's first solid blow to my head. I was almost beside the crumbling entrance of the old mill, my truck tantalizingly in sight.

But I went down.

I tried to roll. Before I could, a second pounding thud creased my back between my shoulder blades.

Again a distant whistle sounded, and I thought my eardrums might be bursting from the blood pumping in my skull.

I managed to turn on my side, eyes wild, watching helplessly as Hiram Frazier raised his iron rod high above his head.

"I am the Alpha and the Omega," he said, clear as crystal, a voice I had never heard, "the first and the last, the beginning and the end."

He brought the bar flying down toward my head, an arc made silver by the searing moon, the last light I saw.

Eighteen

Struggling up through the darkness, I thought I could see a white star, a comet streaking above my head. My eyes opened, blurred, and closed again before I panicked.

I heard a violent explosion of breath burst from my lungs, tried desperately to sit up, arms crossed in front of my face. I could still see, in my mind's eye, Hiram Frazier's iron bar crashing down toward me.

But no impact followed, and I wondered if I might be dead.

I tested my eyes, opened them slowly.

The comet I had seen stood a few feet in front of me: Orvid, his white mane flaring sideways in the cold wind.

"Frazier!" I told him, struggling to get to my feet. "He was here. He was trying to kill me. He's getting away!"

Orvid didn't move, and the serenity on his face made me doubt his sanity. Or mine.

"It's all right," he said soothingly. "I know where Frazier is. Or I'm assuming the man I've got is Hiram Frazier. And he's not going anywhere. Now let me take a look at your head."

He stood sideways, let the moonlight spill onto my face.

"How's your vision?" he asked. "I mean how blurry is it?"

I blinked.

"It feels fine," I stammered, my voice quavering. "It barely hurts. Isn't that a sign of severe concussion? Doesn't that mean I'm about to die?"

"For such a large man," Orvid said, only a slight smile suggested in his eyes, "you certainly are something of a baby about certain things."

"I'm not a *baby*," I chided, "I'm a hypochondriac."

I stood unsteadily.

"You're not slurring your words," Orvid offered. "You can see."

"These are the first signs of impending doom," I insisted. "But the fact is, it's beginning to hurt, now that I'm up. It hurts a lot. What does it look like?"

He stared up at me, squinting.

"It looks like red confetti stuck to your face," he answered, "about three inches long over your left eye. But it's not deep. He's a drunk old man, and his bones are made of cricket sounds."

"Am I hearing things, or are you misquoting the Queen Mab speech from *Romeo and Juliet*?"

"I'm trying to be the sort of companion that your friend Andrews would be if he were here."

I turned to face Orvid directly, hand absently running over the bloody scar on my forehead.

"How would you know about Andrews?" I asked, suspicion edging each syllable like static electricity.

"I told you before, I do my research. I've been studying you for years."

I froze. I was beginning to have a certain suspicion about Orvid's field of study, and it did not bode well for our hero.

"You've been studying me," I breathed. "That's right. I remember your saying that. Why?"

"It's an interesting story," he said quickly, "but wouldn't you rather deal with Hiram Frazier first?"

"My God," I answered, coming to my senses a little, "where is he? He's not getting away?"

"No." Orvid started toward the train tracks. "Let's go."

"Go where?" I said weakly, standing my ground.

"Frazier's down past that thicket of trees," he said, not turning back to me, "where the tracks bend. He was going to hop the train."

"The train," I said slowly. "I *heard* a whistle, but then I thought it was in my head, or in Frazier's howling."

"It was a freight," Orvid said simply. "I heard it coming. By the time I saw Frazier headed into the clearing down there, the train was almost at a standstill. He had a crowbar in his hand, by the way. The one he hit you with, I'd imagine."

"Why didn't he finish the job?" I asked, finally taking the first few steps to follow Orvid.

"The train was coming," Orvid told me, as if it were obvious. "He didn't want to miss it. He only had to stop you from following him. He didn't have time to kill you."

"But he didn't get away?" I said, still trying to clear my mind.

"He's down there in the clearing," Orvid repeated. "He's not going anywhere."

"The train's gone?"

"Gone."

"But Frazier's there?" My voice was a little gravelly.

"Just come on," Orvid answered impatiently. "And don't forget your flashlight."

The night had cleared at last. High clouds still chased past the haloed moon, but the rain was gone. Moonlight spread silver wings, and the spirit of the night soared over everything, blessing bare elm branches with pale benevolence. The flashlight was barely visible where I'd dropped it in the grass.

I collected it, not bothering to turn it on, and followed Orvid into the trees, onto the tracks. The rough gravel bed that supported the crossties seemed a white river. High in the trees a night dove called, and a vague promise of morning was suggested even in the dead of night.

The tracks took an abrupt curve to our right and upward. We came to a clearing on our left half the size of a baseball field. It was empty save for a lone, forlorn figure seated on the ground.

"Is that Frazier?" I whispered.

"You tell me," Orvid said out loud, only a little irritated. "I've never met the man, I'm just assuming."

He picked up his pace. I stumbled behind.

As I got closer, I could see that Frazier was tied with some sort of bands at his wrists and ankles. He was seated uncomfortably on the wet ground, a grimace contorting his face, a mixture of pain and desolation. Despite everything, it was a pitiable sight to my eyes.

"That's him," I said, amazed.

"Let me go," he said weakly, not looking up.

Orvid went to stand behind the figure on the ground, a little to one side of his left shoulder.

I came to a stop a few feet in front of Frazier and stared.

"He charged down the side of the tracks," Orvid began in answer to the questions in my eyes. "I thought to myself, 'Who else could this be? He's got to be Frazier.' The train was already passing, but it was slow. This guy was running faster than it was moving. He had a rusted crowbar in his hand, as I was saying, and he used it to hook onto a flatcar. He was about to heave himself up onto the train when I hit the backs of his knees with my cane. He didn't see me. I'd been standing right there, and he didn't even see me."

"I saw you," Frazier insisted, his voice grating the air. "I just didn't think you were really there."

"He fell, hit his shoulder, might have cracked or dislocated something," Orvid went on, ignoring Frazier. "He would have been crushed under the train if I hadn't pulled his ankles and dragged him away from the tracks."

"I was almost on the train," Frazier sobbed. "I was there."

"What's tying his hands and feet?" I asked, trying to see in the dim light that filtered through the bare limbs.

"I always carry a few police ties." Orvid casually produced a thin, white piece of plastic no bigger than a strand of tagliatelle.

"That's holding him?" I took a step back before I checked myself.

"Riot cops carry something like these to handcuff lots of people in big riots. They work."

"So you hobbled him, dragged him, handcuffed him," I said, touching my forehead again, brushing away wet blood, "and then came looking for me?"

"I was worried about you." Orvid smiled. "If Frazier had killed you, it would have been very difficult for me to take care of your body. You're really big and heavy."

"Yes," I answered drily. "I'll try not to inconvenience you in that manner."

"Okay," Orvid said brightly. "Well, our work here is done."

"Not by a long shot," I insisted. "You understand I have about a hundred more questions."

"Let me go," Frazier muttered with absolutely no conviction.

"What questions?" Orvid asked me amiably, leaning a little on his cane, a generous smile on his lips.

"You've been *studying* me?" I tried not to sound completely dumbfounded. "Is that what you just reminded me of?"

"Where to begin?" Orvid mused.

The moon had freed itself completely from a prison of clouds, and the sky was polished with the soft light. All around us the birds and night frogs kept quiet, anxious to hear what Orvid had to say.

Even poor Hiram Frazier sat mute, breathing through his slack mouth, eyes closed.

"About three years ago, when you first returned home to Blue Mountain," Orvid began, "you had been gone from there a long time."

"Over a decade," I agreed, nodding.

"People were curious about you, about why you were back."

"They were?"

"Lots of people were glad to see you, of course," he hedged, "but you have to know that you're a strange person and people don't quite know what to make of you."

"Conceded." The bloody place on my head was throbbing.

"People thought you might be back to stir up trouble," he went on, "about your family. Even about my family—the rumors concerning your mother and my cousin Tristan. They're still circulating. But that's the thing about gossip, really: everyone likes to talk about it in private, but no one really feels comfortable if it's made public."

"Someone thought I was going to make those awful stories *public?*"

"Some people in my family thought it was a possibility. That's where my interest began, with the gossip concerning my cousin."

"That's really more about my mother than about me," I said, clearing my throat, "but go on."

"Let's just say it sparked an interest. Professionally."

"There it is," I said softly. "The center of your hidden world, your *profession.* I don't know how I would provoke an interest in a person such as yourself."

"What do you think I do?" Orvid asked, his smile turning cold.

"Oh, I know what you do," I said, trying to match his toughness. "I just don't want to discuss it."

"Why not?"

I tried to clear my mind and focus on the exact reason I didn't want to concern myself with Orvid's business.

"Maybe I'm afraid of you," I said. "Or maybe, as I believe I told you, there's enough bad news in my life at the moment and I don't want to sully my subconscious with any more twenty-first-century desolation. Or maybe, finally, I actually do feel some sort of odd kinship with you, a burgeoning friendship of some sort, and I don't want to be disappointed."

"I see." He shifted his weight. "You don't want to be disappointed in me, but you really don't know what I do for a living."

"I do," I insisted, my voice rising. "Skidmore knows too. And frankly, it's as much a mundane cliché as it is a disappointing occupation for a man of your intellect."

"Skidmore doesn't know anything," he assured me.

"He does. Damn." I could feel my temper rising, my face warming. "He's seen you fetch your little packages from the train. I've even pieced together the likely lines of connection: you to Andy

Newlander at the movie house in Pine City, then Andy to Nickel Mathews, and finally from Nickel to dozens of young people in our county. Or is it hundreds?"

Orvid exploded with laughter.

Frazier was so startled he almost fell over, and my adrenaline level shot up, heart thumping, face hotter.

"Oh my God," Orvid finally managed, all but supporting himself on his cane. "You think I'm the county drug lord?"

He dissolved again, ending in a mild coughing fit.

I talked over his wheezing.

"But, see, how would you even know that the subject was drugs simply from my mention of Andy and Nickel," I reasoned only a little weakly, "if you weren't connected with that business?"

"I am an observant sort," he said uneasily, pulling out his inhaler, "as I thought I had demonstrated. I see things; I learn. And with the boys we're talking about, it's not exactly deep-cover spy operations, is it? I mean, Nickel Mathews, God bless him, has the IQ of a radish."

"You're not the drug guy?" I said thinly.

"No." He was smiling again. "That's Eppie Waldrup."

"What?" I felt like sitting down.

"Why did you think Eppie was so aggressive about getting you to intervene with Skidmore on his behalf? Slow as Skidmore is, he's thorough, I'll give him that. He's going to find Eppie out one day, with Deputy Melissa's help."

"He's not involved in stolen cars?" I stammered.

"Not that I know of," Orvid wheezed.

"All those boys who always hang around Eppie's." I swallowed. "They go there for drugs?"

"Drugs and car parts," Orvid said brightly. "If there were handguns available too, it would be the complete American one-stop shopping experience, don't you think?"

"Eppie Waldrup?" I pictured him sitting in his tortured chair in the junkyard.

"What do you think would induce a man to create a musical instrument like the one Eppie made?" Orvid said, his eyebrows arched. "Except for drugs?"

I had to admit it seemed a more reasonable explanation than I'd ever thought of for Eppie's weird xylophone-gamelon setup.

"Sadly," I agreed, "I see that you may be right."

"Oh, I'm right. I've watched him sell weed a hundred times. And recently he's gotten into ecstasy. But I think you know that."

"So you're not the drug supplier in my hometown." I shook my head. "I have to absorb that. For some reason, I do believe you're telling me the truth. Skidmore is going to be embarrassed."

"Not if he catches Eppie," Orvid said reasonably. "Which he will pretty soon now. Especially if you suggest it to him."

"Right."

The wind picked up.

"You'll admit, now," Orvid said after a moment, "that you don't know what I do for a living."

"I guess I would have to admit that. Can I do anything to persuade you to tell me what you really do?"

"Well, as a matter of fact, it relates to our task at hand, as well as my aforementioned professional interest in your return to Blue Mountain. I'm reluctant to tell you everything, but for some reason I have an odd inclination to explain the basics."

"Now I'm not sure I want to know," I said.

Without warning, Hiram Frazier arched his back and tried to get up.

"He's a killer!" Frazier spat. "He's going to slit my throat!"

Frazier tried to wiggle sideways, away from Orvid.

Orvid flicked his cane and tapped Frazier a good knock on the back of his skull.

"Ow," was all the complaint that Frazier made, a weak one at that. "He's going to kill me."

"He's not going to kill you," I assured Frazier, sighing. "We're going to take you back to Pine City, like I wanted to a minute ago.

Only now you're all tied up and hit in the head and everything. But he's not going to kill you."

"Well," Orvid drawled. "Not so fast, Tex."

I met Orvid's eyes. They were amused, but they were made of steel.

"Actually," he continued, "that is what I'm here for. And I mean *here* in the larger sense of the word."

"Sorry?" I thought I was misunderstanding him.

"That's my job." He shrugged. "I'm a Final Solution Technologist."

I stared blankly, I could hear the sound of my own breathing.

"Sometimes in the movies or on television," Orvid explained simply, "a person like me is called a hit man."

"A hit man?" I felt Orvid had tapped *me* in the head with his cane.

"I hate that terminology. I think *Final Solution Technologist* is much better. Funny, you know? Like the new politically correct style speech."

"I don't believe you," I choked.

"It's true. I was pulled into the business by a teetotaler," Orvid said as if he were telling a campfire story. "He was a man named Lincoln Favor, friend of Judy's family in Chattanooga. He never took a drink in his life. He was married to Mattie Jenkins—you know the Jenkins family?"

All I could do was shake my head. Orvid's strange pink eyes sparkled in what little moonlight they captured.

"No," Orvid said cheerily, "I guess there's no reason you would. But Mattie, she loved Lincoln Favor for eleven years. Until she found out why he was so sober. And he was militant about being sober. Every Christmas, for example, Lincoln's brother would bring out a cup of kindness, and every year Lincoln would get into a fight about it, then he and Mattie would go home mad. There'd be a big buzz in the community about it for a week or two, and then the brothers would make up and things would be back to normal. Apparently, one year Mattie even asked Lincoln why he carried on so with his brother, who was by no means a drunk, about something so innocent as a simple Christmas toast. Lincoln said that drink was the devil's tool, that drink clouded a man's judgment and unsteadied his hand. Well, Mattie didn't understand why a man needed that much clear judgment just to collect government subsidy, run a little bitty truck patch, and sit at a roadside vegetable market three months of the year, which was Lincoln's public occupation. But she found out. October thirtieth ten years ago, Lincoln Favor was arrested by the FBI because he had killed seventeen men for money. That was Lincoln's private job, his real work: somebody paid him lots of money to kill people. And that's a kind of work that *would* require a steady hand. Mattie was so scared by the whole thing that she moved back in with her mama in Griffin and hasn't spoken a word, not a syllable, in the years since. She's a mute now. And Lincoln Favor escaped. The FBI put him in prison in Chattanooga, which is where I met him. I was there for cutting up somebody in a fight when I was drunk. Lincoln kind of took me under his wing and got me off the booze. Then some men came and got him out and they took me along. The point is: you never know. Lincoln was just like anybody. Judy talked to him many a time in the store. He seemed to have the same face as most any man. But it was a mask. He seemed a stern member of his church congregation, a hardworking man, a Christian in a little Southern town. But he killed seventeen men for no other reason than money. I learned a lot from him."

The black air around me seemed a net in which I was caught, a dark web, and I felt I couldn't move.

"Does Judy know?" I whispered. "Does she know what you do?"

"Are you serious?" He seemed offended. "We don't keep secrets from one another. I told you this was all her idea, remember?"

Everything in the clearing had gone still. I had to force the air out of my lungs to ask the question I didn't really want to ask.

"How does that have anything to do with me? You said your profession related to your studying me."

"I have an intuition about these things." He took hold of the top of his cane. "I always research interesting people like you."

"What for?" I asked, desperately wanting the answer to be anything other than what it had to be.

"In case someone in my family wanted me to kill you," he said softly.

He drew his blade from its hiding place.

Nineteen

I was too senseless to move.

Orvid displayed the three-foot length of steel; it slashed a silver cut in the black air beside him. His face had not changed expression.

I could feel something struggling in my chest, only gradually realized it was my heart, like a caged animal, beating at the sides of its prison. Blood pumped past my ear in loud explosions. My stomach was made of ice.

Every nerve ending in my body was screaming at me to run, but my muscles were dead, and my brain was paralyzed.

I felt my jaw fall open; heard sounds pour out of my mouth. Were they words? Was I actually talking?

"So what are the bundles you get," I seemed to be asking in some desperate attempt to gain time to think, "thrown from the train?"

"I have my jobs delivered that way," he said brightly, not moving. "Clients send their requests to me in packages that are thrown from the train. A certain conductor is paid very well to deliver what he's told is mail to a rural eccentric at the junction in Pine City. The packages are in a sealed bank courier pack that has a computer-code lock. They contain details of the job, photos, schedules, final decisions. I wait in the abandoned station in Pine City; when I see that the coast is clear, I pick up the bundle and make my final decisions about the job. Does that answer your question?"

"How do you get these clients?" I asked him automatically, exactly the way I would ask a folk informant.

I think I had the idea in mind that if I kept him talking, I would eventually come up with a plan of defense. It was clear to me that Orvid didn't mind talking about his work in the presence of two people who would be dead in a few moments.

"You know," he said casually, "it's mostly a word-of-mouth business. That's really your best advertising. Most of my clients know nothing about me, but occasionally one has heard rumors of a little person with a big knife, and they find it intriguing."

"How many jobs have you had?"

"I stopped counting at thirty."

"You've killed thirty people?" My voice was as thin as the moonlight and quavering.

"Men," he corrected. "No women, no kids. That's one of my rules."

"You have rules?" I rasped.

"Lots of them." He sucked in a deep breath. "I'm something of an avenging angel."

Frazier twitched.

I finally managed a step backward, away from the blade.

"Really?" I'd missed the casual tone I was aiming for, missed it by a mile.

"Without going into too much boring information," Orvid said, his voice solid, "I'll tell you that I only take on jobs when I believe I'll be righting some wrong. I know that may seem idealistic to you."

I didn't have any inclination to argue that murder was hardly, by any conception of the terms, an idealistic pursuit.

"I don't know what you mean." Anything to keep him talking.

"The last few jobs I've taken should suffice as explanation. Let's see. A man hired me to kill two twenty-year-old boys who raped his eleven-year-old daughter and escaped prosecution on a technicality. I researched the case thoroughly, found the boys were, indeed, guilty. They'd even confessed. When I caught up with them, they were in the process of kidnapping another child, I assumed for the same purposes. The strangeness of our judicial system is a labyrinth in which many a Minotaur might hide."

"You killed two boys?" I heard my voice as if it were coming through a tunnel from the other side of the world.

"I killed a congressman who beat his wife repeatedly but was never even arrested." Orvid went on as if he hadn't heard my question. "His wife hired me from a hospital bed, certain that he would eventually kill her."

"And somehow people send you information in a package that's thrown off a train?"

"It's perfect," he answered. "In a high-tech world, my other-century approach usually escapes notice. Not to mention how dramatic it all is. I'm sure I don't need to remind you that our family's always had a flair for the theatrical."

I began to see white spots out of the corner of my eyes, little flares of light. I had to sit down.

I crumpled clumsily to the ground. It was wet, solid; reassuring in the most bizarre way.

"It's a lot to absorb, I'll grant you that," Orvid conceded, acknowledging my collapse. "And I wouldn't be telling you this much if it weren't for the fact that Judy and I are leaving the country together fairly soon."

"You mentioned that," I said as if we were having a conversation over Sunday dinner.

"My point is," he insisted, "that I want to explain why I have to kill this man."

He looked down at Frazier.

Frazier began whispering softly to himself, praying, I thought.

"Judy didn't exactly hire me," Orvid went on, "but you had a hint of how insistent she can be when she sets her mind to something. She believes it's the right thing to do. He took away her girls. I take him away."

"Eye for an eye," Frazier said, more to himself than to us.

"I understand that you think your cause is just," I said to Orvid slowly, "that your work is right. But ultimately it's all semantics and rationalization. Killing another human being, Orvid, takes a toll. It taxes *your* spirit. It leads you down the wrong path. It eventually destroys the fabric of humanity."

"No," he responded simply. "It restores balance. The way I do it."

"Balance," Frazier echoed weakly.

I saw in a flash that, despite Hiram Frazier's previous insistence that I might be his other half, Orvid was Frazier's true mirror. They both believed in the same theory of a balanced universe; though it was clearly a theory born of an unbalanced mind.

"You can't murder this man right here right now in front of me," I pleaded, no other argument coming to me. "You can't hunt down another human being and execute him like this."

"I can," Orvid corrected me gently. "I have. And I will."

He raised his blade.

Night noises ceased, and my temples pounded a violent rhythm. My body weighed a thousand pounds, and I could not move.

"Your high-minded ideals," I said, too high, too fast, "they have no real meaning in this slaughter. You're not setting anything right by killing this man. You're taking revenge. And you're not even taking this vengeance in the heat of the moment, or for a personal reason. You're doing it as a favor to your *girlfriend*! You have to see that it's not right."

Orvid paused.

I could see the shadows of a hundred responses shoot across his face before he lowered his blade.

"Thanksgiving week last year," Orvid said softly, not looking at me, "I went to the school play with Judy. Did you go?"

For an instant I considered the possibility that I had gone mad.

"No." I didn't remotely understand what he was asking me.

"We came late," he went on, "stood in the back. Judy wanted to see Tess and Rory in the show because she had helped them with their lines, even sewed the costumes for them. Rory was the head of the settlers, Tess was the Indian princess. Everyone was sitting in those metal folding chairs in the gym, listening to the words echo around the basketball hoops. Seemed like every soul in the county was there, the gym was packed. The stage looked great: there were trees and houses and clouds; a sky filled with sun. There were stern English settlers gathering in the bounty of the earth's crops: corn, wheat, pumpkins. There were serene Indians, watching, nodding, smoking pipes. Despite the occasion, the settlers looked sad to me. They were all in black and never smiled. The Indians were joking and laughing and making up songs."

Orvid let out a long breath, and his arm muscles seemed to relax.

"The play was running fine," Orvid went on after a moment, "and all the kids remembered their lines except for one boy. Judy told me his line was 'I think I see our red brothers and sisters over the hill.' When he said this, the Indians were supposed to come in from behind the black curtain. Since he never said it, there was a tense moment of silence when nothing happened, but Tess saved the day. She said, loud and clear from back of the drape, 'Come on, my red brothers and sisters—let's go see what the settlers are having for dinner.' Everyone laughed and the Indians came on in. Tess offered an ear of corn to Rory, and Rory curtsied and took the offering. She was supposed to say, 'Thank you, Mistress Farmer, for your gift.' Then the two girls were going to sing 'Come, Ye Thankful People, Come.' But do you know what Rory said instead?"

"No," I answered, more baffled.

"Lucinda never mentioned this to you?" His brow wrinkled.

"No, Orvid," I stammered, "what are you trying to tell me? Why would Lucinda—"

"Instead of the line Rory was supposed to say," Orvid interrupted, his voice grating his throat, "she said, 'Thank you, Mr. Frazier, for your gift.' Judy heard it too; commented on it. Of course it made no sense at the time. Until you told us the name of the man who caused the train wreck."

"The Lord's still whipping me, isn't he?" Hiram Frazier whimpered.

Orvid looked down at his victim.

"Yes, Hiram," Orvid said firmly. "He certainly is."

"You just think you heard that name," I insisted. "You're experiencing a false memory."

Orvid looked back up at me.

"For a second or two at the Thanksgiving play," Orvid went on, his voice thinner, "nobody onstage seemed to know what to do; Judy could see something was wrong with the girls. Then the boy who'd forgotten his line just started singing. Do you know what song?"

I shook my head.

" 'Be Thou My Vision.' And for absolutely no reason, everybody in the gym and on the stage, one by one, joined in. That was the end of the play."

I started to speak, then remembered what was significant about the hymn he'd just named.

Orvid saw the realization on my face.

"That's right," he assured me. " 'Be Thou My Vision' was sung at Tess and Rory's funeral."

I just sat there.

"I'm not a big believer in this kind of thing, as you might imagine," Orvid went on, "this spooky stuff. I fall more to the philosophy of 'How can I use this crap to put one over on the rubes?' But I'll tell you what: this one is hard to argue with. Judy absolutely believes it's the hand of God at work. She heard the name too. I don't know what to make of it. But look right here: this guy's name is Frazier."

Before I could say anything, Frazier spoke up.

"My name is Hiram Frazier," he said, rote, hypnotically.

"He's barely aware of who he is, Orvid," I pleaded, "you can see that. You've got to have a little mercy."

"What the hell would make me be merciful at this point?" Orvid said, his voice a sting on the air.

"You don't make someone be merciful," I shot back. "You can't force it. Mercy drops on you out of the sky, like rain. And listen, it would be good for both Frazier and you, it works both ways. It would save his life, it could save your soul."

"Mercy's the kind of thing you usually ask God for, right? Not a guy like me."

"I swear, Orvid," I said, breathing hard, "if you're looking for justice, or for balance, you'd better start praying, because none of us is going to be saved. You're better off asking for mercy than for justice. That's the way the universe works."

"Forgive us our trespasses," Frazier mumbled, "as we forgive those who have trespassed against us."

"He's an old man," I begged.

"He killed two people!" Orvid snapped back. "Two beautiful, young lives that made a difference in this world. He took them away. It's a debt that's got to be paid."

"He doesn't even remember doing it," I insisted. "God, he doesn't even remember breaking into my house to scare me with a Bible verse not twenty-four hours ago!"

"Well." Orvid's pace slowed a little. "Actually he didn't do that, truth be told."

"What do you mean?" I asked weakly.

"I did that." Orvid sighed, and there was even a hint of apology in his eyes. "Sorry."

"You went into my house," I managed to say, "and left an open Bible?"

"I wanted you to help me," he said quickly. "I thought if you had a more personal stake in finding Frazier, it would speed things up a little. You know you can be slow as Christmas in your work sometimes."

"You broke into my house," I said, my voice a trickle from my lips, "to scare me into helping you find and kill this man?"

"Sorry," he said again, and sounded sincere. "I was hoping Skidmore would investigate the break-in, and that would slow him down enough to give us a head start catching up with Frazier. Which it seems to have done."

"Why did you answer the phone?" I stammered.

"I thought it might be Judy." Orvid bit his lip. "She knew where I was. In fact for a second I thought it was her voice on the phone."

"You scared Lucinda to death," I complained. "And me."

"It worked," he said simply. "You're here."

"Jesus," I moaned. "You're as much of a lunatic as Frazier is."

"I'm going to want that Bible back, by the way," he said emotionlessly. "It's Judy's."

"I'm absolutely certain that I can't let you kill this man while I sit here and watch," I told him, trying hard to make ice of the words. "Not now."

"You can't *let* me?" His chin jutted my direction. "I call that bold talk for the man without the knife."

"That's not a knife." I inclined my head in the direction of his blade. "That's compensation."

"Please!" he exploded, laughing. "You're not seriously trying to undermine my efforts with Psychology 101?"

I felt the heft of the switched-off flashlight in my right hand. I was trying to determine how hard I'd have to throw it to knock the blade out of Orvid's hand. Maybe I could jump up, grab Frazier, drag him behind me, outrun Orvid. I couldn't think of anything else.

Orvid read my mind.

"I've been doing this," he said, a quick glance at his blade, "for almost as long as you've been a folklorist. You don't really think you could outmaneuver me, any more than I could outthink you in the realms of mythological academia. So really don't try. I don't want you to get hurt."

I realized I hadn't exhaled in a while.

"You don't want me to get hurt?" I said, barely breathing. "What do you think I'm going to do if you kill this man? If you don't kill me, I'm going straight to Skidmore."

"I told you that Judy and I are leaving after this," he said calmly. "No one will find us."

"Because you and Judy blend in so well," I taunted, "wherever you go."

"I can kill you if you want me to, but I'd rather not do it."

In that instant, panic forced a fact from the recesses of my memory: albino eyes are light sensitive.

I wouldn't have to throw the flashlight, I'd just have to turn it on. But I'd have to be careful. Orvid was obviously hyperaware, his reflexes were at their peak.

"Yes," I said, struggling to my feet. "I'd rather you didn't kill me, now that you mention it. I thought you were going to."

"Oh, for God's sake, why would you think that?"

"Are you serious?" I stood facing Orvid and stared him down.

"Okay," he admitted. "From your point of view at the moment, I get it. But, damn."

"At the very least, I'm not going to stand here while you kill this man," I sighed, hoping to sound as tired as I was. "If you agree, I'll go back and wait in the truck."

"I don't know," Orvid said slowly. "If you drive off, it'll be hard for me to get home."

"I'll give you my keys," I offered, reaching into my pocket. "A fitting, if ironic, turn of events under the circumstances."

I fished out my keys and held them high in my left hand, showing them to Orvid. As casually as I could manage, I flicked on the flashlight with my right hand, raised it as if I were preparing to light my way back to the factory ruins.

The beam shot a stab of light directly into Orvid's face.

"Christ!" Orvid howled instantly.

I lumbered forward, hand out reaching for Frazier.

I looked up just in time to see Orvid's knife coming directly at me.

Twenty

The hilt of the knife, with perfect accuracy, hit the flashlight so hard that the flashlight broke apart, shattering into three or four pieces, flying out of my hand in as many directions.

"Ow," Orvid said like a kid who'd pinched his finger. "That really hurts."

"My hand." I tried to sound innocent. "Why did you do that?"

I shook the hand that had been holding the flashlight. It was numb.

"Sorry. I broke your flashlight. Reflex. That light in my eyes really stings."

"Oh," I stammered, "the light in your eyes. Really?"

Orvid was already headed my way, rubbing his eyes.

I glanced down.

Orvid's blade was a few feet to my right.

I stepped toward it; scooped it up.

"Look, Orvid," I said, planting my feet as solidly as I could, holding the blade high. "I can't give this back to you."

He stopped, sighed, looked up at me.

"Oh." He rubbed his eyes once more. "You shot me in the eyes deliberately. Good move."

There was actually a hint of admiration in his voice.

"Don't come any closer," I said, but the waver in my voice betrayed me.

"Enough kidding around," he went on, not remotely angry, "give me the thing, okay?"

"No," I pleaded, "I just—I can't."

Orvid took a step toward me.

"I don't want to hurt you," he said, his voice completely calm.

It may have presented Frazier, who gaped at both of us, a fairly amusing image. An oversize man with a big sword in his hand was being menaced by an unarmed person the size of a child.

"I'm pretty fast," Orvid went on. "I could dislocate both your kneecaps before you knew what I was doing, and then you'd have a really hard time moving. Or I could crack your nuts, I'm just about that high. One good punch would mean permanent family planning for the Devilin line. Or."

Orvid reached behind his back and produced a small automatic pistol.

"I could just shoot you a couple of places," he concluded. "Nothing vital, but if you had a bullet in each arm and, say, one in the foot, you'd really be incapacitated. For, like, the rest of this month at least."

He pointed the pistol directly at my right boot.

"All I'd have to do is fall right," I countered, "and I'd smash you."

"I'm faster than that." His gun hand had not moved.

"Or this blade could do you some damage on the way down," I said, hefting his knife.

"Yeah, don't fool around with that. It's really sharp. I cut myself on it all the time."

"I don't know what I'm going to do," I told Orvid honestly.

We might have waited there, locked in our strange standoff, for quite a while, but Hiram Frazier spoke up unexpectedly.

"Which one of you is going to kill me?" he asked, his voice lucid, his words clear as moonlight.

My eyes shot to Frazier's forlorn outline twitching on the ground.

Orvid spoke to Frazier without turning his head toward him.

"Do you remember a couple of nights ago," Orvid asked Frazier, "when you were in Pine City?"

"Where?" Frazier said.

"There was a train wreck," Orvid said steadily. "You were beside the train tracks when a car was hit by a train."

"I don't remember," Frazier said, looked off into the darker part of the woods.

But I could see that he was lying this time. My encounter with him only a few moments before had brought the scene back to him.

"There were two little girls in a car, and you took the keys," Orvid went on carefully. "You were beside a railroad track."

"Sounds like me," Frazier admitted, seeming to picture it. "That's what I'll do sometimes. I usually get ten dollars."

"You caused those girls to be afraid," said Orvid, taking a step closer to me. "And then you caused them to die."

"I did?" his voice was wracked with despair. "I just don't remember. I don't want to."

Orvid's eyes were locked on mine.

"You're all wrong about me, you know, Dr. Devilin," Orvid said quietly. "I hate that I've given you the wrong impression. I don't have vengeance in my heart. Not anymore, at least. I have pity. It isn't exactly the kind of mercy you were asking for, but look at him. Look at Frazier. He's already dead in nearly every way a person can be except for one: his body's still staggering around. What's better for the guy, ultimately? To go on like this, or to end it all here and now? Seriously."

I looked over at poor Hiram Frazier.

Transparent as the silver that sifted from the moon, an old man sat on the cold, cold ground. He was shivering, bone white, dressed in black tatters. He was nothing more than a November ghost.

Orvid and I were both startled to hear Frazier's voice once again.

"The little boy's right, you know," Frazier said, looking at Orvid's back. "You'd do me a kindness if you'd let me die. I'd be grateful if this body could rest."

Orvid lowered his gun. I could see something had changed in his expression. He was trying to come to grips with the exact nature of the thing called Hiram Frazier.

"Usually a ghost is a traveling creature whose body has died away," I said, looking directly at Frazier. "But you're the other kind."

"But I'm the other kind," Frazier said, staring back, completely understanding me. "You see us more often, but you pay us no mind."

"What are you both talking about?" Orvid said, turning.

"He's not the kind of a ghost that's a spirit without a body," I explained, voice hollow. "He's the kind that's a body without a spirit left in it."

"Oh," Orvid sighed.

"A vacant body," Frazier agreed.

That sound, and Frazier's shivering quake, stood the hair on my arms straight up. I felt a flush burning the back of my neck. Everything was edged, like a cutout silhouette.

Preacher Hiram Frazier was, indeed, a true-life, living ghost.

The whole clearing where we stood seemed paralyzed, a place where matter and time were exempt. I had no sensation in my body whatsoever.

Frazier looked up at the black sky, away from the moon.

"You have no idea," he whispered to no one, "what a kindness it would be if you'd only let this body rest. Please let me come home now. Haven't I done enough?"

Orvid's gaze at me was steady.

"Hasn't he done enough?" Orvid repeated.

"I don't know how I can do this anymore," Frazier said, his voice even weaker. "I don't want to suck more life out of this world."

"It may be time," Orvid said to me, "to turn your little *mercy* speech back on yourself. What do you think would be better for this guy? Really, no kidding."

The air all around me was a strange ocean rising and falling, and the threat of drowning in it seemed tangible to me. I had to come up with something to keep Orvid from murdering the old man, no matter what the old man was.

"Tell me again what you heard Tess and Rory say about Hiram Frazier at that Thanksgiving play," I heard myself saying to Orvid.

"I wondered how long it would take you to get ahold of that. They were supposed to say, 'Thank you, Mistress Farmer,' and then sing 'Come, Ye Thankful People, Come.' But instead Rory said, 'Thank you, Mister Frazier, for your gift.' "

" 'Your gift,' " I repeated.

"How about that." Orvid's face was supremely serene.

It didn't take me long to scour the library at the back of my skull and emerge with the facts I wanted.

"Do you know about the alligator god in the ancient Egyptian pantheon?" I said, watching Hiram Frazier's deeply wrinkled, leathery face. "He stands at the gate of death and weighs your heart. He uses one of those old scales, you know, like the scales of justice in that statue? The kind where the counterweight is on one side and the object you want to weigh is on the other? When the god-monster puts your heart on the scales, what does he use as its counterweight?"

"Tell me," Orvid indulged me.

Good, I thought. *The longer I keep this up, the longer I have to figure out how to keep Frazier alive.*

"An ostrich feather." I smiled. "If your heart is lighter than the feather, you get to have your heart back, and you go on to a perfect afterlife. If your heart is heavy, the alligator eats it and you wander forever without a heart in the cold realms between this world and the next."

"Maybe you're referring to the toxicology report for the girls," Orvid realized. "You mean that when the girls died, they were laughing. They didn't realize the peril of their situation. Their hearts were light."

"Yes." I nodded once.

"That *is* a gift." Orvid smiled.

"Just a thought," I mumbled. "Only one of several."

"There are others?" Orvid said, slightly mocking.

"Look at Mr. Frazier's skin," I ventured.

Scales, warts, hard ridges, stood out on Frazier's face and hands, and Orvid nodded. Alligator skin.

"I think it's probably best not to make too much of your mythological observations," Orvid said after a second, "but on the other hand, they do give some import to our business here tonight, don't they?"

"I always think they do," I answered haplessly.

"Well, I get your point in this regard, anyway. Are you going to hand me back my knife now?"

He made a show of hiding his gun away again.

"I don't want to hurt you," I ventured, the words shaky, "but I'm not giving you this blade so you can kill a man."

"Damn," he growled. "Give it to me."

He took another step my way and held out his right hand, motioning impatiently for his blade.

"No, Orvid," I told him firmly.

Without warning Orvid sprang forward, almost horizontal to the ground. His head plowed into my stomach like a cannonball. I flew backward, breath knocked out of me, and hit the ground hard, right next to a motionless Frazier.

Orvid was standing over me instantly, soundless as a beam of moonlight. He kicked and I felt a searing pain in my hand. Orvid pulled the blade away from me quickly and held it a moment to one side of his body, low.

Suddenly he lashed out; swung the blade like a golf club. Before I could move, the motion was complete.

Frazier moaned and fell to one side.

"What have you done?" I cried, trying to sit up.

"Not what you think," Orvid managed calmly.

To my amazement, a second later Frazier put his hands out onto the wet grass and drew in a deep breath. It took me a moment to realize that Orvid had deftly cut the tie that had bound Frazier's hands behind his back.

Moving quickly, Orvid similarly dispatched the white bond around Frazier's ankles.

"Help me get him up, would you?" Orvid said to me.

I found I could barely move, but I somehow got up and trundled in the direction of the body on the ground.

We did our best to get Frazier to a standing position.

"What now?" Frazier asked us blankly.

"Where were you going when I stopped you?" Orvid asked Frazier quietly.

"Home," Frazier's voice ground out. "Catch a train going home."

Orvid stood aside.

"There are the tracks," he told Frazier. "You're going home."

I looked between the ancient preacher and the shorter albino. Neither seemed remotely real in the dim light of the clearing.

Frazier nodded. "Time to go home, ain't it?" He staggered toward the railroad tracks.

"Wait," I interrupted feebly.

"Yes, it is," Orvid answered Frazier, following the man.

"We have to take Frazier back to Skid," I began. "We can't let him go. That's not what I meant."

Perplexed beyond motion, I watched the two of them walk a step or two before I followed to intervene further.

Frazier was humming to himself. I couldn't tell the tune.

"It's coming." Orvid stood directly behind him.

I came to a stop a little to their right and looked down the tracks, trying to sight a train.

"Hear it, Preacher?" Orvid went on.

"I do." Frazier nodded without looking back.

I didn't hear anything.

"What are you doing, Orvid?" I whispered.

I glanced at Frazier. His face was transformed, the moonlight washed it clean, and his eyes were closed in ecstatic rapture.

"Are you ready?" Orvid asked.

"I am," Frazier whispered. "God Almighty, I am."

Tears fought their way past Frazier's shut eyelids, made silver rills down his cheeks.

I craned my neck, strained my eyes to see a train, but there was nothing.

"There's no train coming," I said to Orvid. "Stop this. You're just tormenting him now. What's the point of that? We have to get him to my truck. We have to take him back to the sheriff."

"All right," Orvid sighed.

Orvid took one step backward, and faster than I could see, he raised his blade high in the air, snapping to an etched tableau for a split second.

"No!" I exploded, lunging for Orvid.

"Train's coming," Frazier whispered, softer than the wind, his face shining.

A terrible, swift lightning cracked Orvid's tableau, the sword vanished into Hiram Frazier's back.

The body fell to earth, at long last dead.

There wasn't a single drop of blood.

Twenty-One

I stood frozen, my face inches from Orvid's blade. The crescent moon dangled in the sky, a curl of pale thread. It was a hint of the light that might exist beyond the black sky, a promise of morning.

Sound resumed slowly in the clearing. Doves and tree frogs called, the wind picked up, a draft of cold water washing over everything.

"You're a monster." My voice was leaden; my eyes steadfastly avoided the body by the tracks. "I have to . . ."

But I couldn't finish my sentence. I didn't know what I had to do.

Orvid's blade had disappeared, and he was leaning on his ornate cane.

"You were telling me at Judy's house," he said slowly, "about the character who slew the Minotaur. There was a girl waiting for him at the door that led out of the maze."

"Ariadne?" I mumbled, stunned.

"She gave Theseus a bit of thread to take with him into the labyrinth. He held one end; she stood at the doorway, in the light, holding the other. When he wanted to come home, he followed the thread to her."

"Yes." I tried to focus my eyes on Orvid.

"There you go," he said, his voice a mixture of November air and the scent of last harvest, a warm sound despite the cold that encased it.

There was a rustle in the leaves behind us, and the half-expected voice came pouring into the air, cold and crisp.

"It's done, then."

I didn't have to turn to see Judy. I could tell she was standing a few feet away.

"Done and done," Orvid agreed. "Been a long day."

For the first time his voice sounded tired, but only as if he'd just pulled a double shift at the textile mill.

"It's the end of the slope." Judy came to Orvid. "All coasting downhill from now on."

I had the idea that she meant something quite significant, but I just couldn't force my mind to stay with that idea long enough to explore it.

"You planned this all along," I accused Judy, still unable to look at her.

"I told you this is what I wanted," she said simply.

I glared at Orvid.

"You called her," I stammered.

"Didn't have to." A slight smile was on his lips. "She's been following us."

"What?" I closed my eyes. "I led you both to this man so you could kill him?"

"You have to know," Orvid told me firmly, "that I would have found him on my own eventually."

I could hear the iron in his words and believed him. It was a merciful belief.

"Let's go, honey," Judy said, taking Orvid's hand. "I've got everything packed."

"I have to tell Skidmore what happened here," I began, sounding a little like a child even to myself.

"I know," Orvid sighed. "It doesn't matter. We really are going to disappear. He'll never find us. And, you know, if you try to stop us now, I'll just have to shoot you. I'm too tired to wrestle or anything, right?"

Judy was standing there, beaming at her beau. She took exactly one second out of her adoration to give me a nod and a wave.

"Good-bye, Dr. Devilin," she said. "We won't see one another again."

She returned her entire attention to the man standing beside her. The two of them started off.

"Was that true, Orvid?" I ventured. "The thing you said about the girls in the Thanksgiving play, mentioning Hiram Frazier's name? Or was that just something else to motivate me, like leaving the Bible verse open in my house?"

Orvid sniffed once.

"That's true," Judy said. "They called the man's name. I heard it."

"I don't understand." I could barely see their faces in the moonlight.

Clouds were flying by the moon.

"Weatherman said tomorrow's going to be clear," Orvid announced softly, readying to close the door. "Should be a bright, sunny day."

"I could stand that," Judy told him, smiling.

I couldn't do anything but watch them amble up the hill. Almost before I realized it, they were gone into the woods. A moment after that, car headlights pierced the night, making dancing shadows of a hundred trees. I watched until the light was gone. By then my muscles began to work again, and I headed away from the tracks.

I was afraid to look back at the body on the ground behind me.

Twenty-Two

Somehow I made my way back to my truck, through the old mill.

It seemed less haunted, more at peace. The brick walls were tired, but still managed to bathe themselves in moonlight and a reminiscence of former glory. Even the weeds had taken on a certain uplift, an aspiration to grander flora. Shadows hiding the corners of the building were purple, a royal cousin of the black that had crouched there before. One of the birds that called out might have been a skylark.

The chrome of the door handle on my truck was cold, but I was grateful for something solid, a clear sensation. I climbed into the cab of the truck. I tried for a while to start the engine. It seemed to take forever.

The drive home was perilous. My mind traveled, like Einstein's mind riding his famous beam of light, across the sky in search of any kind of dawn.

Instead, my thoughts were invaded by Promethean doubts and cold new astrophysics. I thought about *dark matter*. Anything to avoid thinking about the long night's events.

The primary dilemma, I mused, was that if Einstein's theory of gravity was correct, galaxies ought to fly apart in more or less the same manner as my flashlight had when hit by Orvid's knife. But clearly the galaxies were not coming unhinged, at least not ours. The road before me seemed uncommonly solid, in fact. But if Einstein's theory of gravity was wrong, then nothing would be holding the universe together—nothing but dark matter. And if initial observations were correct, then the *non*dark matter, the kind that would make up my hand, the steering wheel, the road, the earth, the sky, and everything I would be capable of experiencing in this reality, *that* kind of matter was in the minority. The vast minority. The kind of matter we are, we and the stars and everything we know, may well occupy as little as 5 percent of the universe, barely a speck of all reality.

It was not the sort of thought I found comforting in the black hours before dawn, driving to Lucinda's house.

It didn't help that the image of Hiram Frazier's body dropping across the railroad tracks kept playing over and over in my head like a looped movie.

By the time I pulled my truck in front of Lucinda's, the mood had crystallized, and everything in my body and mind was hard and brittle.

I turned off the headlights.

I sat there in the truck, motor off, lights off, still in the dead night.

In my mind I was digging in the black dirt of Lucinda's garden with a blue-handled spade she had given me for a birthday long ago. I had just returned to Blue Mountain; she hadn't yet recovered from the death of her husband.

"What's that?" She stood over me.

"Fennel and dill," I said without looking up.

"What for?"

"You like dill."

"What about the fennel?"

"I don't know," I confessed. "It was all they had left at Peterson's. It was a going-out-of-business sale. These little packs were only a penny apiece."

"Peterson's is going out of business?" She shifted her weight and the full slant of late-afternoon sun hit me in the corner of my left eye.

"Yes. You don't remember driving by there last week?"

"I had a talk with Hammon today," she told me softly.

Hammon was her dead husband, crushed by a tractor. She often spoke to him in those days, or so she would tell me.

I set down the spade and looked up as best I could in all that light. All I could see was a sepia shadow and a blast of gold. I waited for her to tell me what Hammon had said

"It's all set," Lucinda said.

"What's all set?"

She was staring down at the seed packets. They were faded and wrinkled, even though they had never been opened. Stamped on the bottom in gray that had once been black was the announcement *Lot Packed for 1998 Season.*

"You know these won't come up. They're expired."

"Seeds don't expire." I looked down at the packets. "Do they?"

"You'll never get dill out of those little black dots." Her voice was ghostly.

"Maybe not. But I like being here with you, and digging up the dirt, and sitting out here in the sun."

"I know. How many times do we have to have the 'process over product' conversation?"

"As many times as it takes." I smiled.

"I'm going in. I just wanted you to know that I had the talk with Hammon." She was a shadow again, silhouetted in the setting sun.

"Okay," I said quickly, "what talk?"

"Hammon said he's moving on now. He said it was our turn, yours and mine. It was okay with him."

That was all. She went back in the house. She never brought it up again, and I never asked.

The seeds did come up. They appeared before Thanksgiving that year. The packets had been mislabeled. They were tarragon and mint. They were the first things I planted in Lucinda's garden, and still growing there. The tarragon was a perennial, and the mint had only taken over one small corner of the raised bed she'd reserved for spices. We never discussed that I thought tarragon belonged in every dish, so I always wanted a fresh supply; or the recollection that Hammon had made mint juleps, his favorite dinner-party concoction, and so he always wanted plenty of mint growing in the garden.

I pried myself away from those thoughts, sitting in the dark in my truck, and tried to stare around the side of the house, see if I could see that raised bed. But everything I saw in the dark landscape, and most of the things I couldn't see, were haunted, wracked with longing memories.

I was startled from my melancholy reverie by a soft voice.

"Fever?"

I peered toward the house to see Lucinda standing in the open doorway, squinting.

"Yes," I answered, disoriented.

"What are you doing sitting out there in the dark?" she asked me, amused.

I glanced at my watch. It was close to five in the morning.

"What are you doing awake at this hour?" I asked.

"Waiting for you," she answered as if it were the most obvious thing in the world. "When you didn't show up for dinner, I called Skidmore. He said you were out working."

"I was supposed to have dinner with you," I remembered, half-dazed.

"You okay?"

"I don't know." I stared at her.

"Well, come on in the house," she said, a gentle irritation edging her words. "We'll sort it all out together."

She turned and headed into her living room.

"I don't know why a person would sit out in the cold and dark," she continued, mostly to herself, "when there's a perfectly good fire in the fireplace."

"There's a fire?" I called out weakly.

"I saved you some supper too. And a piece of that apple tart you like."

That got me out of the truck.

I felt my legs move the rest of me across her lawn, up the porch steps.

"Damn it," she said from inside.

"What?" I quickened my pace.

I shoved through the door and into the living room. Lucinda was sitting on the floor, poking at the fire. Her hair was pulled back and the blaze made her face flushed. The room was warm and dry; hickory and cinnamon apples filled the air. She was wearing one of her old shirts and a pair of faded gray jeans.

"I tore my favorite shirt," she groused, "stoking this fire. Look."

She held up the frayed shirttail, a long thread hung from it, and the heat from the fire made the thread dance upward in my direction.

"I see." I rubbed my eyes. "I've had kind of a tough day myself. I have to call Skidmore."

"Not right this second you don't. Sit down and have a little bite to eat. You'll feel better after that."

The fire was bright, and I felt its heat on my face and hands, stinging a little. Lucinda was up, headed into the kitchen.

I sat down on the sofa, staring into the fire.

"Tess and Rory were laughing when they died," I said, marveling at how exhausted my voice sounded. "And the man responsible for the accident has been killed."

Lucinda dropped something in the kitchen, a plate or a glass; the sound tore into the air. She appeared in the doorway, face drained, staring.

"What?"

"I saw the man who was responsible for Tess and Rory's accident." I wondered if my face looked as blank as hers. "I watched another man kill him."

Lucinda started to speak three times before she decided on the perfect sentence:

"Maybe you did have a worse day than I did."

"Maybe," I agreed.

She paused a moment, then returned to the kitchen.

"Well, eat first," she called gently, "then tell me all about it."

I never ceased to marvel at the way the people in my hometown handled shock: always pulled back, always burying something under mountain rocks.

A second later I could hear the musical sounds of plates and silverware and glasses. I tried to let the pleasant noise take my mind. Lucinda appeared soon with a huge plate in her hand. I reached into my inner coat pocket and laid two photographs on her table.

"Here," I said softly. "I brought your pictures back."

"Look at those faces," she sighed.

"Beautiful."

A smile touched her lips, an expression of sublime acceptance, if not complete forgiveness.

"I'm glad I knew them."

Lucinda set the plate down in front of me, a full quarter of an apple tart filling a large part of it, and joined me on the sofa. She put her hand on the side of my head for a moment.

The food filled every sense: warm acorn squash with butter and brown sugar, fresh steamed chard with pine nuts, and a whole Cornish game hen that had clearly been slow-smoked over mesquite all day. The steam rising from the plate curled invitingly, and the fire in the hearth was a perfect backdrop, hissing pleasantly, casting its amber comfort over everything.

I went straight for the tart and had a bite of it in my mouth before I noticed a light disturbing Lucinda's front windows.

"Hell," I mumbled, starting to rise from my seat. "Did I leave my truck headlights on? Can't I even sit still for one minute and enjoy this food?"

Lucinda gave the windows a slow glance.

"No sugar," she said softly. "That's dawn."

"What?" I said, sitting back, not quite understanding what she'd said. "It is?"

"Yes, Fever." Her hand effortlessly slipped into mine. "It's morning."

Twenty-Three

By the time the sun was high, I was standing in Skidmore's office. He'd found Hiram Frazier's body just where I'd told him it would be in my 5:00 A.M. phone call. He'd wanted more information, but I was too dazed to tell him much over the telephone, so he'd made me promise to come in and see him. I wasn't feeling much more coherent in his office at noon. I hadn't been able to sleep much. At least I'd had a shower.

The day outside was clear. A polished copper light careened amid the last of the leaves, and the air was a crisp bite, a cold apple. Autumn's light and air were, however, shut out of Skidmore's lair.

He closed the office door, sat behind his desk, and indicated an insistence that I take the chair opposite him. His face was a mask of exhaustion and skintight nerves.

"I called Tennessee about Frazier this morning," he began. "Actually spoke to a real live person this time. Know what they said?"

"They probably didn't know who you were talking about." I guessed.

"Pretty much. I asked if they wanted the body. Nobody did."

"What are you going to do with it?"

"I don't care." He measured out the syllables, barely controlling his ire. "Where are they, Fever?" His voice was a stranger's, his eyes wild and disoriented.

"If you mean Orvid and Judy," I sighed, "I wouldn't know. Do you have any idea how you look at the moment. How you sound?"

"How I *sound*?"

I sank back into the chair, breathed in the stale air of his shut room, and closed my eyes.

"You have to tell me what the hell is the matter with you," I said softly, "or I can't talk to you at all."

"Are you serious?" His voice was suddenly spiny. "You'll talk to me when I say you will!"

I opened my eyes, but didn't move otherwise.

"That's not you," I said simply. "That kind of sentence, that tone of voice."

I slapped the arms of my chair and hauled myself to a stand.

"What do you think you're doing?" Skid growled.

"I've had it," I shouted at him. "I'm going to see if anyone in this town knows about exorcism, because you've obviously got a demon in your clutch housing!"

His head snapped back only slightly, and there was the merest second of a crease at one corner of his mouth.

"My clutch housing?" he said, calming. "That's what you went with? Clutch housing? You don't know thing one about cars, you realize. Where did you come up with that?"

"It's from an old cartoon in the *New Yorker,* actually," I admitted, only a little embarrassed.

"Yeah," he followed instantly, "*that* I believe."

"You need a priest," I insisted.

He let out a long, heavy breath.

"I need a vacation," he corrected me at length. "That's surely true."

I sat back down.

"So are you going to tell me what's going on with you?" I prompted quietly.

"It's no big mystery, Dr. Drama," he told me, squinting. "I don't believe I'm doing this job of sheriff right. I don't think I'm running my life especially well at the moment."

"What are you talking about?"

"Everybody thinks I'm doing terrible," he managed to say. "I hear the talk."

"I think you're hearing incorrectly."

"I'm saying that I've discovered it's a whole lot easier to complain about the boss than to *be* the boss."

"Well," I began.

"For one thing, I should have known about all this drug business in town a long time ago," he interrupted. "I just didn't want it to be true. I didn't want our town to be that town."

"You mean about Nickel Mathews. I had the same reaction."

"I mean that *Melissa* knew about it before I did," he said, self-mocking. "You know, God bless her and I think she's great, but she's not the brightest bulb in the store, and she's not half the seasoned law enforcement professional I am."

"But she *is* Nickel's cousin. You said yourself she had a personal stake in the matter, and that's what compelled her."

"Maybe," he allowed.

"So." I shifted sideways in my chair. "Speaking of Melissa."

"God, Fever, I know what everybody thinks," he said, softer. "It makes me mad, and it's made me stupid. I'm afraid I've been—I don't know—daring people to think the worst. You can't tell me you don't know what that feels like. I happen to know that in your life you've gone out of your way to exaggerate people's worst opinions of you just for some weird version of spite and righteous indignation."

I smiled.

"That's a significantly astute observation," I told him. "Must be the seasoned law enforcement professional in you."

"You don't know where Orvid and Judy went." He leaned forward.

"I do not," I said plainly.

"We found tire tracks from Judy's car in the woods where you said they'd be. We know from the mud that they turned left onto 186. Other than that, they could be anywhere."

"Still," I said, "as I pointed out to Orvid, they don't exactly hide in a crowd."

"If Orvid's been a hired murderer like you said, he's figured out a lot about *hiding*."

I had to admit that would be true.

"You're telling me," I said slowly, "it turns out that you're not having an affair with Melissa."

"I am not."

Skid's eyes were bright, and he might have been on the verge of an actual smile.

"Good," I said. "You need to straighten things out with Girlinda, though, don't you?"

"Girlinda's not worried about that." Skid laughed. "She's worried about my losing sleep and eating poorly and, well, being less interested in her in general, you know, since I've been sheriff. She doesn't think I'm after the wrong girl, she thinks I've taken the wrong job."

He let that sink in. Of course Girlinda wouldn't believe town gossip about Skid. She knew him better than that.

"You're better at your job than you realize," I began, mustering a pep talk.

"I did arrest Nickel Mathews," Skid went on matter-of-factly, "with an ounce of pot and ten hits of ecstasy."

"What?" My eyes widened.

"All a part of the big drug bust—and do you have any idea how much I enjoy talking like the policemen on television?—that went down yesterday." Skid sat back proudly. "You'll never guess who's the drug kingpin of our little East of Eden."

"Eppie Waldrup," I shot back. "You got him!"

"I did," he went on less certainly, "but I thought that would be more of a surprise to you. I had to sweat it out of Nickel."

"Orvid told me. What about Andy Newlander?"

"Got him too." Skid nodded. "All in the jailhouse. How did Orvid know?"

"His job apparently lets him in on a plethora of secrets."

"I'll want to know more about Orvid."

"I don't know much more," I said, "but of course I'll tell you the whole story. Some of it's fascinating. For instance, did you know the girls were dating Nickel and some boy named Tony Riddick?"

"Yes, Fever, I knew that," Skid said wearily. "Sometimes a teenaged girl will do just about anything to prove to her parents that she's beyond their control."

"Oh," I said, disappointed. "I thought I'd be telling you something there. Well, do you remember that strange preacher over in New Hope?"

"I can tell this'll be a long story." Skid slumped in his chair, obviously calming. "You know it felt good to tell somebody that me and Melissa weren't fooling around."

"Maybe you should tell more people."

"Don't want to say it too much," he responded more softly, eyes downward. "People think you're covering something if you talk about it too much. Besides, everybody important knows what's the truth."

He didn't look up.

"Right," I agreed after a second. "So, what I was getting at with Nickel's dating one of the girls—"

"You want to know what about the drug screen that Millroy had to run," he interrupted.

"Right."

"That damned Millroy," Skid sighed. "Does he remind you a little of the pea-brain football coach we had in high school?"

I knew whom he meant and shook my head.

"I thought more Sargent Friday from *Dragnet,*" I said.

"Well, he's worthless, Millroy is," Skid said as if it were a total explanation. "He made me stop that funeral so he could run more tests, and then those tests were as inconclusive as the first ones had been. But it doesn't appear that the girls had any drugs in them. The best explanation we can give is that they were laughing when they died because they had something to laugh about. That's how I told Millroy to write it, and shut up."

"Good. That's a good thing to say to everyone."

"Amen."

"So the funeral is . . . ?" I ventured

"Tomorrow morning," he answered. "And only the family is invited this time, so you're off the hook. I know you hate those things."

"Except for the food."

"Exactly."

"Lucinda will want to go."

"She's family," Skid said simply.

"Yes." I shifted in my seat.

The way Skid had said that Lucinda was *family* made me realize something about my relationship with her. I didn't have words, exactly, for what I was feeling. Maybe I thought she was my family too.

"Look, could we finish all this later?" I said. "I am still a little vague about everything, and you were right: it is a long story. Besides, I'd like to get back to Lucinda at the moment. I don't like to leave her alone, what with everything that's happened. Could the rest of it wait?"

"All right." Skidmore stood. "I want to go to lunch anyway."

I stood too.

"One more thing," I began. "You know how the police on television tell people in stories like this that they're not to leave town?"

"Yes." He cocked his head, amused.

"I thought I should tell you that Andrews has asked me to come to London with him and work on a project of his." I shrugged. "I'd like to go. I wouldn't mind getting out of town for a while anyway. A short while. Shouldn't take more than a couple of weeks."

"When would you leave?"

"Whenever you say we're finished with this business," I answered contritely.

"Good." He smiled. "You could come over to dinner tonight."

"Not tonight. I really do want to talk a few things over with Lucinda. Maybe she'll go to England with me."

He stood frozen for a moment. I assumed he was trying to decide what to say.

"Bring me back a surprise from London," he offered wanly after a moment.

The light outside was blinding, more like a summer afternoon than late autumn. But when my eyes adjusted, I could see how clear the air was.

All the way back up the mountain, in fact, I had the sensation that I could see better, see farther than I ever had before. You can always see farther in late autumn, of course, when the leaves are gone from the trees. In June the maples along the road to Lucinda's were filled with green that blocked out everything behind them. But that day you could see rows of bare dogwoods, and, once, a stand of vacant pear trees. You could even make out the mistletoe hanging in globes all over the huge oak boughs.

The sun slipped behind smoke-gray clouds, but I could still see all the way to the bottom of the slope where I'd started the upward climb. And at the edge of one sharp turn I could easily find the house where I was born. Down that way, past blackberry thickets, was a stream where I'd first kissed a girl who would later become my sweetheart. There were great granite rocks just beyond. That's where we'd sat to talk about my leaving, and cry and cry.

I felt if I strained my eyes a little, I could almost make out the footprints of every last traveler who had crossed my winding path on that climb. Even overcast, the sky allowed—or did it encourage?—the sober examination of the way up the incline.

You can always see farther in autumn, and there's comfort in that, knowing spring is a trick, realizing summer's deception. What could be more important than that clarity?

I had a sudden urge to stop the truck, pick a gentle spot, get out, and roll down the hill, arms folded across my chest, the way I had when I was seven. It was nearly too great to ignore. But I ignored it that day.

I needed to see about something over the ridge, a little farther up the slope.